The Crumbling World

James Kirst

World Castle Publishing, LLC
Pensacola, Florida
Copyright © James Kirst 2021
Paperback ISBN: 9781955086448
eBook ISBN: 9781955086455
First Edition World Castle Publishing, LLC, July 19, 2021
http://www.worldcastlepublishing.com
Licensing Notes
Editor: Maxine Bringenberg

Chapter 1

Down towards the bowels of hell, five adventurers descended. Their goal was to end the reign of the giant winged, fire-breathing monster that terrorized the local village above. Leading them was the knight Lance, whose white armor remained unblemished even in those deep, dank caverns. At the age of fifteen, the king dubbed him to be the "Chosen One," for he exhibited the combined skills of several venerated soldiers, exceeding the great Guston and perhaps even rivalling the legendary warrior Artus. According to prophecy, the Chosen One was the one who would lead the kingdom of Evermore to eternal bliss. Never would the kingdom end if the Chosen One remained vigilant in his duty.

With him were his four most trusted allies. At the rear was the healer Alizon. Her short brown hair peeked through the hood of her white robe that covered her small and dumpy body. In front of her was the wizard Strefonio, who wore a blue robe that extended past his ankles, thus covering his entire frail frame. Taking the middle was the rogue Sanders, with short brown hair and wearing a black coat with a multitude of pockets that augmented the pouches hanging from his clothes.

The elven maiden Nerissa stood next to Lance, wearing her signature green tunic that went down to her knees. The small tree colored boots and similarly colored stockings allowed her legs to remain agile. Though her bosom was slightly exposed due to a slit near the top, she covered herself by tying the tunic's small strings together. She also wore a brown shirt underneath to preserve her modesty. This tall young woman with long flowing flaxen hair could not resist holding the knight's arm and hand as they traveled deep into the lair. She was Lance's betrothed, after all.

They were moving through a labyrinth of tunnels after defeating all manners of monsters, wraiths, and beasts to reach the innermost sanctum where the firedrake dwelled.

"How much deeper does this hole go?" Sanders asked, twirling his handlebar mustache.

"Quite rude for the flying lizard to live in so deep of a hole," Alizon said, raising her arm over her head, ensuring the spell she'd cast provided illumination. The torches that lined the cavern had disappeared by this time. "Shall we discuss the matter with him when we meet?"

"The villagers seemed to think the winged beast is quite powerful," Strefonio said and pulled out a pair of oddly colored mushrooms from his bag. "Mayhap, I should partake of these mushrooms to enhance my spells in case those rumors be true."

"My beloved's muscles be all that we need to succeed," Nerissa said while her fingers played with the amulet dangling around Lance's neck.

"Does that amulet only work if the wearer be pure?" Strefonio asked.

"I believe that is but a myth," Sanders answered.

"We should hope it is a myth, as I doubt he still be pure after all this time with her," Alizon sneered.

"Bite your tongue, woman!" Nerissa snapped.

The smell of sulfur and brimstone, along with the rise in temperature, silenced the argument. Lance raised his hand in the air. "The beast be near."

Lying curled like a dog in the cave's gigantic, awe-inducing final chamber was a dragon, several buildings tall, horned, red, and scaly. Its giant feather-like wings wrapped around its back. Small flames shot from the creature's nostrils as it loudly snored.

"Mayhap, it would be prudent to take a stealthy approach," Strefonio whispered.

The large encrusted eyes of the beast opened before anyone could answer. The lizard rose sharply, its head only a few feet from hitting the ceiling of the cave. It let out a mighty roar towards the heavens. Fire streamed from the beast's mouth as it encircled the cave. Lance and his companions dove into nearby rocks for cover, each of them barely able to dodge the attack.

"I blame you for this," Sanders said, pointing at the wizard. "He must have heard you."

"No need to assess blame," Lance said. He pulled out his sword and shield and lowered the visor of his helmet. His voice echoed yet still maintained its authoritative cadence. "To arms!"

Lance leaped over the rock barriers and charged the foe. Sanders joined him, relying on his quickness to avoid the attacks as opposed to Lance's heavy armor and brute strength. Nerissa provided cover fire with her bow and her magical quiver that had unlimited arrows.

Alizon and Strefonio poked out from their cover just enough to cast their spells. Alizon cast white magic to protect the warriors, healing when necessary and making their skin more resistant to the flames and more impervious to the beast's razor-sharp claws. Strefonio cast several aquatic-themed offensive spells to douse the winged lizard's flames.

The beast flayed when he attempted to keep up with his more fleet of foot attackers. True, he was on his home turf, but restricted space proved to be a challenge. He shot flames at Lance. Each attack was deflected by his shield. The dragon tried to stomp on Sanders several times, but each time completely missed. Once he tried to stomp on Lance, but the knight's superhuman strength allowed him to deflect the blow.

Defensively they were sterling, but their offensive efforts were met with great resistance. Though their blows annoyed the creature and provided some pain, no meaningful blows were landed.

Nerissa's aim was mostly true, but her arrows were constantly deflected. The creature was much too large for Strefonio's spells to have any meaningful effect, outside of, judging from its winces, a bit of pain and a slight distraction.

Lance tried to cut down the creature at its feet. No more success was met when he stabbed the tail. Several blows to the body bounced right off. Lance's blade, though mighty, could not penetrate the scales. If his blade could provide no wounds, Sanders' daggers had no hope of doing any better.

The six of them were at an impasse, which would have remained indefinitely had it not been for Lance's sharp eyes and quick thinking. One of Nerissa's arrows barely missed the beast, flying mere inches from its nose. The bolt deflected off the ceiling and landed on the dragon's head. The dragon let out a high-pitched howl for no more than a second and stopped its attack for an even shorter period of time. Yet this brief change in behavior was enough for Lance to suss out the creature's weakness.

"I have an idea!" Lance shouted. "But a distraction is necessary! Strefonio! Sanders! Attack him directly from the front!"

"'Tis what I'm already doing," Sanders sighed.

"Methinks 'tis folly, but for you, I shall do so, my dear friend." Strefonio reluctantly moved from the rocks and positioned himself appropriately.

"Why do you not order Alizon and me to do the same?" Nerissa growled. "Are you still under the illusion that we are the weaker sex?"

"This is not the time for such a discussion!" Lance screamed.

"Alizon and I shall show you that we are just as capable." Nerissa hopped from behind the rocks and joined Strefonio and Sanders, much to Lance's chagrin. He had no time to argue, though.

"I wish to remain here," Alizon said, not joining her female counterpart. "In such perilous circumstances, I do not mind being called the weaker sex." Nerissa glowered but was too concerned with dodging the falling foot of the dragon to protest.

Lance dashed to the dragon's tail and began his ascent. In response, the beast attempted to shake off his adversary. The knight managed to maintain his grip. The dragon increased his effort as Lance made his way across his back. His amulet provided him the necessary boost in strength, though let it not be said that the three companions did not assist greatly. Their attacks proved to be painful enough for the creature not to abandon them, the necessary diversion for Lance.

Straddling the dragon's neck, Lance was rocked violently from side to side. His grip on his sword remained true, though just barely, and he struggled even with both hands to lift his blade over his head. Pointing the hilt of the sword towards the heavens, he thrust the blade into the back of the firedrake's skull, penetrating its brain.

Each companion covered their ears as the dragon let out a bloodcurdling cry. His skull rapidly fell towards the earth. Sanders, Strefonio, and Nerissa managed to escape by jumping behind the rocks they had just abandoned. The ground quaked, and debris fell from the ceiling onto the floor when the head landed. Lance was thrown off the neck and landed with a thud.

Lance got up no worse for wear. After a quick confirmation that everyone was all right, Lance checked to see whether the beast was still moving.

He wasn't. The dragon had been slain. They were victorious.

"Victory is ours!" Nerissa exclaimed as she leaped into Lance's arms. She lifted his visor and gave him an impassioned kiss.

"Don't make us do anything like that ever again," Sanders admonished. He stretched and cracked his neck. "I wonder what kind of loot they have here." He began to explore the cave.

"That was quite the experience," Strefonio said, rubbing the back of his neck. "Methinks I'll treat myself to a treat to unwind." He pulled a couple of magic mushrooms from his bag.

"I shall treat you foolhardy lot that chose to expose yourselves to danger." Alizon walked around and healed the party's wounds.

"Now do you see we are not the so-called weaker sex?" Nerissa scolded playfully.

"True, true, you did outstandingly, my beloved. I shall not make that mistake again."

"I believe the deeds of the foolhardy should be admonished rather than praised," Alizon jeered.

"Shut your mouth, woman!" Nerissa yelled.

"Ladies, please," Lance pleaded. "No need to argue. We have succeeded in our undertaking. The focus should be on the celebration of our victory, not on petty disputes."

The ladies glared but acquiesced.

"Do you believe the king shall be satisfied with our endeavors?"

Nerissa covered her mouth as she giggled. "Always concerned with what the king will think."

"We defeated the firedrake," Alizon answered. "Need you ask?"

"Indeed," Sanders concurred. The pockets of his black pantaloons, as well as the various pouches he wore around his personage, were filled to the brim with treasure. "The people of Maldonia shall sleep soundly tonight. He shall be more than pleased."

"Thank you all for your help," said Lance.

Sanders smiled. "You can always count on us. My primary goal is to help people. It is almost as much fun as collecting loot. Almost."

"My friends are what's most important to me," said the wizard.

"I would do anything for my beloved," Nerissa said.

"Just never forget to be careful, okay, Lance?" said Alizon.

"Let us return to him," Lance said.

After confirming there were no more spoils to be had, the party headed back into the tunnels. In the lead was Lance, with his beloved clinging to his arm. His three other companions followed closely behind.

As Lance reached behind his love to make a one-armed embrace, he noticed something. "Nerissa, your bow and quiver are missing."

The elven maiden loosened her grip on Lance's arm and reached behind for both. "They must have fallen off when the creature attacked. Worry not. I shall retrieve them."

Lance grabbed her arm. "No need. I shall retrieve them in your stead."

"Have I not already proven I am not made of porcelain?"

"'Tis nothing to do with a perceived weakness. I wish to do it to make amends for my previous crass behavior."

"If you insist."

"Shall I go with you?" Alizon asked. "To provide light?"

"No need." By this time, they had walked far enough that the torches that lined the walls had returned. The knight pulled one off. "This should provide adequate light. Worry not. I shall join you all outside." The five bid temporary adieus as Lance made his return into the final chamber.

The trip was mostly uneventful. A stray small mandrake or two did make a couple of feeble swipes at his ankles but were nothing a few strokes of his sword weren't able to handle. He soon arrived back in the chamber where the recently deceased dragon now lay.

Lance searched behind the rocks where his companions previously hid. On the ground were the items he was looking for. After setting the torch down, he picked up the quiver and the bow and carried them on his back. Lance picked up the torch and headed back towards the tunnels.

"How long do you plan on maintaining this illusion?"

The knight turned suddenly in shock. A mysterious man had appeared. His voice was surprisingly familiar. Lance examined him closely. Most of the details remained hidden by the brown cloak, including the face, which was obscured by the hood.

"What do you mean? Who are you to say such things?" Lance demanded.

"My name is Al Kahim. You will soon grow quite accustomed to that name."

Suddenly, Lance's vision was obstructed — the cavern had filled with smoke. Lance covered his face to protect it from debris that swirled toward him. The ground rumbled, and the sounds of thunder filled the room.

Soon afterward, the room was clear, and the noises dissipated. Lance darted his head frantically around the chamber. The stranger was nowhere to be found. He was alone save for his fallen, scaly foe.

"He's no more than a manic wizard," Lance muttered to himself. "No need to pay his imprudence any heed." As he left the room, Lance could not help wondering why the stranger's voice — nay, his very essence — seemed so familiar.

Lance rejoined his allies at the entrance of the cave and was greeted by smiling faces and a sunny, cloudless sky. He handed the bow and quiver to a grateful Nerissa. When asked whether he met any difficulty, Lance spoke of mandrakes but neglected to mention the cloaked figure. He did not feel it necessary to stir what he perceived to be unnecessary panic among his friends.

They were greeted with open and jubilant arms by the people of Maldonia, the town closest to the dragon's lair and the one most terrorized by the fiend. Though no lives had been lost due to the menace of the monster, many thatched-roof cottages were. They were resilient people, though. They would rebuild.

For now, though, it was time to rejoice. The townsfolk

celebrated with the adventurers for three days and nights. It was a humble celebration with as many foods and wines as they could spare. Though this was but a mere precursor to the festivities that awaited them when they returned to the capital, the adventurers still expressed their sincerest gratitude.

The best minstrels of the town joined the adventurers as they made their trek home through the pastoral countryside. They alerted each town they passed of the party's triumph. Many cheers were elicited when the people heard of their deeds. They could not help but shower the adventurers with gifts, often more than they could spare. Though these presents were always humbly denied, Sanders did have difficulty at times making this moral decision.

They moved past Stonewall, through the small town of Tortuil, and past the hidden elf village of Ylaserine. Finally, they walked by the growing town of Sheepshead until they arrived at the capital.

A messenger alerted the king of the adventurers' pending arrival, which allowed him to prepare a lavish greeting for them when they arrived in the city of Angenehm, the capital of the kingdom. The best musicians of the land played their instruments loudly when the party entered the city. They continued to play jubilantly as they followed the five. All of them were accompanied by throngs of the cheering crowd.

Merchants offered their finest wares. Chefs approached to provide their most succulent foods. Owners of chateaus delivered their finest wines. Metalsmiths and armorers showed their latest advancements in weapons and shields and told them they would be honored if they were used in their next adventure.

Young maidens approached to offer their hand to the eligible bachelors. Mothers and fathers thanked them for keeping their families safe. Children approached to express how much they would like to be just like them when they grew up.

From amongst the crowd, a familiar face dashed to Lance. The two of them shared a warm embrace.

"I am so glad your journey was a success," the middle-aged woman in modest clothing and a shawl said to the young man.

"Mother! It is so good to see you! Will you be joining us in the festivities?"

"No, I just don't have the time. The cat needs feeding, and I have other matters to attend at home. Besides, I wouldn't feel right being amongst royalty. Enjoy yourself, and be sure to visit me afterward." Lance promised he would as the two exchanged farewells.

The joy and merriment, this celebration in the streets, continued past the castle gates and did not relent. Servants bowed, and ladies curtsied as they walked by.

Several knights were in the castle. The younger ones were especially quick to express their admiration. Though the veterans were more reluctant, even they could not help but mutter begrudging respect for the adventurers' endeavors. Despite their friendly demeanor, Lance knew of their incredible skills and hoped he would never have to face them in combat, though he was still pretty sure he could best them.

As they entered the room, several guards stood across from each other over a plush red carpet. It led to where King Rudolph sat on his throne up a three-step stairway. The guards' swords were drawn high in the air, as was the custom of the kingdom, a tradition dating back several generations. It was used to signify that those who entered were worthy of the utmost veneration.

The chancellor greeted them as they entered and led them

to the bottom of the steps. King Rudolph's golden crown and red jewels sparkled, and his red and purple robe was immaculate. His long hair and beard were trimmed and clean.

Though Lance's senior by at least four decades, there was an energy to the man. Even his royal face had hardly a wrinkle — stern yet soft features, soft blue eyes, golden-brown hair. His face displayed what seemed to be a perpetual smile, at least when Lance was present.

"Greetings, Your Majesty," the chancellor began. "These humble five would like to request your audience."

Lance removed his helmet, letting his long wavy hair flow out to his shoulders. His three cloaked or robed companions lowered their hoods in unison. They all bowed toward his grace. King Rudolph bade them cordially to rise.

"A kind greeting to my most loyal and beloved subjects," the king began. "Word of your triumph has spread throughout the kingdom like wildfire. We have grown too accustomed to your victories, so I dare say we may one day no longer revel in your success as it is expected." The entire room let out a hearty laugh. "Fear not," the king continued, "That day has not arrived. An extravagant celebration has been arranged. My royal chefs, please bring out your most delectable cuisine. It is time for a feast!"

The king clapped, and from behind and to the right of his throne, where the kitchen was located, came numerous carts used to serve their meal. The attendees seated themselves at the various oak tables spread on either side of the red carpet.

Guests were treated to the finest cedar chairs. The king's seat was at the dining table closest to the throne. It was not quite as ornate as his golden and jeweled throne. However, it was still quite the sight to behold, with royal red cushions and a top that was a full two heads taller than his majesty standing upright.

Lance took his seat next to the king, an honor he had earned seemingly eons ago. Next to him was the lovely Nerissa. Next to her were Strefonio, Sanders, and Alizon, respectively.

Their delectable banquet consisted of the most extravagant food in all the land. They were served the most savory hams, the most succulent beef, the juiciest fruits, and the finest vegetables the kingdom could grow.

The knight regaled his liege with his latest adventure. Several hearty laughs were shared, and his royal highness was quite literally on the edge of his seat when he reached the climax and conclusion of his tale. Lance continued with several more afterward, as it was his habit to reminisce.

Lance discussed his first adventure as a squire, where he protected his master when the man was ambushed by the black knight. He then told the tale of when he protected villagers, who were walking home, from bloodthirsty brigands single-handedly during his first expedition as a knight. Lance excitedly expounded on his mission into the wyvern caverns, how he managed to clear them out but still find time for tea.

He recalled how he met Sanders. Lance caught him when a woman reported his theft of her things, but upon further scrutiny, he realized that Sanders was truly a man with a heart of gold. The knight asked for his assistance in exchange for exoneration from a jail sentence. Sanders eagerly agreed. Yet after ridding a dungeon of evil trolls and more than meeting his obligation, Sanders chose to stay, partly out of loyalty and friendship that was birthed from the enterprise and partly due to the loot he realized he could take.

Alizon and Strefonio were originally part of an academy. When it was under attack by a griffin, their headmaster requested aid from the king, so Lance was sent, believing he was all that they would need. He was mostly right, but the battle did prove to be a bit more difficult than initially thought. Thanks to the wizard and the healer, though, they prevailed. Lance asked for their assistance afterward, and they — or that is to say, Alizon — eagerly agreed. Strefonio agreed too but was as tranquil then as he ever was.

Then there was the tale of how he met Nerissa. The evil goblin king Trekz had found the elven village of Ylaserine and sent his troops to attack. The characteristically secretive and prideful elves refused to ask for help, even though their bows were no match for the goblins' cold steel, strength, and sheer numbers.

Only Nerissa thought to seek aid from Lance and his then party of four. She had heard the tales and knew the roving band of adventurers, who had been granted such special privilege from the king for their myriad successes, could defeat that malicious army.

Her faith did not go unrewarded. Lance and his adventurers, along with Nerissa's impeccable aim, were able to drive the army back. With his army reduced to rubble and not used to such resistance, the goblin king and his men were forced to make a hasty retreat.

Lance did not expect her to be such a fantastic archer. She did not expect him to be so valiant. Neither expected to find someone they would be so attracted to. The two of them almost inevitably fell in love.

All these tales had been told before. King Rudolph had heard them all. Yet, he remained captivated with these stories. Hearing them always filled him with pride.

There were times these stories even got the king incredibly

excited, and he could not help but regale Lance with stories of how he was an excellent swordsman back in his day, specializing in the broadsword, just like the young knight. He even suggested they spar a couple of times after the festivities, which the young man politely declined. When he did, the king would laugh and say he should not underestimate him just because he was old. His skills had not diminished, as he still practiced every day. Upon hearing this, the two of them would share hearty banter, discussing their past achievements in an affable game of one-upmanship.

That is not to say the rest of his crew did not share in this storytelling. Their adventures were shared with perhaps only slightly less enthusiasm and vigor and received accordingly, though this was no indictment of Lance's friends or the audience. The knight was so adept at reciting tales it was difficult for anyone to compete.

King Rudolph raised his hand. Silence befell the room. "There is something I must announce." He bade Lance and Nerissa to rise. "It is my pleasure to announce that Lance and Nerissa shall be wed at the end of this month! It goes without saying how much these two mean to me. I will be the solemnizer of this wedding. I bid you all to join me in congratulating the happy couple!"

Nerissa and Lance blushed and held each other's hands over their heads. The crowd roared in response. Each guest stood and gave a rousing cheer. Everyone went particularly wild when the two shared an impassioned kiss.

Everyone, that is, except Alizon. She was noticeably absent from the frenzy. Though she managed to will herself to stand and clap for the pair, albeit a slow and almost sarcastic one, she did it while wearing a distressed grin.

Good fortune abounded for Lance. He could imagine no better life. It was as if he were living in a dream.

Suddenly, a large bang was heard at the entrance, interrupting the merriment. The doors had been flung open and had crashed against the wall. Several guests were startled, and more than a few jumped with fright. A lone messenger dashed through the doors, then knelt next to the king.

King Rudolph growled. "I hope you have good reason to interrupt the celebration of the hero Lance and his allies."

"Sire, my apologies for the disturbance, but I come bearing terrible news! The soothsayer Senna has just received a vision. An evil wizard from Stonewall plans to end the world."

A collective gasp and murmurs escaped the mouths of the crowd. Lance knew Senna quite well. She was the one who had given him his amulet. The soothsayer didn't often have visions, but what she perceived was always correct.

"Egad," the king said. "And in Stonewall of all places. Who is this wizard?"

"It is a name you have heard, though I've no doubt it will still surprise: Al Kahim."

"Of course," the king said. "I presume he lives on Mount Posledna."

"Yes, sire," the messenger confirmed.

A shiver went down Lance's back. "Did you say Al Kahim?"

"Is that a name you are familiar with?" Alizon asked.

"How could he be?" the king answered, his face looking pale and ashen. "Only our wisest and most revered scholars have even heard the name, and even then, he was considered a mere legend. His power is said to dwarf all of our most powerful wizards combined."

Several of the more fragile guests plopped themselves into their seats upon the revelation. Some others passed out upon hearing this grave news.

"What's worse is that Senna told us Al Kahim has already cast the spell, and she can feel the world beginning to change." Almost as if on cue, the ground shook. It didn't last very long, nor was it particularly powerful. Nevertheless, it was enough to cause panic.

"The end is near!" one of the partygoers screamed.

"Not yet!" the messenger explained. "The soothsayer says there is hope. The world cannot crumble, as the spell is not quite strong enough. It still needs a final ingredient."

"What is it?"

"We are not sure. The premonition became cloudy at that point. She could see no further. Our most intelligent scholars are already perusing ancient texts for clues. We have considered sending our best knights to confront the evil wizard, but even they have yet to find the courage."

The king fell to the back of his chair and closed his eyes. His hand rubbed his temple, sweat dripping profusely from his brow. He said meekly, "We must stop him."

Lance put a foot on his seat and announced, "Worry not, my liege! We shall stop him!" He shifted his weight and looked over to his four companions. "Are you with me?"

An almost tangible silence befell his most loyal confidantes.

Alizon stepped forward and raised her hand to her heart. "Of course I am." She did her best to look into Lance's eyes and force a confident smile.

Strefonio, having already seated himself again, took an extra couple of bites from his mutton. "I guess I have to. Another one already. I know it's the end of the world and all, but it doesn't seem fair." He sighed. "Maybe I'll feel better after I finish my meal and, of course, pop a couple of mushrooms to take the edge off."

Sanders rested his head in his hand and leaned against the table, darting his eyes in every direction but the knight's. "I was really looking forward to the break. We always get a break after a mission. I wanted to spend some time with the gals in the tavern and spend some of the loot. I also wanted to look for some potentially lucrative opportunities for the future. There better be a good reward."

Nerissa looked down and shook her head before standing and eeking out a pained half-smile. "If it is what my beloved wants," she said through gritted teeth.

"I knew you would, Nerissa," Lance stated proudly. He reached for her waist, but Nerissa moved away.

Lance was in near shock. He didn't know how to respond. His confusion only grew when he heard her mutters. "We have a wedding to plan, and he wants to set off on another life-threatening expedition. What is his obsession with adventure, anyway? Makes me think we're rushing into things. How well does he know me anyway?"

The young knight wondered what she meant, how she could even be concerned with such matters as a wedding considering the circumstances, and what she meant about rushing into things. These things concerned him, deeply and emotionally, but he did not know how to express himself, nor did he know how to refuse the king. Thus, when it came to his betrothed's frustration and anger, the knight chose to remain mum.

Instead, Lance looked at his friends, bewildered. "Be you not excited for another rousing adventure? I admit the stakes are dire, but we must remain steadfast! Let us venture on with exhilaration and faith that we shall—"

Nerissa screamed and interrupted Lance's diatribe. "We said we'll go!" After a short pause, she continued speaking in an almost whisper. "We said we'll go."

Lance looked at her for a moment. He wanted to ask her so much, yet could not find the words. Instead, he addressed the king.

"My gratitude for an excellent meal, my liege. We shall be off. Worry not, for we shall succeed."

"I doubt it not, Sir Lance. Seek Orbo, our wisest scholar, at our royal library to learn more of Al Kahim and then be off. Hurry, and do not dally, for the fate of the kingdom rests on you and your companions' mighty shoulders. We eagerly await your return."

With that, the five companions set off to what would become their most important adventure yet.

Chapter 2

The wizened scholar adjusted his thick, wide-rimmed glasses that sat awkwardly on his face. He leaned forward in his chair and squinted at the young man standing in front of him. Orbo looked slightly to his left. Beside the young man was a white-robed young woman.

He observed the three others that had accompanied them. The man in a blue robe seemed anxious to access the contents of his pouch and was looking for a good place to be discreet. The man in a black hood stroked his chin as he gazed upon the valuable paintings and baubles that adorned the room, seemingly lost in thought.

The young elf-woman was restless and agitated. She wandered around the room and occasionally sat restlessly at one of the tables spread across the copious library before looking towards the scholar and the young duo, then continuing on her angry and purposeless stroll.

"Ah yes, Al Kahim. I've indeed heard of him. You are familiar with Artus's Prophecy, yes?"

"Obviously," the elf answered in his stead.

Orbo grimaced. It was a rhetorical question. Naturally, the young man was familiar with the prophecy. Everyone in the kingdom was. Even the smallest of school children were familiar with Artus and his prophecy.

Centuries ago, Artus had served the good king Gunther. Utilizing his exemplary swordsmanship, the knight protected this peaceful kingdom from scores of monsters that flooded the land, including the colossi that threatened to smash the kingdom into dust.

Of course, his greatest adventures involved the Takas, a race of shapeshifting beings that took on human form. The legends said they used terrible yet incredibly powerful magic, unlike anything the world had seen since, to enslave the kingdom. Though Artus was much more skilled than they, their skin was impenetrable. They eventually won through attrition, and Artus was left for dead.

Even Artus's wife, the powerful mage Alathea, who accompanied him on all his adventures, could not bring him back to life with her spells. It took the good gods' grace to revive him. They did not wish to see the world's greatest hero fall to such creatures, so they took pity on him, bringing him back to life.

When Artus returned, his sword was suddenly able to penetrate the monsters' skin, allowing him to defeat the Taka and free the world from their oppression. No one was quite sure why his blade suddenly had this power. Most credited the gods, especially Knarrenheinz, the god of fire and steel. They said he forged a blade he dubbed Artus's Sword, after the hero, and gave it to him to save the world. Others believed a different type of magic was involved.

Regardless, shortly after this victory, Artus placed the

sword in an enchanted stone amongst trees within a grove near Stonewall, which could only be opened with three magical gems. He entrusted his closest companions with these jewels. Artus told them that one day the kingdom—nay, the world—would face a cataclysmic threat, but a Chosen One would emerge to protect the land. When this Chosen One appeared, it was their duty to give him trials of their own discretion to ensure he was worthy of his sword—Artus's Sword, as it became known. Their descendants were now the ones tasked with protecting those gems.

Then he vanished. Artus and his wife Alathea were never seen again. His omen became known as Artus's Prophecy.

"Artus's apocalyptic premonition has been the subject of much debate amongst scholars. The consensus is that the catastrophe predicted would involve some sort of monstrous invasion, maybe a return of the colossi or a gigantic wyvern. Perhaps even several of such powerful creatures would invade our beloved kingdom. Yet the scholar Mortimer felt differently."

"What did he believe?" Lance asked.

Orbo stroked his grey beard. "He was a different sort of scholar, more an adventurer like yourself than your typical sage. He was completely obsessed with Artus, too, going so far as to actually use the ancient texts to trace his journey exactly. Mortimer was convinced that there was knowledge to be gained, something other scholars had missed. For nearly ten years he traveled, perpetually retracing the legendary hero's steps over and over again. None of his outings ever bore fruit. He was about to give up when he happened upon an almost innocuous tale by pure accident.

"There's an old library in Stonewall that serves as its historical landmark. It dates back to the time of Artus, after all, and he undoubtedly visited it at some point, being the intellectual he was. Mortimer was finishing combing through the texts, as he was wont to do, and he must have done this countless times prior. As he put those texts away, he noticed, almost by chance, a small piece of paper tucked behind one of the corners of a bookshelf. He picked it up almost dismissively, thinking it was a note left by and for a small child, a secret message or perchance merely a confession of crush. Instead, he found something that has been in dispute for nearly a century, though I dare say the skeptics, including myself, now have no choice but to accept the veracity of what he found."

Orbo stood and turned towards the large bookshelf.

"What was it?" Alizon asked.

"It was a note," Orbo answered while he examined the bookshelves. "Or I suppose it could have been a diary entry or part of a larger manuscript. It is difficult to say exactly. It was recorded as part of an anthology. I can tell you what the note said if only I could find it."

After another scan, Orbo looked up and nodded in confirmation. He wheeled over a large ladder and asked Lance for some assistance. With the knight holding the ladder, the scholar climbed and pulled down a large volume from the shelf, then very carefully descended. Orbo placed the text on the table and opened it up to the relevant passage.

"Ah yes, here it is."

***

After climbing the unclimbable Mount Posledna to prove to the people of Stonewall that he still possessed his massive strength, despite his advanced years, Artus was compelled to find the god Thor to have his blade strengthened by the fires of Odin. It was not widely known why. Some speculated that he saw a vision atop that mountain. Others believed it was divine intervention. Neither was true.

Let it not be said that Artus was not courageous, but contrary to belief, he did feel fear. On the peak, he found a decrepit hut. The knight went in thinking it was abandoned but instead found a man sitting by himself in the middle of its only room. Having not taken even two steps into the room, Artus found himself paralyzed. It was as if the gods were gripping his chest. Artus fell to the floor, barely able to lift himself to all fours. He began to shake uncontrollably. An unfamiliar feeling overwhelmed him. The knight was not used to such emotion. He was used to instilling them into his enemy.

Artus somehow sensed that the man in the room possessed a power that defied comprehension. The knight had faced mighty wizards in the past, hundreds of them, sometimes all at once, yet none of them collectively had a fraction of this man's magical prowess.

"Who are you? What are you?" Artus gasped.

The wizard stood and turned towards Artus. "I am Al Kahim. Pray you never hear my name again." With a flick of his wrist, Artus was returned down to the village.

The villagers found him convulsing on the ground. In a panic, they assisted him to a nearby hut, where Artus spent three days and nights in bed with an intense fever. Even his wife Alathea, with her exemplary healing abilities, could do little to ease his discomfort. He complained incomprehensibly about the terror he'd observed when he bore but a glimpse at "his face."

On the fourth day, he suddenly sprang out of bed. He told his wife Alathea nothing of this experience, only that he needed to find Odin to strengthen his blade. He was successful. His sword, refined by the metals of the gods, proved to be an invaluable asset in several of Artus's remaining adventures.

Yet, the experience proved to be too much. He never found the nerve to scale that mountain ever again. His sword was bequeathed to the royal family. They had kept it under the throne ever since. It could only be given to the one that proved himself worthy to the keepers of the gems.

***

Orbo looked up from the book. "This story was largely thought to be the machinations of an overactive imagination. There were too many holes. No mentions in any other texts of convulsions or powerful wizards. It is difficult to believe the village could be sworn to secrecy for this many generations. Yet Senna tells us that Al Kahim is threatening the world. We can no longer doubt its legitimacy."

Orbo excused himself and walked into the archive. He returned with a list of names and locations. The scholar handed it to the young knight.

"Here are the names of the current keepers of the gems and where they are located. I think it's clear what you must do. Prove yourself to be worthy as the designation Chosen One and worthy to hold Artus's Sword. It is our only hope."

Lance put his hand to his heart. "Fret not. We shall succeed in this noble task."

The scholar adjusted his glasses. He mentally noted with disdain the wizard attempting to discreetly consume some multi-colored mushrooms, the hooded figure deftly hiding some trinkets in his coat, nearly escaping Orbo's remarkably sharp eyes, and the elf woman's frown as she sat and rapidly tapped her foot against the ground, her body shaking.

Orbo muttered, "I wish I shared your confidence." Orbo reached onto a nearby shelf and handed Lance a large, rolled up piece of parchment. "This is a map that will show you where to go to retrieve the gems. It lists the locations where the keepers currently reside. You can trust the map. The king pays many emissaries a lot of gold to keep track of this sort of information. Good luck."

Lance and his mage friend bid the good man adieu, his three other companions hardly paying attention at all to their surroundings, and the five left the library and the castle, onward to the city's streets.

Lance opened and checked the map. Sheepshead, though quite a distance away, was still the closest locale on the map. He closed the map and told his crew where they were headed. This was met with a few mumbles and very little fanfare. The knight did not appreciate the lack of enthusiasm but ultimately chose to say nothing instead of focusing on the adventure.

As they walked, Lance's ears perked as he heard the mutterings of the townsfolk as he passed.

"Do you really think the world is in danger, or do you think it's another excuse for the king to tax us heavily?"

"Does he ever need an excuse?"

"The best part is, after the 'Chosen One' is successful in another one of his frivolous ventures, you know the king will force us to have yet another lavish celebration."

"Gods. Can't afford it none. Can't give away no more free items."

"Other towns are feeling it too. I mean, I'm grateful, and all, but the expense to keep them fed and armed is really starting to take its toll."

"Guston never asked for a reward. A true hero, he was. Slayed many a dragon in his day yet was always humble. Always had time for a chat."

"If he was so great, where is he now?"

"I would not be surprised if the king had a say in his disappearance. Guston could have become king."

"Are you kidding? The son of a farmer could never be king."

"The people loved him. We loved him. Why not?"

Lance looked at them askance as the words escaped their lips. They were guileful. The knight could easily hear them. They even made it clear that they knew he heard them. Yet, they were able to gossip in such a way that obscured exactly who was talking. The knight could never determine to whom he should direct his grievance.

No matter. Lance had other matters to attend to. Chiefly, as he was wont to do, visiting his mother before his latest adventure.

The affluent homes of Angenehm were located in the central part of the city. Their size rivaled only the castle itself. Branching from those houses were the more modest homes. These were hardly anything to be ashamed of. In fact, they required a decent wage to afford, yet still lacked the size or the amenities their more expensive counterparts possessed. As the city branched out further, the dodgier residents resided. Some of them did not actually have a home, choosing to dwell on the streets or the various seamier establishments as a de facto domicile.

Lance's mother lived on the edge between the modest and the seedy. Her home was more of a cottage than a house. It was made of wood, but Lance still pictured it in his head as being made of straw, perhaps because he conflated it with the image of the home he grew up in before becoming the Chosen One.

His mother had moved to the city shortly after Lance had been granted his coveted title. Though her son could afford to provide a much more opulent home, she preferred to live in her tiny residence. After all, she said, it was just her and her cat Albert now. There was no reason to live in a mansion. It would take forever to clean, if nothing else.

"Do I really have to go in there with you?" Nerissa asked when they arrived at the home. The question baffled Lance so much that he froze in place while reaching for the door. He turned and faced the elven woman. "It seems a visit like this should be personal between mother and son. We'd just get in the way."

Lance stared at her for a moment and then at his other four companions. Three of them had what the knight would describe as expectant looks on their faces. "I'm sure she wouldn't mind. I especially think she'd want to see you, Nerissa. You are my betrothed."

"Yeah, but I don't think it's a good time, with the end of the world coming up and everything, you know? I'm just not in a good headspace. Maybe when we've killed the evil wizard or whatever, I'll feel more like seeing her, but right now is really not a good time. I really just need to go somewhere and clear my head." She then muttered just loud enough to be heard, "Besides, I don't want to deal with that cat."

"Yeah, that cat is a jerk," Strefonio concurred.

"He's nice to me," Lance said quietly. "And my mom."

"He knows you," Sanders said.

The knight took off his helmet and scratched his head. "Do you want to wait out here?"

"No. I mean, I don't want you to feel obligated to cut your visit short because you're worried about us standing out here."

"I don't believe my visit will take very long."

"I think it'd just be better if I just did my own thing. If we did our own thing, I mean."

"Agreed," Sanders said.

"If they like, don't have to go, then I don't either, right?" Strefonio said.

Lance sighed. "All right. If that's what you all really want, I won't stop you. Where shall we meet when I'm done?"

"Don't worry, I'm sure we'll find each other. You're a smart guy — you'll figure out where we are." Nerissa's voice faded as she said this. She, Sanders, and Strefonio had practically disappeared by the time she finished her sentence, not bothering to do more than a half-hearted wave as they departed.

Alizon remained with him. "I can go with you if you'd like, Lance."

"No, it's okay. No reason for you to get roped into my visit. Besides, this is a personal thing between a mother and son. You'd just get in the way." Lance bit his tongue immediately. "That is not what I meant." All attempts to placate the incensed Alizon were futile. She stomped as she stormed off towards his friends, leaving the knight in a huff. "I suppose I shouldn't fuss over injudicious word choice," Lance muttered to himself. He turned around and opened the door. "Hello, Mother!"

The thin woman with a mottled face and soft brown eyes, wearing a long white dress and an amaranth stained chemise, faced the knight. A wide smile formed on her lips. She abandoned her work at the stove momentarily to run over to the young man and give him a gigantic hug. Though her arms were pressed against metal, they both could feel the warmth.

"Don't just stand there. Come here and sit." She led him to a seat by the kitchen table. Lance set his helmet and gauntlets on the table and sat as gently as he could on the chair. His mother's calico cat rubbed against his feet, and the knight gave him a quick stroke, as was his habit.

"Where are your friends?"

"They had other matters they wished to attend to, it seems."

"Even Nerissa?"

"Unfortunately, yes."

His mother paused for a moment. "Pity." She shrugged. "No matter. I can see them some other time. Dinner is almost ready. Would you like anything?"

"No, thank you. I have eaten enough."

"Are you sure? There is plenty. I know how much you love my cooking."

"I regret to say I do not have the time. I have something to tell you."

His mother looked at him solemnly. She took the stew from the stove and placed it on the table, then turned her attention to her son. She held both of his hands and looked him in the eye. "What is it, Lance?"

Lance struggled to find the words. "Mother, the evil wizard Al Kahim threatens to end the world. This will by far be my most dangerous adventure yet. We may fail this one."

The woman patted her son on his knees and smiled. "You've thought that way about every adventure you've taken part in. You told me this when you had to retrieve the chalice for the king. And what about the time you had to fight those trolls? You even told me this recently before you fought that giant dragon, and look how that turned out."

"This time is different. The end of the world is nigh. Does this not scare you, Mother?"

"My world may always come to an end whenever you go off to fight. Yet, I do not try and get in your way. Do you know why?"

"I'm too stubborn?"

"Perhaps that's part of the reason, but I also know you have a talent for this, and more importantly, this is something that drives you, fills you with a burning desire. I would rather have you home with me, where it is safe, but I know it would be unfair to try and keep you here. Plus, you have talent beyond anyone's imagination. Everyone says this. We all can't be wrong."

"This seems to be more than even I'm capable of."

"You are capable of anything, Lance. You just need to believe in yourself. Not just for you, but your friends and the people of Angenehm."

"I feel overwhelmed."

"Have you given any thought to how you are going to defeat this evil wizard?"

"I need to get a sword."

"Well, then get the sword and whack that evil wizard over the head." His mother stood briefly to awkwardly pantomime swordplay. Lance laughed upon the sight. His mother smiled and resumed sitting next to her son.

"It's not that easy. I have to go to various towns, pass their exams, and acquire gems to unlock the sword. There isn't even a hint as to what those tests will entail."

"Just take it one town at a time. I'm sure you'll succeed. You're the Chosen One, after all."

"Don't tell anyone, but sometimes I don't feel I truly am."

"You are. At least you'll always be the Chosen One to me." She gave the knight another hug.

"Thank you, Mother."

"Do you feel better?"

"Perhaps a little bit. I'm glad you were here."

They conversed some more on all sorts of topics of various importance until it was time for the knight to resume his mission.

"Farewell, Mother," he said as he hugged his mother one more time at the doorway.

"Visit me anytime, son. Farewell, and Godspeed." The two waved as he departed. "Oh wait, don't forget these!" Lance turned to see his mother struggle to lift his gauntlets and helmet from the table. Lance walked over to her. "These are much heavier than they look," she conceded.

Lance smiled. He took the gauntlets from her hand and put them on, then took the helmet and placed it atop his head. The knight left.

Feeling melancholy yet somehow invigorated, Lance needed to regroup with the rest of his party. He searched for them in what he believed to be the most likely places.

Lance went to the archery range to find his beloved Nerissa. She was nowhere to be found. He turned his sights towards the thief's guild to find his companion Sanders. The thief was missing.

The royal library was next. He hoped to find Strefonio and Alizon. One of them was there, the mage, but the wizard was absent. Alizon sat at a table near the entrance of the monolithic place while she perused an ancient text discussing the nature of shapeshifting wizards.

"At least you are where I expected you to be," Lance said. "I could not find the others anywhere."

"That's probably because you didn't look at The Wretched Swallow."

"Is that a place?"

Alizon slammed her book shut, which elicited an angry stare from the head librarian. "Sorry," Alizon said sheepishly to the man. He shook his head and continued with his work. The mage resumed her conversation with Lance. "It's a tavern.

Nerissa suggested they have some fun. They wanted to celebrate our victory over the dragon."

"I did not realize they enjoyed such establishments."

"Yeah, they do. You just never noticed. You often imagine what you want rather than face the truth."

"Regardless, this is hardly the time for merriment."

"That's what I said. They don't listen to me."

"We should go and retrieve them."

Alizon shrugged. "If we must."

The two traveled from the royal library in search of the locale. They asked around but had difficulty finding information from the more respectable people in town. There was either genuine ignorance of the location or, strangely enough, an almost hasty dismissal, combined with irritation that Lance would even suggest they knew of such a place.

One of the seedier residents happened to be walking by when they overheard Lance's inquiries. They were happy to guide him and his companion. The unsavory suggestions the two men made toward Alizon made her want to immediately rebuff their offer and give the pair a couple of fists to the face. Lance convinced her that they should follow them, as unpleasant as that prospect was since they were the only ones that seemed to know where the tavern was located. She reluctantly acquiesced.

The duo led them past the affluent houses, past the modest homes, and continued until they reached the empty alleyways that were dark, even though it was just past noon. After stepping over some disheveled, wretched men passed out on the sidewalk, lying in their own vomit, and after being accosted by some desperate-looking men looking for change, they eventually arrived.

"Welcome to da Wretched Swallow," the man rasped,

"An oasis of debauchery in an otherwise wholesome Angenehm. A place where you can whet your whistle and get certain services from the ladies if ya know what I mean." He laughed riotously. Alizon and Lance looked at each other, baffled. "No need ta be shy. Let's go in, then." The man opened the door. A body flew through the opening.

A tall, muscular man stood at the door. "And stay out of my bar!"

"Looks like another fun time." The man looked towards Alizon and Lance. "Come on, come on, let's go in already."

The duo walked in with their unsavory host, only for their olfactory nerves to be assaulted with the smell of cheap liquor and strange perfumes wafting in the air. Raucous noises reverberated throughout the edifice. Chaos was everywhere.

Men chased women of ill repute up the stairs—not to imply these women were unwilling participants in the chase. Fights occurred all over and seemingly at random. In one instant, a pair of friends would be sitting at a table, enjoying a drink. In the next instant, they'd be exchanging blows. Perhaps something was said that made the other feel slighted, or perhaps it was some sort of bizarre ritual, as the fighters would often resume drinking afterward, bruised and battered but otherwise acting as if nothing had occurred.

A flaxen-haired woman with flowers in her hair, wearing a tight lavender and white dress, made her way over. Her skirt barely covered the top part of her upper thighs, and her bodice hardly covered her chest.

"Can I do anythin' for ya, love?"

Lance, with a slight amount of perspiration gathering on his forehead and a bit tongue-tied, described his friends.

"I know who yer talkin' about."

The knight was aghast and horrified at the scenes she directed him toward.

Strefonio sat in a dark corner of that dank establishment. On each of his arms was a woman, both of whom were dressed as well as the hostess. The wizard wore a wide grin as he attempted to awkwardly drink from two pitchers of beer he carried in his hands to the amusement of his new friends.

The slack-jawed knight was led to the bar. Sanders was there, along with a group of men and more scantily clad women. Each of them was clapping, laughing, and drunkenly encouraging the woman dancing erratically on the bar.

It was Nerissa.

"Strefonio! Sanders! Nerissa!" Lance screamed. "What is the meaning of this? Cease what you are doing right now. It is time to go!"

All eyes turned to the knight. An almost unsettling silence filled the room.

Strefonio sheepishly set down the beer and unwrapped his hands from the ladies. He plopped down some coin and moved toward the entrance.

Sanders scowled and stopped clapping. Nerissa danced a little more until she realized the party was over. She shrugged, reached out to the thief, who helped her down from the bar, then shuffled with him to where the knight stood.

"I knew Lance was allergic to fun," Sanders said.

Strefonio chortled. "We better do what Dad says."

Nerissa giggled. "Time to venture off for king and country."

Lance demanded an explanation as to what was so funny while Alizon looked on sympathetically. No explanation was provided.

The young knight stormed out, with his party not far behind. There was an awkward silence as they walked toward the exit of town until Lance decided to break it in a clumsy fashion.

"You're missing the shirt you normally wear underneath your tunic."

"What's your point?" Nerissa asked.

"Did you take it off at the tavern?"

"So what if I did?"

"I'm just curious."

"Not that it's any of your business, but it is sweltering today. I just wanted to cool off."

"I didn't notice it being particularly warm today," Alizon said.

"Nobody asked you," Nerissa hissed.

Sanders intervened. "It's not up to you to decide. It's her choice."

Strefonio concurred. "Yeah, man. I mean, if you're not hurting anybody, you should be able to do what you feel."

"Thank you," Nerissa said. "At least the two of you get it." She glared at Lance and Alizon. Alizon glowered back. Lance made several vain attempts to apologize. Each attempt was met with silence.

The young man was confused. His friends had never acted in such a manner before. Lance wondered what might have spurred the change. As they approached the dirt trail leading towards the next town, he sighed and looked into the cloudless, azure sky. He noticed, though, that the sky seemed somewhat darker, a little closer to black. However, that did not bother him as much as what else was in the sky.

It was small, almost imperceptible, but further inspection made it undeniable. A small crack, black as if it were an opening to space, had formed.

"Everyone! Look! The sky has a crack!"

A collective gasp was inhaled, and their eyes immediately darted to where Lance's finger was pointing.

"I don't see anything," Nerissa said. She shook her head.

"It's not like, cool to try and scare us like that or something," said the wizard.

"Do you not see it?"

"No, I don't, Lance," said Alizon, almost apologetically.

"There's nothing up there," Sanders said.

Lance made several attempts to show them but was only met with denial. Soon he came to the conclusion that either everyone was lying, or he was the only one who could see the phenomena.

"I suppose I was mistaken," he said sheepishly. The party muttered their forgiveness.

Yet, he could not take his eyes off it. The knight pondered these revelations and what it could all mean as he led them out of town toward Sheepshead.

Chapter 3

About one hundred miles to the south and a bit south of Angenehm, through the beautiful but small Shertham Woods and across the Glistening Valley, and through the towns of Sojourn and Respite, is the small town of Sheepshead. The town borders a large river shaped similarly to an upside-down "U," named, appropriately enough, the Ewe River, a play on words that is both a reference to its shape and an allusion toward the abundance of sheep the community raised, though it is worth noting that the community also provided a plentiful supply of wood and wheat.

The western and the eastern parts of the river lie parallel to each other. The latter is about three hundred miles long, while the former is 450 miles long. Connecting the two, which ultimately forms the "U" shape, is a northern river that is only about one hundred miles wide. It is not a particularly wild river, but it is long and very deep. Fording is impossible. This provided the town with incredible protection from invaders but also caused its isolation.

When the party arrived at the edge of the town, they encountered large caravans full of various stones.

"What's going on here?" Lance asked one of the drivers.

"We're from the city of Stonewall. We have agreed to trade with Sheepshead. In exchange for brick and ore, they will provide wood, wheat, wool, and meat."

"Why do you wait out here?"

"We've looked around, and though there are several bridges that allow access to the town, we haven't been able to find any that are strong enough or wide enough to handle the weight or width of even one of our wagons. As I'm sure you know, the river is deep enough that we can't exactly ford it either. One of our men went into town to ask the mayor where we can find a good bridge to cross. We are waiting for his return."

"We are also headed into town to see the mayor. We will let you know if we learn anything."

The driver thanked the knight, and the party headed to the nearest bridge that could lead them into town.

Lance looked down and observed the wooden bridge. He was a bit taken aback. It was rickety and only a couple of inches above the water. It was barely wider than an average man's shoulders. A couple of rope supports on either side provided people something to hold on to as they walked across, but there was little more.

Nerissa scoffed. "How pathetic. You would think they'd be able to find one person that could build a proper bridge."

"They sure ain't as good as like, the capital's bridges," Strefonio said.

Sanders concurred. "No excuse for this."

"That's a little unfair," Alizon said. "Angenehm has a plethora of resources and people compared to this town. The situations aren't exactly comparable."

"If they're going to start trading with Stonewall, they had better learn how to build a bridge," Sanders retorted. Alizon apparently did not feel like prolonging the argument, so she remained mum.

Lance led the way, taking cursory steps forward to see whether it could support his weight. Realizing it could do at least that and more, he moved his way forward, motioning to his companions to do the same.

Alizon went next, followed by Strefonio, Nerissa, and Sanders. They each walked cautiously in a single file, gripping the rope tightly as they inched their way across.

It seemed like even a gentle breeze caused that bridge to swing back and forth violently. With each step, Lance felt that the wood beneath him would crack. He swore he smelled rotted wood. River water splashed against his knees and even reached his face.

An occasional scream would cause Lance to look back to find that one of his four companions had lost balance, either due to the wind or the wet, and fallen to their knees with both hands clutching the rope. With little he could do for them except to say an encouraging word, which would mostly be ignored, he would then press forward.

The young man did not know how long the trip was taking, but it seemed to be going on forever. Whether this stood as a testament to the length of the bridge or to how slowly they were going, he could not say. As much as he suffered, his companions had it worse. Lance's steel armor prevented most of the wet from penetrating, keeping his skin relatively dry. His companions were not so lucky. All of them were soaked.

Fortunately, the summer sun-dried them well when they

finally reached the other side.

"This town is utterly appalling," Nerissa muttered while she dried in the sun.

"Another backwater," Sanders said as he rung out his damp clothes.

"This is like, the only robe I got, man," Strefonio complained.

"This is my only robe too, but it's not like we had much of a choice," Alizon explained.

"We made it, though," Lance said. "Since we are here, we may as well look around."

Contrasting sharply with the metropolis that was Angenehm, Sheepshead was best described as a disparate set of farms connected by crude dirt roads. A few dissimilar cottages did decorate some of the mottled landscape but were few and far between. Sheep dung and barley were pronounced smells that drifted in the wind. Seas of white wool and amber fields of grain were the chief tourist attractions. Pastoral, one might call it, or rural, or for the more cynical, dull.

Sanders, Strefonio, and Nerissa made condescending comments as a herder momentarily and apologetically blocked their path while leading a flock of sheep. The three were having difficulty containing their disdain of the less than cosmopolitan inhabitants.

After his party had finally dried off, Lance asked the herder for directions to the mayor, and the friendly man directed him to the brick house in the middle of town, which served as both a home and the town hall. Compared to the typical wattle and daub homes of Sheepshead, it was a mansion. Yet, it would have hardly been more than a modestly sized home in the big city.

When they arrived at the wooden door of the town hall, Lance asked his group whether they wished to join him or go off on their own.

"We might as well join you," Sanders said. "Do you really think there's anything to do in a one-horse town like this?"

"I doubt this town even has one horse," Nerissa snickered.

Lance shrugged and led his party to the mayor.

A late-middle-aged, heavy-set bespectacled man with tufts of brown hair dangling above his ears of an otherwise bald head greeted the adventurers warmly from his desk as they entered his abode cum office. He rose to shake each of their hands.

"Well met, adventurers. My name is Jebediah Brown. It's so good to meet you, folks. We aren't used to getting visitors in this town." He then noticed his uncleanliness and did his best to wipe the crumbs off his white shirt and use some spittle to wipe off some of the stains of his brown vest. The sight slightly nauseated some of the more squeamish party members, chiefly Strefonio and Nerissa.

"I apologize. I'm chained to my desk these days, so all my meals are consumed here."

Lance insisted that none of them were offended. He then explained the purpose of their visit.

The mayor fell back to his chair and wore a nostalgic smile. "Man alive. How long has it been since I've thought about the Chosen One, or even heard the phrase 'Keeper of the Gem'?"

"So you know who it is?" Lance asked.

"Know? I am the 'Keeper of the Gem.'" The mayor pulled a key off a ring connected to the brown leather belt that was having difficulty keeping his brown pantaloons up around his waist. He opened one of the drawers and pulled out a small chest. "This here contains an emerald my father entrusted unto me just like his father entrusted unto him, and so on and so forth."

"Can we have it?" Sanders asked.

"I'd love to just give it to you, but tradition dictates that I give the Chosen One a test."

"Can't we just forego tradition for once?" Nerissa asked.

"I'm afraid not. It's important to ensure that this gem is given to someone truly worthy of the moniker 'Chosen One.'" He pointed at Lance. "For all I know, this gentleman is a charlatan."

"Fine, but what would you have him do?" Sanders asked.

Mayor Brown paused. "That's a good question. I haven't thought about it for years, and I don't mean to be rude, but you haven't exactly come at a great time. We are in the middle of a pretty dire situation right now."

"Are you referring to the caravans?" Lance asked.

"Exactly. The upshot is we have an agreement with the city of Stonewall. They have a surplus of building materials, and we have a surplus of wood, food, and other like resources. We want to expand the city with more modern homes, and they want to eat. Things aren't exactly going to plan right now, though."

"A driver told me the bridge cannot hold even a single caravan."

"He's right. I thought they knew this. However, I talked to Frank, the leader of the caravan, and he was incensed to find out he's going to add some time and distance to his trip. He's going to have to go down about three-hundred miles south, come around, and go another three-hundred miles north. It's at least two months of extra travel."

"Is there nothing else he could do?"

"It's our only option right now. The men of our town are hardly capable of building one that can sustain the weight of several people, nevertheless hold a wagon."

"I'm sure he must have been disappointed to hear that," Alizon said.

"I'm not thrilled either. We're going to have to supply them with food and water, so it's not going to be cheap for us. It'll be worth it overall, but the profit won't be as great as I had hoped. That's not even the worst of it, though. They didn't bring security in the form of militia or mercenaries with them. Instead, they are going to have to move through hostile territory unprotected."

"Hostile from whom?" Lance asked.

"Orcs. They are indiscriminately attacking people who infringe on what they are calling their territory. Undoubtedly their fangs will be salivating when they hear the caravan is from Stonewall."

"Impossible," Lance said. "King Rudolph's great-grandfather signed a treaty with them after they were defeated a century ago. Attacking traders would be considered an act of war."

***

Almost a hundred years ago, a fierce war was fought between the dwarves of Stonewall and the orcs. The dwarves were the clear victors and drove the majority of the orcs west, where they wound up in the woods just outside of Sheepshead. A treaty was signed shortly afterward where the two parties agreed that the hostilities would end if essentially neither side aggravated the other, and so it was thought they would leave each other alone.

During that last century, the people and dwarves of Stonewall had all but forgotten about the old enmity they once had toward their orc rivals. They were far more concerned with trade and mining than they were past wars.

Unlike with their counterparts in Stonewall, though,

all was not forgiven. For the most part, the orcs had been so consumed with the effort of merely surviving that they could not entertain any ideas of reviving old conflicts. Instead, they were waiting for the right time when they had been able to rebuild and then attack anew.

Under King Knaugh, things were once again looking prosperous. There were rumors that the people of Sheepshead and the traders that traveled near served the perfect test bed for their warriors, a sort of dry run to see whether they were ready to fight Stonewall once again.

***

"That is what you say, yet they are attacking us anyway," the mayor continued. "Guston did not care about treaties when he drove the rogue dwarves off our lands fifteen years ago. He always did what was right!" Mayor Brown took off his glasses and rubbed his eyes. "There's a rumor that they are getting away with it because King Knaugh disavows these orcs, claiming they have gone 'rogue.' They are bandits acting outside of his purview. Whether that's true or not is debatable, but it is what's happening." The mayor paused again. "As I speak of this, I have come to know how to test you, and I think it's pretty obvious by this point. Escort the caravan. Defend them from the orcish bandits."

"We accept."

"Seriously? Are we really going to waste the next two months playing wet-nurse?" Sanders asked.

"The wilderness will certainly be good for my hair," Nerissa concurred.

"Though I would have worded it differently, they have a point," Alizon said. "Will we have time to take on this task?"

"The end of the world is looming," Lance said, rubbing

his chin, "Are there no other tasks that would satisfy the exam?"

"Delivering those supplies is imperative for this town's future. I can think of no greater test."

Sanders pulled out his dagger. "I can certainly think of a much better way of getting that gem."

Mayor Brown almost instinctively scurried backward in his seat as the thief inched forward.

Lance stepped in front of Sanders to intervene. He forced an awkward laugh. "Sanders, you loveable rogue, your sense of humor will be the death of us all."

"I wasn't kidding."

Lance forced an even louder and more awkward laugh. He demonstrably put a hand on the hilt of his sword. The thief glared.

Mayor Brown pulled out a dirty handkerchief and wiped his brow. "Quite the sense of humor this young man has."

The sound of the door and a shrill voice interrupted the proceedings. "Hello, darling! How are you?" A dumpy, bejeweled woman in a lavender dress, around the same age as the mayor, with blonde hair and brown eyebrows, entered the room.

"Oh, it's my wife Eleanor," Mayor Brown said. "Hi, honey."

Her presence seemed to deescalate the situation. Sanders sheathed his blade and flashed the woman a smile. She was charmed.

"Who is this dashing young man?" she asked her husband. "Oh, and the rest of his friends."

"I believe that man is Sanders, and the man in front of me is Lance. They have volunteered to escort the caravan so they may deliver their goods, and in exchange, this group shall receive the emerald."

"So this man must be the 'Chosen One,'" she said, playfully placing a couple of crimson fingernails on the thief's chest. "I can see why."

"I'm the Chosen One," Lance corrected.

"Oh. How nice for you."

Sanders scoffed, "He always gets tied up with semantics."

Eleanor's ruby lips curled into a smile, and her hazel eyes gazed on the thief's physique.

Mayor Brown coughed. "Anyway, thank you all very much for your help. I now bid that you please wait by the caravans. We will give you the rations you will need shortly. I wish you all the best. Good luck."

The party clumsily adjourned, though Sanders stayed behind for a moment after the rest of his crew had already walked out the door.

"It was a pleasure to meet you," he said, shaking the mayor's hand. "And you, my dear, it was especially nice meeting you." He grabbed the woman's hand and gave it a gentle kiss, and rubbed her hand and forearm. The woman giggled like a schoolgirl as the mayor hurriedly rushed him out the door under the guise of having a pressing deadline.

The prospect of crossing the bridge again pleased none of the five adventurers. They did so, though, facing the same difficulty as before and the same amount of dampness, perhaps slipping once or twice less than before. Once again, their venture necessitated a quick dry in the summer sun. Afterward, it was time to start their mission.

Lance and his adventurers met with the caravan leader Frank, who was grateful for the assistance he was about to receive. Shortly after, several large men from town crossed the bridge carrying huge sacks containing the promised supplies.

These men seemed to have significantly less difficulty crossing, possibly due to a combination of their strength and being more used to the swaying and the waves, being as they were natives of the town.

Lance could not help but notice the bridge buckled a bit when those men crossed with the extra weight and that Nerissa seemed to be enraptured by a couple of them and made no attempt to hide her enchantment. He brought up his dissatisfaction with this revelation, only to be met with denial and righteous indignation for even being accused. Further attempts at discussion were met with silence.

They moved south. Lance and his party were atop horses that were lent to them. He led the caravan, followed closely by Nerissa and Sanders. Strefonio and Alizon held the rear. Behind them were the wagons. Frank led the first.

Not a day had passed when Sanders reached into his pocket and pulled out a diamond bracelet that sparkled. Nerissa's eyes were drawn to his ill-gotten goods. "Look what I lifted off of that old bag." He handed it to the elf woman. "I think it'd look awfully good on you."

Lance interjected. "Sanders! How dare you steal from that kind woman? She trusted you!"

"Did you see how poor everyone was there, and she dares to flaunt the royal jewels? No doubt Mayor Brown's got his nose in things that would make me look like a choir boy. Besides, I only stole a bracelet. It's not like she'll miss it."

"That is flimsy rationalization."

"You'd feel better if you just think of it as civil disobedience."

"I happen to approve of what Sanders did for me. I think what he's doing is very sweet," Nerissa said. "When's the last time you bequeathed a gift unto me?"

"Nerissa, he stole that bracelet. And besides, I thought you hated gaudy trinkets."

"What do you really know about me, Lance? Sometimes I swear the way you imagine me is different than who I really am. Besides, an exquisite bracelet is hardly a gaudy trinket anyway." She took the bracelet and wore it proudly around her wrist, taking some time to noticeably display it. "I am grateful for the sweet gift, Sanders."

"Lance is right. Stealing is wrong, and gifts are unnecessary when you share each other's love," Alizon asserted.

"What does a fat cow like you know about love? Who could love you? All men love me."

Alizon attempted to whisper to Lance. "Of course they do. She'd spread her legs for anyone who gives her a gift, apparently." She was overheard.

"What did you say, you fat whore?" Nerissa shouted.

***

"Dear gods," Frank muttered to himself. "Our escorts are a bunch of school children. Did we really need to bring them?" He would find his answer much sooner than he expected.

From a distance came green-furred figures with sharp white fangs, riding large horses. Swords and axes were drawn high as they rapidly approached. There weren't many of them, ten at most, but they were crazed and inflamed with anger. Blood seemed to pour from their mouths. Their banshee-like screams filled the air, which forced the drivers to cover their ears.

Frank panicked. He made some meager attempts to get the caravan to act, to form a circle, to do something, but his orders were incoherent. Though he had attempted to mentally prepare himself for this kind of thing, he had never been attacked before and was not prepared for what it truly entailed. His cadre of drivers felt the same.

They would have been doomed if not for Lance and his adventurers.

"To arms," Lance growled. His party drew their weapons or began casting their spells as appropriate to attack.

The orcs were dispatched with ease. Lance rode to a pair and cut them down with a single swing. A flurry of arrows dispatched nearly a half dozen. Strefonio's flames burned a couple more to cinders. Even Sanders got in a few good swipes with his daggers. It was so quick that Alizon found herself with nothing to do.

"That should do it," Lance said once the orcs were defeated. When the drivers realized the threat was over, they let out a jovial and appreciative cheer. A few of the younger men personally congratulated the warriors, especially Nerissa.

"Thank you very much," Frank said. Immaturity aside, at that moment, he was truly glad the group had agreed to accompany his caravan.

***

Yet as the days moved forward, tensions only increased. Sanders constantly derided Lance for his leadership ability, and the knight retorted with criticism of his pilfering ways. When something would appear to be missing, it would cause an argument between the two of them. Finding out where the item had been misplaced did little to ease the anger.

Nerissa often came to Sanders's defense, which never helped the situation, especially when Alizon would come to Lance's defense, spurring a fight between the four of them that would often last the day and well into the night.

Strefonio seemed to be in his own world. He started a friendship with some of the less motivated drivers, and often they would wander off at night only to be missing at dawn. The caravan once burned up an entire day looking for these men and eventually found them in a mushroom field miles from the trail. An extra day was needed to allow them to recover from the fungi's effects.

Things came to a head when Nerissa wanted to take a bath. Over a month had passed. She was dirty and more than a little aggravated. Outside of some infighting and Strefonio's excursion, the trip had been mostly uneventful after the first orc attack, and frankly, to her, seemed like a complete waste of time. The elven woman believed a bath would calm her frayed nerves.

Lance objected. Strefonio and his friends had already cost the caravan some time, and he didn't want any further delays. Plus, though he wouldn't admit it, he did not like the looks some of the younger men were giving her or that she was returning their lascivious leers. Try as he might, he could not slay the green dragon of jealousy.

Alizon agreed that it was a waste of time, which caused yet another shouting match where it was implied that one was too uncivilized and frumpy to be concerned with cleanliness, and the other implied she really liked accompanying men into their beds. Sanders came to her defense and even offered to join her, which made Lance about as happy as one might expect. Strefonio attempted to justify his past behavior to an audience who was growing increasingly apathetic towards this justification.

Frank was attempting to shout down the group, protesting their constant bickering, not just that day but the entire trip, when he saw, coming over a hill, a score of green-haired creatures approaching rapidly, riding their large stallions. Their mannerisms were even more crazed, more intense than before. Their hostility was greater, as were their numbers. There were at least three times as many as there were in the previous attack.

The squabbling had left them vulnerable to the impending orc attack.

Frank made an effort to order his caravan to take evasive maneuvers, but his orders were even less effective than last time. Terror gripped their hearts even more so than during the last attack because it was readily apparent that their guardians were unprepared, and the orcs quickly surrounded the caravan.

Nerissa made a mad scramble for her bow. She tripped a bit over the clothes, as she had partially disrobed, and her running was interrupted by her pulling up her pants. When she finally managed to reach her bow and quiver, she could not find an appropriate distance to shoot her bow. Effectively, her contribution to the fight was running away as well as possible, which proved especially difficult as she was on foot while her foes were on horseback.

Lance did not attempt to get to his horse and instead flailed wildly at the orcs on foot. His sword reached a target rather consistently, whether it was a horse's head or an orc's arm. Regardless, it was an effective method of reducing their numbers. His amulet also aided quite a bit during this skirmish.

A few of the orc's attacks did land, but the quick-thinking Alizon cast a spell that protected that young man and the rest of her companions, which in turn bought Strefonio enough time to cast a burst of flame spells that rapidly vanquished the marauding horde.

Sanders mostly played support this battle. He apprehended a couple of horses from fallen riders and rode them to Nerissa and Lance, which provided the elf the ability to gain some distance on her foes and play a part in the battle, and made the knight much more effective.

Attacks came from all sides. Screams were coming from everywhere. Lance had difficulty discerning which ones were coming from his allies or the men he and his group were supposed to protect and which were coming from the orcs. The whole scene became engulfed in a fog of miasma.

Yet, their vigilance eventually paid off. Their actions soon made efficient work of the orcs. More and more continued to fall until a couple of arrows from Nerissa downed the final two enemies. The battle was over. Lance and his group were the victors.

"Excellent work, everyone," Lance said when things had settled down.

"Considering I was literally caught with my pants down," Nerissa said, "I think I did as well as was expected. I'd like to thank you for bringing me that lovely stallion, Sanders."

Sanders beamed. "Anything for you."

"I'm just glad I could like contribute this time," Strefonio admitted.

"As am I," Alizon said.

"Both of you did wonderfully," Lance said. "All of you did. Now, let us report to Frank." He led the group back to the caravan, somewhat expecting to receive accolades.

However, there was no cheering.

Instead, they found the drivers formed in a circle. Lance asked them the reason why they gathered in such a manner, but none would answer. Their eyes were transfixed on what was in the center of their circle.

Lance pushed a pair aside and moved toward the center, followed closely by his companions. They stopped in their tracks when they witnessed the grizzly scene.

Frank stood over two men. One stared into the sky with

lifeless eyes and a deep gash across the throat. The other lay on his stomach, a leg and an arm missing. His face was mutilated to the point it would have been difficult to recognize him as human. Both were obviously dead.

"This is your fault," Frank growled.

"How is this our fault?" Sanders asked.

"If you weren't bickering with each other like children, you would have been paying attention and prepared for an attack."

"That is complete and utter balderdash," Nerissa snarled. "You knew you were riding through adverse territory, and we were ambuscaded. We are not responsible for your deaths. We're the only reason most of you are still alive!"

"We're like, sorry about the dead dudes and stuff, but this isn't our fault," Strefonio said.

"These aren't just dead dudes!" Frank screamed. "These were friends! These were fathers with families! What will I tell their widows in Stonewall?"

"I assume they knew the risks," Sanders said.

"They expected to be home over a month ago! They expected a bridge! They expected you to be able to protect us!"

"And like, we have," Strefonio said. "Er, mostly."

"We're doing you a favor by accompanying you on this journey," Nerissa said. "We could have left you to fend for yourselves. We're doing you a favor."

"No, you are doing this for a gem." He rubbed his eyes. "If you want to do me a favor, hunt down those orcs, so we may receive justice and vengeance."

"We can't," Lance said. "King Rudolph signed a treaty."

"They violated that treaty. It is now null and void."

"These were the actions of wayward orcs. I do not wish to cause another war. My hands are tied."

Frank sighed deeply. He stared at the corpses that were once colleagues. An awkward silence enveloped. "Fine," he finally said. "I suppose I have no choice. Give us some time to honor the dead, and we'll figure out the rest."

A proper burial and a short ceremony were given to the deceased. Afterward, Sanders and Strefonio had to take over the driving duties. This delayed the journey a little bit more than it had already, as the two awkwardly fumbled their way through something they had never done before. The travel delays meant Frank, the most experienced with such matters, had to further ration supplies. This left everyone hungrier, thirstier, and crankier, yet at least able to survive.

***

After slightly more than two months and two weeks, their journey was complete, having gone below the river and back north to the main part of town. Frank led the party into the town hall. Mayor Brown wore a large grin when he first noticed them. When he saw the expressions on their faces, though, his smile quickly evaporated. He stumbled over the words as he spoke.

"W…welcome back, everyone. How'd…did it go?"

"Two of my men died. I want financial compensation."

"B…but, I mean, I'm sorry for your loss, but you were riding through hostile territory. I don't think it's fair to—"

Frank slammed his hands against the table, interrupting Mayor Brown mid-sentence. The man stared daggers into the mayor's soul. He growled, "We were only going through there because your backwater little burg couldn't build a proper bridge. The adventurers you sent were supposed to protect them. Now, I'm going to have to tell two wives and their children that their husbands and fathers won't be coming home. I just want some money to give them so they can last through the winter, all right?"

The mayor nodded. He reached into his pouch and started placing coins on the table. He did not stop until Frank told him he had been properly remunerated.

"Thanks," he said coldly, "I suppose that'll do. Once everything's been unpacked, we'll be leaving."

"Shall we make arrangements for the future?" the mayor asked.

Frank scoffed. "No, we shall not. It will be a cold day in hell before Stonewall agrees to trade with Sheepshead again."

"Surely you cannot let one bad experience taint —"

Frank held up his arm. "Stop. It's not just the loss of lives. The trip is simply too long and way too costly. Because I can't trust these escorts anymore, we're going to have to take the long route home to the southeast, which will mean we're essentially trading at a loss at this point. To do this again is completely impractical."

Frank turned and left the distraught mayor without saying anything else. As far as he was concerned, the conversation was over, and there was nothing more to say.

***

Lance and Alizon helped the men unpack while the rest of the party and Mayor Brown watched. After everything was unloaded, the leader of the caravan purchased food and supplies they would need on their trip home and, as he said he would, led his caravan toward the southeast instead of the southwest. It was much longer but also much safer.

A dejected Mayor Brown led the party back to his office once all else was complete. His wife had made it back to the office by this time, having earlier been visiting a friend. Her overt flirtation toward the thief was this time met with a cold, bitter glare. She backed off, wondering what had made his eyes seem so hateful and full of disdain.

The mayor opened the drawer, pulled out the chest, unlocked it, and handed Lance the stone.

"Well done, Lance," the mayor said unenthusiastically. "You and the rest of your party have passed the test. You have proven that you are worthy of having this emerald and are worthy of the title 'Chosen One.'"

"Are you all right?" Lance asked.

The mayor sighed. "Of course. I suppose we have enough brick and ore for one windmill at least. It would have been nice for this town to advance, but then again, there is nothing wrong with it being the same as it ever was, as it has been since time immemorial." He paused. "If only we had an engineer."

Lance stared, trying desperately hard to come up with comforting words. Nothing sprung to mind.

"We have the stone, Lance. I think we can go."

Nerissa's words woke Lance from his trance. The adventurers left the town hall, and the knight checked the map. It showed an arrow leading to question marks with a label that said Hidden Elf Village. Only a native elf or those who knew one would have any idea where to go next.

"I think the next place we need to go is Ylaserine," Lance said. "Luckily, we've got you, Nerissa, to lead us there."

"Yes, lucky us," she sighed.

Lance looked toward the sky. Another crack, a small one, had formed. The sky was an even darker hue. He made a feeble attempt to point it out to his companions, only to be met with the same resistance as before. The knight quickly dropped the subject and continued onward.

They exited the town the same way they had come in,

across that long, wretched bridge one last time, one stone richer and one step closer to unlocking the sword necessary to defeat the evil Al Kahim.

Chapter 4

A few miles from the city of Limegate, about seventy-five miles north of Sheepshead, was the beautiful Shelcouche Lake. Adjacent to it was the sprawling Evergreen Forest, large enough to be considered a type of city unto itself. Within that forest was a glen, and within that glen was a very specific grove that encompassed the hidden elven home of Ylaserine.

Finding that village was a daunting task, even for the most experienced trailblazer. Navigation required deciphering very specific landmarks, which was an incredibly difficult task as these markers were so carefully placed it was virtually impossible to determine whether a certain fallen tree or rock formation was a guiding needle or the random placement by Mother Nature herself.

There was no true entrance. The village was only accessible by an unmarked trail through a specific set of trees at the end of the grove. Arcane magic lost to the current generation of elves prevented random visits, as travelers that did not follow a specific path were whisked out, oblivious that anything had happened, thinking only that they had reached the end of the forest. A countless number of individuals journeyed through that forest, unaware that such a town existed within.

A guide was a necessity. Preferably someone who had been there before, a native if at all possible. They had one in Nerissa. She had guided them before when her village was in trouble a year ago and agreed to do so again that day. That is not to say she was exactly joyful about it, though.

"I got you here. I can't believe you couldn't remember anything."

Lance took one last look at the crude map he'd scrawled from the last expedition. "The trail is incredibly difficult, my love, and I guess my cartography is lacking."

"It's all right, Lance. We found it easily enough," Alizon said.

"Shut up! It's not that tough. He needs to learn to map already."

The knight promised he would work on his skills.

There was something magical about the elven village. Perhaps it wasn't true magic, but there was certainly something enchanting. Homes appeared to have originated from a bygone era, using only the most efficient construction techniques utilizing as little wood as possible. Ornateness seemed to be a foreign concept. Everything was centralized. There was a communal atmosphere. It could be best described as a quaintness that would be foreign to any city denizen.

Many villagers looked at the outsiders quizzically. Undoubtedly they were thankful for their assistance not even a year prior, but the historically isolated villagers still felt diffident toward uninvited, or for that matter, invited, guests. Lance made several attempts to hail them and start a discussion, but they would often dart their eyes away and feign they were busy with some trifle.

A few friendly ones did emerge. Friends the party had made during their last outing were more than happy to welcome them back to their homes, though they were disappointed that three of the knight's party seemed to not share their exuberance.

After a brief reminiscence of past adventures, Lance discussed his predicament. They led him to the royal courtier, who introduced himself as Eldaerenth. He was a late middle-aged elf with long, thick silver air and age lines across his face, wearing a dark blue button-up coat, a white undershirt, and beige pants. After a brief discussion of the issue, he agreed that this was a matter that needed to be attended to by the king.

"That is to say," the courtier added as he led the group to the regal home, "His son Prince Nasir. I'm afraid King Kymil has fallen quite ill."

"Dreadful!" Lance gasped. "How bad is it?"

"It is not my place to say. I will let Prince Nasir explain." He stopped and called out through the door. "Lance is here, my lord. He wishes to speak to you."

Lance noticed this the last time he visited, but he was still struck by its modesty. In most places, especially in the expansive metropolis that was Angenehm, the facility would hardly have been considered anything more than a hut, yet it was nearly twice the size of the Ylaserine's other homes. The only edifice that rivaled its size was the tavern, which doubled as the town center.

"Allow him to enter." Lance's elven friend motioned toward the door.

There was only room for one other person. Three others were inside, so the home was near capacity.

"Do we have to wait out here?" Nerissa asked. "Or can we do our own thing while we wait?"

"I suppose you can go off on your own," Lance said, removing his helmet so he could scratch his head.

"Great, there's an old friend I want to visit. A man I am sure is still in great physical condition."

"Ah, so you wish to see whether he'll aid us in our quest."

"Um, yeah, sure, why not?" With that, the elven maiden practically ran to a nearby home.

"I guess I'll be off too," the wizard said. "I heard a rumor of someone here who has some, let's say, wares I might be interested in." He set off, seemingly in an aimless direction, and disappeared.

Sanders excused himself as well. He said he had some business expenditures to discuss at a nearby tavern. What this entailed, he refused to elaborate.

Alizon assured the knight she would wait outside for his return. The knight thanked her and entered the home.

King Kymil lay in a bed in the middle of the room. He was in terrible shape, not at all than the vibrant man he had been when Lance had last met him. The knight remembered him sitting on his throne proudly, virile and strong, donning his flowing viridian and gold robe and a wooden branch crown resting upon his head. Previously he was healthy enough to gather an army, to lead a charge, to guide his people to victory. Now, he looked near death.

The beautiful Queen Axilya, wearing her lavender gown, her flaxen hair covering her eyes, sat next to her husband, gently weeping on the opposite side of the bed. A royal seal with a gnarled oak tree hung over the bed. Other humble trinkets made out of wood decorated the walls, and a wooded mat lay on the floor.

Prince Nasir was standing tall and proud next to his father. The black and gold tunic displayed his unusually, for an elf, muscular frame, and even his legs and feet seemed to bulge from his black pants and brown boots. Strength exuded from the man, as well as a recognizable dignity and integrity. The prince was somebody one would be proud to have as a leader or a friend.

"Welcome back, Chosen One," the prince said. "As you might have guessed, we are still not used to visitors, nevertheless regulars."

"I've only been here once before."

"Anytime anyone visits again within a year is considered a regular in Ylaserine."

"Worry not, Chosen One, we trust you, like we haven't trusted anyone since I was about my son's age," the queen said. "Not since the Goblin Slayer have we trusted someone as much as we trust you."

"Who was this Goblin Slayer?" Lance asked.

"He was before my day, but I have heard the stories, and his exploits are legendary," the prince explained. "He's the one that drove the invading goblins out of our homes when my father first took the throne. I'm sure you've heard of him. His name is Guston."

"Indeed, I have heard that name many times."

"We know not where or why he disappeared but know this. Should he ever return, we'd welcome him with open arms. Now's not the time to reminisce, however. We should discuss the matter at hand, as difficult as it is for me to talk about it. We do not know the cause of my father's sudden malady, nor have our healers been able to find a cure. Alas, hope is all but lost." The prince paused for a second, taking a moment to look at his father before his eyes returned to Lance.

"Our legends speak of iocilsoo root, which is said to be a panacea that can cure any ailment. It is said to be about the size of a child and purple. The veracity of such a claim is dubious, to say the least, but it may be our only hope. I regret to say the only place iocilsoo grows is Orianna's Grotto, which, due to its nefarious reputation, has been nicknamed by many as 'Death's Alcove.' It is located on a beach not far from here. In the past, we have sent several search parties for the root, but I dare say none have ever returned."

His eyes turned toward a locked chest in the far corner before he continued. "My father entrusted me with the gem two years ago on my sixteenth birthday. I am quite familiar with its legacy, and it is not something I take lightly. Responsibility mandates that I provide you a trial, and though this is a selfish request, I believe you'll agree it is adequate. Instead of sending more young men to die, I will send you in their stead. Bring me the root, and I shall grant you the stone."

Lance enthusiastically agreed.

The prince had a short discussion with the courtier at the door. He set off and returned with another man. Prince Nassir told Lance that this man would serve as his guide. Much like the entrance to the village, finding the alcove required taking a very specific path. Prince Nasir wished the knight luck, then returned to his father.

Lance needed to gather his party. Alizon was easy to find. She was where she said she would be. Sanders bumped into Lance walking out of the town's tavern after having shaken hands with a shady individual. The young knight inquired about the nature of their conversation, but the gentleman thief was able to dodge his questions.

Strefonio wandered into the trio, not noticing them until he literally bumped into the knight. His mind was preoccupied with the contents of his bag.

A large elvish man emerged from a nearby home, accompanied by Nerissa. One arm was draped over his shoulder. She leaned and whispered something into his ear that amused him to no end. However, upon seeing her group, she displayed not surprise but more of a mild disappointment. She wore the bemused smile of a child having to return to class after playtime ended.

"Is he a suitable ally for our adventure?" Lance asked.

"Hmmm? Oh yes, right, of course. Um, no, he's not suitable at all. A terrible fighter. More a lover — a pacifist, I mean."

"I see." Lance shrugged, not quite sure what to make of her statement. He had more pressing matters to deal with regardless.

The elven guide led them through a narrow patch of woods, over a very specific rock formation, and across a few specific parts of a stream to lead them to the edge of the woods, where it opened up to a red-sanded beach. "This is as far as I will take you," the courtier said. "If you can find a path to your right, there is the cave we have nicknamed Death's Alcove. It is right next to the ocean."

Danger was readily apparent. The beach crawled with giant crab-like creatures with human-faced shells. Their razor-sharp claws made mincemeat out of a poor gull that foolishly landed on the beach, hoping to find a discarded fish carcass for a meal. Its corpse was greedily devoured by several of these creatures, exhibiting that these weren't typical decapods.

Accompanying them were gelatinous creatures with long tentacles. Their appendages bent at awkward angles that somehow produced horizontal locomotion. Small, electric bolts were generated with every motion.

One of the gangly things bumped into one of the crabs. Incensed, the crab attacked. A large bolt of electricity shot through the tentacles in retaliation. An electric corpse was all that was left. None of the other crustaceans were foolish enough to provoke another of the strange jellies.

Lance and his party noticed some large objects next to the water. They gasped almost collectively when they realized they were decaying elven corpses.

On Lance's orders, the adventurers set to work. Nerissa reluctantly shot her arrows, insisting the hard shells and gooey nature of the other sea creatures would make such efforts futile. She was correct. The arrows went right through the viscid upper bodies and deflected off the hard shells.

"Told you it was pointless," Nerissa muttered. The knight insisted that it was useful to determine the types of resistances these monsters possessed.

Lance then told Strefonio to cast fireball spells at the enemies. After consuming a mushroom, he did as he was told. The flames were met with resistance. Fire had no more effect than the arrows when it came to penetrating the shells. The viscous nature of the other made it as if Strefonio was trying to set ablaze the ocean.

The knight took a swing at one of the crabs with his sword. His blade was met with claws. A bit of a struggle occurred, but Lance managed to flip one to its back, exposing its soft abdomen. Lance plunged his blade. The creature was no more.

"Hard shells, soft body," Sanders said. The thief hopped from side to side, narrowly avoiding the claws and quickly flipping over each crab with his dagger before they had a chance to resist. Then, he ordered Nerissa to fire her arrows to quickly dispose of her enemies. She complied, and dozens of the creatures were slain.

"At least someone is smart enough to come up with an actual plan," Nerissa said. "He looks so graceful too."

"Lance is the one who actually figured it out, though," Alizon insisted.

"Whatever, wench! Sanders is also graceful as he moves," Nerissa swooned.

Soon all the crabs were dispatched, and all that was left were the gelatinous creatures.

"How do we deal with those things?" Nerissa asked.

"If fire doesn't work, what about ice?" Sanders suggested. "Strefonio, freeze the creatures. Lance, grab a tree branch, and bash them when they are frozen."

Lance paused for a moment. He considered ignoring these orders and coming up with new ones. He wondered whether it was prudent for a leader to take commands from his subordinate.

He relented. It was a good plan, and he didn't want to let pride get in its way. He'd just ignore the besotted look on his beloved's face as she stared at the thief.

Ice flew from the wizard's hands, and the branch fell atop the frozen hydrozoans, shattering each of them into a thousand little pieces. The knight tossed aside his makeshift club when the last creature was defeated.

The courtier watched the systematic decimation of these creatures with awe. He started to think that perhaps they stood a chance against the creature in the cave.

"We won!" Alizon exclaimed.

"What are you so happy about?" Nerissa scolded. "You didn't do anything."

"I mean, if anybody is hurt, I'd be happy to —"

"We're fine."

"Harsh words are unnecessary, my beloved. We should take joy as a team that our foes have been vanquished," Lance said.

"Let's just go. And why do you always insist on speaking that way? Not everything requires flowery speech."

The adventurers followed the coast until they reached the cave, doing their best to ignore the horror that was the putrefying bodies. A low rumble was heard, and the ground shook slightly. Overhead, seagulls were flying in erratic patterns as if avoiding something. A couple of the birds fell suddenly. Lance dismissed it as his imagination, but he could have sworn they bumped into something.

Alizon cast her light spell, and the fivesome entered the cave.

Several unusually fast black tortoise-like creatures with razor-sharp teeth attacked as they made their way ever deeper into that cavern. A slice of the blade through the creature's heads made by both Lance's sword and Sanders's dagger made quick work of these foes. Despite the cave's foreboding name, the cavern seemed relatively serene, if not a bit too quiet.

Then the danger became readily apparent.

"Ow, son of a—" Lance tripped, but he did not know over what. He was in front of his group, and in his haste, walked too far away from Alizon, which negated her spell's illumination. When she and the rest of his party caught up to him, the knight was startled by the revelation.

It was an elven cadaver. How long it had been dead, Lance could not even begin to guess, but judging from its smell, it could not have been for very long. The body was damp to the touch. As Alizon shined her light deeper into the cave, an increasing number of corpses in varying states of decay began to appear. Some were skeletons, some were only visible from the remnants of the clothes that lay on the ground, and some were still decomposing. Lance presumed that the most recent corpses were those trying to fetch the root for their king. All the bodies were soaked.

A palpable apprehension consumed the group. Lance reminded them they had been through worse. This did little to reassure them. Luckily for them, they did not have too much time to dwell on their dire situation.

A large, concentrated stream of water shot toward the party of five from the final chamber. They desperately dashed aside and placed their backs against the walls. The water barely missed them, but they were able to avoid this first attack.

"What was that?" Strefonio asked. His allies were too busy concentrating on keeping their backs against the wall, acting more out of instinct than rationality as they shuffled forward to answer his question. The wizard would receive his answer when they reached the final chamber.

A giant terrapin met them, which let out a gigantic, nasally scream. A strange thing was growing on its back, a thick and twisted purple and brown plant. It appeared to be half as tall as Lance. Its shape and how it grew evoked the image of distorted human limbs.

"The root," Alizon suggested. She was right. The iocilsoo grew on the creature's back. How such a thing was possible baffled them, though they did not have long to think about it too deeply.

A concentrated beam of water shot from the terrapin's beak. The party of five barely managed to avoid the stream, moving deftly to the side. Lance assisted the two women, while

Sanders and Strefonio did their best not to get in each other's way.

"Spread out!" Lance instructed. It was a good plan. The creature's large stature in a relatively small cave made it practically impossible for it to maneuver. Moving to various corners of the room would ensure they would avoid the head. As long as they managed to avoid going underneath one of its appendages, there was time to think of a plan—or so one might assume.

The terrapin pulled its four limbs and its head into the shell, which fell hard, causing a loud crashing noise to reverberate off the walls as the ground shook violently. Nobody managed to stay on their feet. Its head and feet then reemerged, none of the parts where they originally were.

Strefonio, who thought he was safe by the creature's left leg, now faced its head. He leaped but could not completely avoid the rushing water. The wizard was slammed against the cave's walls, his left leg and right arm bent awkwardly. Strefonio could then do nothing but lie on the ground and moan.

A panic ensued. Alizon dashed toward him to get in range to cast her healing spells, only to be thwarted by the creature. He had shuffled his limbs once again, and now his head faced the white mage.

Nerissa fired in a stupor. Her wayward arrows deflected against the carapace. Some hit their target, but even the softer legs and head seemed unfazed by her bolts.

Lance hacked away but had little luck as well. His slashes were like pinpricks or stepping on a child's toy, annoying but nothing more.

Sanders was the only one thinking rationally. He had assessed the creature's weakness. "Like I said earlier, hard shell, soft body!"

Drawing his dagger, the thief rolled under the terrapin, merely about a foot from the creature's body. He stabbed it. The creature let out a manic scream. The thief rolled back before he was crushed when the creature retracted its four limbs and head and slammed against the ground.

"Lance, we'll need some time if we are going to slay this creature. You're going to have to lift it when it pulls its body parts inside."

"Are you giving me orders again?"

"We have no time to argue! Just do it!"

"I'm not sure I'm strong enough."

"Don't you remember? Your amulet will provide you extra strength!"

Lance reluctantly crawled under the creature, scuffling on his stomach as he barely had room to do anything else. He used his elbows to lift himself up and slowly moved his hands underneath the creature as he raised the terrapin over his head.

The creature, as predicted, moved its four appendages inside its shell. Lance managed to hold him up, barely. He was not completely upright. His knees were bent, and his legs and arms shook. The amulet around his neck glowed and provided him extra strength. Yet even then, he would not be able to hold the creature upright for very long.

"Do it now!" Lance growled.

Sanders crawled under on his knees and made several cuts with his dagger. Nerissa joined him, using one of her arrows as a makeshift knife.

Alizon, after using the distraction to heal her wizard friend, also joined to cast a couple of her spells to provide whatever boost she could provide the knight and to heal the muscles and nerves that were tearing under that enormous weight.

Strefonio, on the other hand, was still recovering from the attack. Physically he was fine, but mentally he needed a break. At least that was how he justified partaking in a few mushrooms rather than accompanying his friends.

His assistance was ultimately not required. The creature's abdomen was soon ripped to shreds. As its innards fell on the floor, the creature became lighter, which made it possible for Lance to flip the creature against the wall, exposing its stomach as it lay awkwardly on its side.

Lance proceeded to finish the job. The terrapin let out one more exasperated howl before it breathed its last. The knight fell to a knee, gasping for breath. It was a hard-fought but well-earned victory.

Nerissa ran over. Lance extended his arms in anticipation, but she passed him. Her arms wrapped around Sanders. The thief, the knight, and the mage stared, befuddled. Strefonio was still oblivious.

"That was brilliant!" she shouted.

"Thanks," Sanders said, rubbing the back of his head.

"Don't I get one, my love?" Lance asked. He did do the bulk of the work, after all, and, more importantly, she was his betrothed.

"Yes. Of course." She unwrapped her arms slowly and lumbered over to her fiancé, putting her arms around him briefly. For a moment, nothing was said.

"What'd I miss?" Strefonio's head finally cleared enough for him to join them. None of them bothered to explain.

"We should retrieve the iocilsoo," Alizon said, piercing the awkward silence. Lance and the rest of them agreed.

The knight shoved the creature off the wall. It landed with a nauseating and hollow thud. Lance carefully scaled the slimy carapace. When he reached the top, he had trouble with his footing. A sword swipe proved to be impossible. Instead, he had to use his sword as an improvised saw. It was akin to cutting through bone. The endeavor unsettled Lance's stomach.

Once the deed was done, he slid down with the shell root in hand. Now on solid ground, he hacked the root to pieces with his sword, an endeavor he found quite simple now so that it could fit in his pack. It was time to go.

They exited the cavern. Strefonio laughed to himself as they walked. Sanders swaggered. Alizon's face expressed concern. Lance attempted a conversation with his future wife. Nerissa had none of it, seemingly more interested in the thief than her husband-to-be. She remarked that Lance was not the only one who could come up with imaginative plans.

The courtier was flabbergasted to see them again and even more surprised at their success. This time he really did cheer. Lance and his crew had difficulty keeping up with him as he dashed through the complicated trail to return to Ylaserine.

"Sire! Sire!" he shouted as he reentered the village. "They have returned with the root!"

The prince popped his head out the door. "They have?" He summoned his best healer to retrieve the various parts of the root from Lance. The medicine man went into his home, and after a brief period, emerged with a powder. In the king's anemic state, the root's parts needed to be ground down so they could be consumed.

Prince Nasir took the powder and dashed to his father's side, with Lance right behind. His father was in terrible shape. The king's complexion had worsened. His breaths were few and far between. His mother, Lance was told, had to be removed from his father's side. She had become hysterical with grief.

The prince bade his father to open his mouth. He had to ask several times before he complied. King Kymil's mind was fading. He struggled to hear his son's words. Comprehension was even more difficult.

Like sands from an hourglass, Prince Nasir poured the iocilsoo powder onto his father's tongue. He pushed it in gently, lifted his father, and massaged it down his throat.

King Kymil's eyes widened. He sat up, completely upright, and stared at his son for a moment, then at Lance, then back to his son. He smiled. For but a brief second, the prince was overjoyed.

Then the king fell back down to his bed. He was dead before his head hit the pillow.

A sorrowful wail escaped the prince's lips. He fell to his knees by his father's side and held him in his arms. He could do nothing but sob.

Lance fled the room, avoided his friends, and moved toward the back of the home, his emotions overwhelmed. He wasn't sure why these feelings emerged. The young man had not known either of them for long, and though the incident was sad, to be gripped with such sorrow surprised him.

It took him a while, but eventually, the knight was able to shake it off. He wiped his eyes and took some time to breathe, letting the sadness pass. The knight reminded himself that he needed to be strong for his elven companion.

Several minutes had passed when Lance reentered. He found that the prince had composed himself, though his eyes were still puffy from the tears.

"I appreciate you leaving me alone in my time of grief. I also would like to apologize for my lack of composure there. I am pleased that my mother is not here if only so she would not have to witness that horrible display. Breaking the news to her will not be a pleasant experience, I must confess."

"Perhaps I could do it for you?"

"Quite kind of you to offer, but no, this is something I must do. However, there is a matter I must attend to first."

He pulled a key from his pouch and unlocked the chest sitting in the corner. The prince pulled out a ruby and handed it to Lance.

Lance was flummoxed. "You're still giving this to me?"

"You fulfilled your end of the bargain admirably. It is not your fault our legend turned out to be false. My father was quite unwell. I was merely hoping for a miracle."

The knight thanked the prince for his generosity.

"If you will forgive my rudeness, I must ask you and your friends to leave. I have many matters to attend to now that concern my people specifically, and I believe your presence will only conjure unnecessary stress."

The knight agreed. Besides, he had other matters to attend to as well.

Lance exited the home. He informed his party of the death.

"That poor man and his family too," Alizon said.

"Yeah, poor guy, so sad," said Nerissa.

"I'm surprised you are not more affected. Does this matter not concern you specifically, having been originally from this town?"

"Look, you flabby tart, I have been out of this town for over a year now, and even then, I never really had much love for it. I only fetched help because I didn't really feel like dying that day, you hear me? It's sad that he's dead, but I don't really care much about politics, okay?"

"Okay, I'm sorry. I didn't mean to hit a nerve."

"The only nerves you hit were in my ears whenever I have

to hear you screech."

"Enough," Sanders interjected. "Let's just get going. We've wasted enough time."

Lance silently agreed and checked his map. The next and last town they needed to travel to was Tortuil.

He looked up at the sky. A little bit darker still and another crack had formed. This time he did not even bother to inform his group.

The five of them left the village, a pair of them with heavy hearts. They were one stone richer and one step closer to unlocking the sword necessary to defeat the evil Al Kahim.

Chapter 5

About a hundred miles to the southeast of Ylaserine was the tiny little burg of Tortuil. Though it was on the main thoroughfare and was able to sneak its way onto a few maps here or there, it was so remote that to most people, it may as well have been another hidden elf village. It was so small that Sheepshead seemed like a bustling metropolis in comparison. Tortuil was only composed of a few cottages to the east and a couple of homesteads to the west. Those who knew about the town thought of it as the eastern edge of the kingdom, with Angenehm being the western edge, though this was not literally true in either case, as there were a few little hamlets to the west of the capital and a major town, Stonewall, to the east of Tortuil.

There was an expression that the sands of time moved oppressively for all but the town of Tortuil, owing to its languorous nature, being the most reluctant of the kingdom's towns to gentrify. This was not necessarily out of protest or any sort of moral conviction. It was simply unnecessary. The crops were plentiful. The seclusion made it resistant to invaders. The people were by and large happy. There was no reason to change.

A common expression amongst the other towns of the kingdom was there were only three guarantees in life — death, taxes, and Tortuil being the same farming community it always was.

"This place must be free of crime," Sanders groaned. "There's nothing worth stealing."

"It's the perfect place to hide something," Nerissa concurred, "Because who'd want to be here?"

"Is there, like, anything to even do in this town?" Strefonio asked rhetorically.

"I don't know. I kind of like it," Alizon said.

"You would," Nerissa sneered.

"What on earth could you possibly like about this place?" Sanders asked.

"It's quaint," the mage said. "It seems like the kind of place where someone could raise a family without worrying about the stresses of modern life. It's the kind of place where everyone knows everyone else. I bet you everyone here is friendly too."

For the most part, she was correct. Several people greeted them, and most of them could talk the party's ear off. Lance's multiple pleas to excuse themselves were ignored. Not out of malice, but due to the excitement of having someone new with whom to converse.

They discussed at length the new addition to the Carver family. The Miller's older of their two sons was already showing interest in swordplay and horse riding. Young Alan's attempts to woo the fair Catherine was a hot topic of conversation.

Lance was polite but made every effort to steer the conversation toward his objective. "I don't mean to be rude," he said. "As I am sure under different circumstances, we would love to talk to you more about these topics at length."

"Speak for yourself," muttered Nerissa to a laughing Sanders.

Lance ignored them and continued. "But I must insist that you lead me to the Keeper of the Gem. We must speak to him."

"He must be referring to Roger," said one of the elderly women.

"What he puts his wife Megan through is criminal," said another elderly woman.

"Hush, you two!" a third woman said. "We don't know it to be true, and we should not discuss such matters with strangers." She pointed to a nearby house in a row of cottages. "He be over there."

Lance thanked her and summoned the rest of his party to the man's home. He raised his gauntleted hand into the air and gave the door two solid knocks.

A middle-aged woman opened the door slightly. Only her head was visible, as her body seemed to be hidden in the shadows. Her brown hood obscured much of her face. Her most noticeable feature was her left eye. It was black and swollen, with bruising all around. The wound seemed fresh.

"Hello?" she said meekly.

"Are you all right?" Lance asked.

"I'm fine," she said quickly. "Everything's fine. Is that it?"

"Well, no. We were told that a man named Roger lived here. I presume he's your husband?"

"Yes, he is. I'll go get him." She closed the door abruptly.

Lance and his companions could hear a male voice yelling through the walls. "Now, what the hell are you bothering me for? Can't you see I'm busy? I'm not drunk. I just had a couple of drinks! Yeah, I drank there too. It's a tavern. What do you expect?

Some people at the door? Why didn't you get rid of them? I have to do everything, don't I? Keeper of what now? That nonsense my father used to tell me? They're here for that? Of all the stupid things."

The sounds of furniture colliding with the ground were heard before the door was opened. A mussy brown-haired man with a gruff face and piercing hazel eyes spoke through the crack. "What do you want?"

"Are you Roger, the Keeper of the Gem?"

"Nope, goodbye."

Lance's hand caught the door before it could close. "Please, an elderly woman directed me here and told me this is where I could find the Keeper. My name is Lance. I have been ordered by the king to collect the gems, so I could retrieve Artus's Sword and save the world from Al Kahim."

"Lance. Where have I heard that name before?" The man's head jerked suddenly. "Ah, crap, you mean King Rudolph, right? You're the guy he's been calling the Chosen One. Shit, all right, you caught me. I'm Roger, Keeper of the Gem, or whatever. It's an amethyst. I can get it for you."

"Aren't you supposed to give me a test?"

Nerissa slapped him on the shoulder, and Sanders slapped him on the back of the head, and then reeled a bit when he realized he'd hit his helmet. Both of them called the young man an "idiot."

"Ah, right, test. Shit, Dad told me about that. Let me think." His eyes darted all over until they focused on an area of land just outside of town. He pointed to it.

"Got it. There's a catoblepas not too far from here in that prairie over yonder. He's been terrorizing the town. Kill it, and the gem is yours."

"Why didn't any of the townsfolk bring it up, or even yourself for that matter?"

"Oh yeah, I mean, we're so scared of it that none of us like talking about it, and we didn't want to involve strangers, you know, 'cause uh, it's our problem, not yours. It doesn't feel right to drag anyone else into it, you know?"

"Ah, yes, of course. How very noble of you. We shall gladly accept your task. We shall return victorious and provide you the horns of the creature as proof of our victory."

"Okay, sure, whatever."

Alizon voice piped up. "Excuse me. I know it's not my place to ask, but I'm wondering, is your wife all right? What happened?"

Roger growled. "You're right. It is not your place to ask, so hush woman!"

"Answer her question." Lance glared into the man's eyes with such ferocity that he began to shake.

"Yes, okay, um, so that catoblepas or whatever attacked my wife, and she fell on her face."

"Why didn't you mention that?" Alizon asked.

"I, uh, didn't want you to, uh, think this task was like, personal, or anything."

Alizon glared skeptically. Lance smiled with a relieved obliviousness and said, "I must confess you exhibit nobility that your initial appearance belied."

"Nah, I'm just a farmer, not noble at all."

Lance tried to explain what he meant, but Roger's eyes glazed before he could finish his explanation.

"As lovely as all this is, we're burning daylight, so let's just kill yet another creature," Sanders said.

"He's right. We shall return soon."

"All right."

The five rode their way toward the prairie, and as they did so, the members conversed.

"We could have avoided this all had you not insisted on a test," Sanders chastised.

"You are such an idiot, Lance," Nerissa concurred.

"He's not an idiot, Nerissa. He's just trying to do the right thing," Alizon defended.

"Like, I'm shocked you're defending him," Strefonio, the sardonic wizard, answered.

"I apologize for what may seem to be a miscalculation on my part, but the tests are part of the prophecy," Lance explained. "I worry what might happen if we do not follow it precisely."

"If you say so, Chosen One," Nerissa sighed.

"Hey, guys, what do you think about Megan?" Alizon asked.

"Like, who?" asked Strefonio.

"Roger's wife."

"What about her?" Sanders asked.

"Don't you find the story a bit suspicious? I mean, how do you think she got hurt?"

"What do you mean?" Lance asked. "She fell when the catoblepas attacked."

"And landed on her face and hurt her eye and nothing else? And the supposed dangerous creature just let her walk away? Plus, those old women didn't want to talk about her husband, and didn't it seem like Roger was reaching for something for us to do? Doesn't it all seem weird at least?"

"To be honest, I don't really care," Nerissa said. "I just want this over with."

Sanders concurred. "We've wasted a lot of time already

that we didn't need to, and really for no reward outside a gem we cannot even sell." The thief muttered to himself, "We've been doing a lot lately for no real reward. These backwaters don't even have anything to steal."

Alizon appealed to the knight. "Lance, you understand, right? Unlike these fools, you have an excellent imagination. You can picture what really happened, right?"

"Actually, Alizon, I too think it'd be best if we just focused on our mission," Lance said. "Besides, the man seemed credible and explained himself quite well if you ask me."

Alizon sighed and rolled her eyes. "If you say so, Lance."

The party remained silent until they reached the prairie. There they saw the creature. It was a mid-sized creature about the size of a cape buffalo. It walked around the field sluggishly, its head always pointed to the ground. Its head and tail were reminiscent of a wildebeest.

If looks or smell could kill, the five would have been dead upon arriving on the field. Lance immediately placed his visor down to cover the assault on his olfactory nerves while the rest of the party had to make do with their hands.

"Don't you have a spell that can make that smell more pleasant?" Nerissa asked Alizon.

"I regret to say I possess no such thing," she answered.

"Then what good are you?"

Lance dismounted his steed, drew his blade, and cautiously approached the creature. Step-by-step he grew closer. The idea was for him to run his blade through its head before the beast noticed him or any of his companions. His group of adventurers observed him from just far enough to be out of the creature's immediate line of sight but close enough that they could observe the beast and the knight's every move.

Lance walked until he was only a few feet away. That is when the creature's head jerked up. His eyes stared directly into Lance's.

The catoblepas approached rapidly. Lance readied his blade. He could hear Alizon and Strefonio in the distance conjuring spells. Sanders and Nerissa dismounted their steeds and were approaching, ready for a fight.

Then the creature stopped. It shoved its nose into Lance's chest, nuzzled its head against him, and started to snuggle.

"Aww, would you look at that?" Alizon said. "He's friendly."

"He is incredibly docile," Lance observed. He removed a gauntlet to pet the creature on the head. The knight was at a bit of a loss of what to do. A couple of his companions, though, were not.

Lance could feel something fly under his hand. At first, he thought it was an insect, but it was too big and much too fast to be that. He looked down and noticed blood pouring from both sides of the creature's head. An arrow had apparently been lodged into and through his skull.

The catoblepas let out an anguished cry as it fell limply. He was dead before he hit the ground.

"What did you do that for?" Alizon cried.

"Because we have a mission to do!" Nerissa yelled. "We have to collect the gem, and thanks to that idiot knight over there, the only way to do that is to kill that beast!"

"But he was friendly!"

"So what?" Sanders sneered. "Nerissa is right. Did you forget? The world is in danger, and if slaying the beast is the only way to get the gem, she was right to do so."

"Besides, like, Lance said that one dude was like,

trustworthy or whatever, so maybe the beast would have liked, I don't know, ate him, cut his armor open like a tin can once he let his guard down, or something, I don't know," Strefonio said.

Alizon fumed and said nothing.

"Lance, get the horns so we can get out of here!" Nerissa ordered.

"Ah, yes, right, of course." He used his broadsword and did as he was instructed.

Afterward, the five of them returned. While the others groused some more about the town and the odor of the creature, the mage was noticeably silent.

Lance knocked on Roger's door. The man answered. "Oh, you're back already."

"Here are the horns you requested."

"Uh, thanks. Not sure I actually asked for them, but whatever."

Roger opened the door wide enough that he could receive the knight's gift. He tossed them aside. It made an audible bang as it collided with the floor and against his wall. Paintings and other decorations fell. The melody of cracking vases played within the house.

"Shit, shit, shit. Now I have to clean that up. It never ends." He sighed. "Anyway, congratulations for passing my test. You have done good work protecting the people of Tortuil. As Keeper of the Gem, I thank you for your great work."

Roger patted his pockets and then looked inside the house. "Where did I put that damn thing? Megan! Where's the amethyst?"

A frail voice answered. "I think you left it on the table."

"So what the hell are you doing? Bring it to me now!"

The sounds of rummaging emanated from the home. A

meek hand reached towards the man and handed him the gem.

"Here you go," Roger said as he dropped it into Lance's hand, "Once again, congratulations, thank you for all you've done, good luck, I hope we never see each other again." He slammed the door without saying goodbye.

The knight looked at his hand, baffled.

"Okay, so now we have all the gems," Nerissa said. "Now we can return to the king, right?"

"Yes," Lance said. "This is true. Let us return to him now."

"That's it?" Alizon asked. "You're not going to do anything else?"

"What else is there to do?" Sanders asked. "We were here for the gem, and now we have it. We can now get Artus's Sword. There's nothing else to do here."

"He's right," Lance said as he mounted his horse. "It is time to return to the king. Let us be off!"

They rode through the day and night, pausing only to eat, sleep, and take care of their most basic biological needs. Like the wind, they traveled through towns and forests, through rivers and the prairies, for days and nights, for weeks and months, until they finally arrived where it all began. The adventurers had the gems. Now they would be able to unlock the sword, rid the world of Al Kahim, and prevent him from ending the world.

The party of five met with the chamberlain shortly after they arrived at Angenehm. He granted them immediate access to the castle. There they rushed to the royal chamber, where they moved past the familiar plush red carpet to meet with the king.

"Your Highness, King Rudolph, Lance, and his companions," the royal chamberlain announced. The five of them bowed as the king greeted them.

King Rudolph looked like a changed man. It wasn't just

his face that looked a little bit different than before. It was a little more wrinkled, which was to be expected considering the deep concern he now seemed to permanently carry. It was as if his entire physique had changed, almost as if he were a little shorter and a little more frail.

No, it was not just these little changes. It was as if the entire structure of his face and his physique had changed, albeit only slightly. Only a close friend like Lance could have noticed. Such was the cost of wearing the crown and having to rule in such a precarious climate where the world could end at a moment's notice, the young man assumed.

"Lance, have you good news?"

"Yes, my lord," Lance said, holding the sack which contained the gems. "We were successful."

"Excellent. I will grant you access to Artus's Sword." The king pressed a button underneath the cushion of his chair, behind a hidden panel in the back and underneath the seat.

Three servants were summoned. Each of them went to the chair's left side and pushed it to the right. It revealed a large hole connected to an ominous, long, spiral stairway that was carved from the rough-hewn stone of the castle's foundation.

Lance traversed those damp and odorous steps, with his companion Alizon the only one who accompanied him. Her assistance was required to provide illumination with her craft.

The cavern underneath the castle was a place where light came to die. Water dripped from the ceiling. Their boots made splashing noises as they moved through the pools that had collected. Lance's metallic armor seemed to especially resist his navigating the place, as it was not at all suited for such an environment.

In addition to the wet, they had to deal with the cold. A

chilling, almost supernatural breeze was gusting towards them. This compounded an already chilly atmosphere. Alizon used her free hand to cast a flame in her palm to keep the two of them warm, though this yielded little success.

There was only one direction to move in, straight. The hall of the cave was barely wider than Lance's shoulders. Alizon walked slowly and awkwardly, almost sideways. In one hand, she carried the light, and in the other, she carried the warmth. To position herself properly so she could provide both was an endeavor that took deftness neither of them realized she had.

This laborious slog seemed to take ages to complete, but the duo eventually reached its terminus, which was a room that was both wide and high. A single ray of light descended from the ceiling, landing upon an obsidian stone base shaped in a pentagonal prism, tall enough that it reached Lance's armpits. Carved in its middle were three holes aligned perfectly horizontally. They were in the shape of an emerald, a ruby, and an amethyst.

Lance reached into his bag and placed each in their respective slots. At first, nothing seemed to happen. Then, a low rumbling sound emerged. The ground shook though not intensely, just enough to be felt.

Out from the slot ascended a longsword still in its brown leather sheath, with a silver tip. Lance stared at it, awestruck. It wasn't just how the weapon made its appearance that filled the young man with wonder. Artus had once wielded this blade. It made the young man feel simultaneously trepidation and exhilaration. He questioned whether he'd be worthy of wielding such a sword, but at the same time, he was eager to prove he was.

He grabbed the silver and black cruciform hilt with both hands, pulled the blade from the stone, unsheathed it, and raised into the air the double fuller blade, which appeared to shine. It was flawless even though it had spent an indeterminable amount of time in this cave.

It felt much heavier than he had anticipated. True, he used a broadsword more often than a longsword, but it was not as if he did not have any experience with the latter. He remembered only a slight weight variance between the two, not a drastic one.

As proof of the sword's inordinate weight, the light around his amulet shone brightly as he gripped it, filling the room with its glow, causing Alizon to cover her eyes. It was a testament to Artus's strength that the legends stated he carried it with ease.

The two returned from the cavern. King Rudolph smiled upon seeing the Artus's Sword suspended from the young man's waist and congratulated him on its retrieval. Lance handed the king his old broadsword. He didn't need it anymore. Perhaps the king could find someone else worthy to wield it.

"You know what you must do, Lance," King Rudolph said. "The fate of the world depends on you and your friends."

The knight nodded in silent affirmation. There was nothing more to say. He gathered his party.

A guard had caught Nerissa's attention, and it seemed the two were engaged in some coquettish conversation.

Strefonio was sitting at a table shaking while he chewed on something, presumably one of his mushrooms.

Sanders appeared to be searching for something, placing the palm of his hands against the walls and slowly sliding them across, occasionally knocking in certain places.

Each seemed a bit disrupted when Lance returned, almost as if he were interfering with activities they preferred to engage in. They reluctantly rejoined the knight, though not without a little bit of banter.

"Onward to Stonewall," Strefonio said.

"I heard it is quite nice of a place this time of year," Sanders followed.

"With a name like Stonewall, what sort of place could it be but paradise?" Nerissa rhetorically asked.

"Perhaps we should send Al Kahim a letter announcing our arrival?"

Lance grunted but otherwise did not reply. There were far more pressing things on his mind, including the state of the sky, which was somehow darker still, with not one but two more cracks formed. The low rumbles had become so commonplace at this point they were hardly notable anymore. He wondered how long the world could persist in such a state. He wondered more about how he was the only one who seemed to notice.

He also wondered why his companions acted in such an erratic manner. Their personalities seemed to have completely changed without any explanation. Was it that they were under the influence of something he could not quite comprehend?

No matter. The adventure was near an end. Only one more task to complete, then the world would return to normal. His companions would return to normal as well, he was sure. He led his group of adventurers out of town toward Stonewall so that he could confront the evil wizard Al Kahim on Mount Posledna.

Chapter 6

The knight focused solely on the mountain range adjacent to it as they walked through the city of Stonewall. One of those mountains was surely Mount Posledna. Somewhere up there was Al Kahim's home. He was concerned with the dangers that awaited him at the top of that mountain and the sort of power the wizard was said to possess. Deep down, he wondered whether he was truly skilled enough to defeat him.

These sorts of thoughts had dwelled in the back of his mind since the adventure began. At first, they were whispers, but each subsequent endeavor caused those voices to crescendo to the point that they were now shouts.

Lance looked down at his waist and tapped Artus's Sword with his hand. It was not time to think of such things. The blade would be enough to defeat the evil wizard Al Kahim. It had to be.

A friendly dwarf greeted Lance and his crew upon their arrival. He introduced himself as Jacob Dance, but everyone around those parts called him "Old Pete," chiefly because "Old Pete" rolled off the tongue much better than "Old Jacob" or "Old

Roger." The man carried a pipe in his mouth. Not that he smoked. He just believed if a prospector went by the handle of Old Pete, he should also carry a pipe to complete the picture.

He served as the town's de facto mayor. They called him "old," but he had barely reached thirty years of age. Some believed he was given the moniker by humans, who were notoriously bad at determining a dwarf's age due to their long white beards. Some believed the brutal sun and tough working conditions had done the man no favors, causing him to have prematurely wrinkled skin and thinning hair.

The fact was, though, he was old compared to the majority of the town. Most of the inhabitants were young, very young, with the median age being around nineteen years old. The youth of the residents was easily explainable. Dust flew in the air and invaded the lungs whenever a cart was pushed by, or a horse galloped through town. Combined with the hastily constructed wooden buildings that provided little refuge from the oppressive heat, the constant influx of wagons moving to and from town, the lack of amenities save for a small shop that provided basic goods like food and tools, this was hardly the ideal place to raise a family. Only those seeking fortunes before they could move to greener pastures had a chance to survive.

Much of the mining community consisted of dwarves. Long forgotten were the conflicts they had with the orcs. No longer did they care about the ax. All they cared about was the pike. Their skills with it were so legendary that some claimed they lived in those mountains, as ridiculous as that notion was. In truth, most lived in Stonewall's hastily constructed wooden edifices they called homes. Those with families, as few as there were, lived in one of the many houses outside of town where the environment was less harsh.

Humans worked alongside them, and though some of the heartier gentlemen did assist with the actual labor, most either worked in the offices doing the number crunching or the transport of material to their trade destinations. This suited the dwarves just fine. They preferred doing real work.

Old Pete was a little bit different than the typical dwarf. He had a vision for the future. True, the mayoral position may have been unofficial, but he took it seriously. The man wished for the city to evolve beyond a small mining community reliant on the tributes of the kingdom's capital.

This is why he attempted to find other cities with which to trade, but their seclusion made things incredibly difficult. Much of the populace considered Tortuil to be the edge of the world. Stonewall was almost thirty miles east and forty miles south of that town, so for most people, it may as well have been in a different world.

No matter who they bartered with, the venture would be expensive. Any such undertaking would require a great return from whoever their partner was. Very few cities could afford such expenditure, and the kingdom's capital was one of them, and thus far, the only one.

Lance had witnessed firsthand their one attempt to trade with a new city, Sheepshead, which actually lay closer than Stonewall — at least it would have it a decent bridge. Indeed, they would have made an ideal partner.

"Angenehm takes advantage of us. They built their large homes and even the castle with our precious brick and ore, and they really didn't give us what it is worth. It has been barely enough to cover the costs." Old Pete shook his head. "A lot of places could use our stone, but very few can afford it. I thought we had something with Sheepshead. They wanted to expand,

and we had the material for them to do it. Unfortunately, their bridges can't take our loads, and we can't afford to make those long trips across the river. The city would actually be much more convenient and closer to trade with if not for the Ewe."

Several hearty young men passed Old Pete, and they greeted each other with reciprocal warmth. A couple of them shared a glance with the elven maiden, who did not particularly attempt to even feign modesty.

"Enough of your life story, old man," Nerissa said. "Let's just cut to the chase. Where's Mount Posledna?"

"Yeah, man, like, we have to go up there and kill some wizard or something," Strefonio said.

"I apologize for my companions', shall we say, frankness, but they are correct," Lance said. "It would be beneficial to know where the evil wizard dwells."

"Evil wizard? What are you talking about?"

Lance explained the situation.

"I'll be damned, so I'm talking to the Chosen One," Old Pete said. "I thought that whole thing was just a myth. Then again, I suppose that explains what a knight's doing in my town, as well as his motley crew."

"Tell us where Mount Posledna is," said Sanders.

"Again, I apologize," Lance said. "This has been an incredibly stressful time for all of us."

Old Pete played with the pipe in his mouth. "Mmm-hmm. Well, I heard some rumors that a man is living on top of Mount Posledna. It seemed too fantastic to check out, and if there is a man up there, he doesn't seem to be bothering anyone. Personally, I think the evil, shapeshifting wizard story is a lark, an old wives' tale, if you will. But you seem like a decent guy, Lance. I'll guide you over there."

"Finally," Nerissa said with a sigh.

"Your friends, on the other hand," Old Pete muttered, "Leave a little to be desired." Old Pete led them to the largest mountain in the range. He raised his hand. "This is Mount Posledna."

Lance was overwhelmed. The mountain went higher than the eye could see.

Nerissa asked, "Do you really expect us to scale that mountain?"

"None of us have the proper equipment," Sanders observed.

"Aren't mountains, like, really cold or something?" Strefonio complained.

"This one doesn't appear to have any snow, so I suppose that counts as good fortune," Lance said.

"Still, we're going to have to climb it with just our bare hands at this rate," Nerissa said.

Lance wandered aimlessly along the side of the mountain. His friends were correct. The mountain seemed impossible to climb. Many scenarios played through his head as to how they were to confront this challenge, and most of them resulted in them falling to their untimely deaths.

When he made a third pass along the base of the mountain, he saw it. There was a small and narrow trail, difficult to notice but impossible to miss once observed. It seemed too good to be true.

A shiver went down Lance's spine. Someone must have carved the pathway—but for what purpose? Stonewall wasn't exactly a tourist attraction, so it was not as if someone was likely to use the mountain for a hike. No mining operations were happening on Posledna. Therefore, the prospectors of this town were not likely to have created that trail. Lance could only think of one man who would have done something like that.

He called over Old Pete, along with the rest of his companions, to confirm.

"Yep," the prospector said, "That is new. At least, I don't recall seeing anything like that in all my memory. Of course, I don't make it a habit to take a good hard look at any of these mountains."

"It would have taken a powerful wizard to carve such a trail into that mountain unnoticed," Lance said.

"Or someone just had a lot of time on their hands," Old Pete said.

"Could you really hide something like this?"

Old Pete shrugged. "We have been very busy lately."

Lance turned to his companions. "Should we follow that trail?"

"Do you have any better ideas?" Sanders asked.

"It probably leads to a trap."

"Artus's Sword is supposed to be magical or something, right, and like, defeat the wizard?"

"He's right," Nerissa sighed. "Look, Lance, we've got to get up there, and it's the only way. I don't know what you're worried about, anyway. That sword is supposed to be able to defeat any enemy, and you're the Chosen One. Let's just get up there and defeat him so we can finally go home."

"I agree," Sanders said. "Stop thinking about this so much."

"All right," Lance said. "Let's follow that trail."

Old Pete insisted they were crazy but still wished them the best.

The knight was about to lead the group up to the mountain

when he noticed something. "Wait a second. Where's Alizon?"

"Oh, who cares?" Nerissa moaned. "Her fat ass would probably slow us down anyway."

"Our climb would likely be more efficient without her," Sanders said.

Strefonio scratched his head. "I mean, we could like, use her help, but at the same time, wouldn't she slow us down too? I don't know."

"Come now, do not speak that way. What of your loyalty to a companion?" Lance asked. The group muttered but did not answer. The knight shook his head. "I will find her. We will need her. Please wait here for my return."

"All right," said Sanders.

"It's not as if we have anything better to do," Nerissa said.

Lance thought for a moment. There was only one place she could be.

"The library of Stonewall has such a rich history," Alizon had said to her companions on the way over. "Did you know that Stonewall was once capital to the ancients? I don't believe I could resist perusing those antediluvian manuscripts." Her comments were met with the excitement of someone having to pay their taxes.

Lance asked Old Pete for directions to the library. He led him to the entrance in front of the most derelict structure in town. The wooden panels were old and had not seen a coat of paint in years. Some of them were beginning to fall. The sign above was missing the second "R" and the "B," such that it read "LIRAY" instead of "LIBRARY." Each wooden step creaked as Lance walked on top of them. He swore he felt loose nails. One of the boards rose when he stepped on it, and he hastily put it back in place.

Inside was even worse. Dust invaded his lungs, making it difficult to breathe. The megaliths of books in the sprawling sea of bookshelves were covered in dust. Light could hardly penetrate the thick coat of grime through those semi-translucent windows. This place may have once been a palace of information, but now it sat as a relic of a forgotten time.

Alizon sat at the least dilapidated of the tables, which was, all things considered, an incredibly relative term. Her hand hovered just above a thick manuscript. From her hand shone a light. Her eyes devoured every word. She was enraptured.

"I thought I'd find you here," Lance said.

She jerked in surprise. "Lance! I'm sorry, I didn't hear you enter. I've been fascinated with this book. See? It has a plethora of information about the old world and magic and wizards who could change their shape. It's wonderful."

"It sounds like a good book, and I don't mind you reading, but you should have let us know you were here."

"I did. I told everyone I was headed to the library. You even grunted at me in response, which I assumed was acknowledgment."

"I apologize. I think I was so concerned about the mountain that I really wasn't paying attention."

"It's all right, I suppose." Alizon sighed. "Must we really scale that mountain?"

"Unfortunately, yes. I can think of no alternative."

"I understand. But can I have just a few minutes more to finish this passage?"

"We are in a hurry."

"It won't take long, I promise!"

Lance paused for a moment. "I suppose that will be fine."

"Really? Oh, thank you, Lance!" She resumed her studies.

While she read, Lance looked through the bookshelves and read the spines. Mountains of information were at his fingertips, yet nothing seemed particularly interesting. That is until he saw a red book with golden letters that read *Apocalypto*.

Lance opened it and thumbed his fingers through the pages until he landed on a random passage. He could not believe his eyes.

It described the end of the world—or more specifically, how a spell of such cataclysmic power could affect the world's very environment and even begin to alter people's personalities. Everything began to make sense.

"I'm done!" Alizon shouted. "Are we ready to go?"

"Yeah," Lance said as he peeled himself away from the book. "Let's go."

The knight led the mage to where the rest of the party was gathered underneath the mountain. Strefonio was stuffing mushrooms into his face. Nerissa was busy cleaning her nails. Sanders appeared to be in mid-conversation with the wizard.

"Don't those mushrooms have a specific purpose?" Sanders admonished. "Should you really be eating so many?"

"Like, I can't help it. When I'm stressed, I eat, and it can't be more stressful than this."

Nerissa sneered. "At least close your mouth." She noticed the pair of adventurers walking toward her and alerted the wizard and the thief.

"So, the prodigal child's returned," Sanders said.

"Where have you been?" Nerissa demanded.

"At the library."

"And you did not feel the need to tell us, cow?"

"I told you! You weren't listening."

"Did you really think it was prudent to leave now?"

"You leave all the time!"

"That is none of your business, and I only leave when we have the extra time to kill!"

"She's right," Sanders concurred. "Your timing was awful."

Alizon looked at Lance pleadingly, then to the rest of the group. "I'm sorry, everyone."

"You should be," Nerissa sneered.

"All right, that's enough," Lance ordered. "It is time to go."

They all begrudgingly agreed. Lance led the group as they ascended the mountain, following the trail they hoped would lead them to Al Kahim. The trail was long, sandy, and narrow. There were times the adventurers had to walk in a single file. Dust flew as the wind ceaselessly blew, getting into lungs and eyes, causing fits of coughing and ocular irritation.

"This sucks. This really sucks," was the constant complaint. Lance, for once, was not inclined to argue.

Large rocks were a constant chore to climb around, as were small cliffs. Lance would lead when they were encountered. He'd scale the obstacle, then assist his friends.

Sanders had the least difficulty following his companion. Though his upper body strength was not comparable to the knight's, it was still formidable, and the two men were similar in terms of overall athleticism.

The same could not be said for Strefonio, Nerissa, and Alizon. Nerissa of the remaining trio was in excellent shape, but her thin frame made things difficult for her when brute strength was necessary. She'd needed the assistance of the two men to scale the rocks or other such impediments. Strefonio and Alizon, being far less athletic, required even more help.

The first major obstacle was met about halfway up the mountain. The path narrowed and jutted outward in a curved direction such that to have any hope to traverse, one would have to put their back against the mountain and slide across. It was not a particularly long stretch of land, but a single misstep would cause a most unfortunate plunge.

It would also feel very isolated. There was only room for one person at a time, and the walker would momentarily be blind on both sides due to it protruding. There was more than a little bit of apprehension.

"Should we like, turn around or something?" Strefonio asked.

"Not the worst idea I've ever heard you say," Sanders said.

Nerissa pointed at Lance. "You know he wouldn't let us."

"Good point," Sanders said. "So, who wants to go first?"

"I think Alizon should," Nerissa said. "Age before beauty, after all."

"I'm only a month older than you!" the mage protested.

"Then fat before beauty."

"Nerissa!" Lance scolded. "That is completely uncalled for!"

"Sorry," she said with a wry smile. "It just slipped."

Alizon glared. Her hands formed into fists. She was ready to let the woman literally feel her wrath.

Lance stepped in front of the two, preventing conflict. "Now's not the time for this, ladies."

Sanders interjected, "I'll go first." The thief placed his back against the wall and started shimmying carefully along the path. For a moment, he disappeared.

"Nerissa, we're really going to need to talk after this whole thing is over," Lance said.

"We'll talk only if I feel like it, and I have to tell you, right now, I won't feel like it."

"Okay, I'm here!" Sanders' shouts interrupted the knight before Lance had a chance to argue with Nerissa over her pugnacious retort.

"Strefonio, would you like to go next?" asked the elven maiden.

"Ladies first."

"You're such a gentleman. Well, I suppose I'll go next. The path is likely to break under Alizon's weight."

Lance held Alizon's arm before she could take a swipe at Nerissa. The elven maiden failed to notice, as she was too busy laughing at her own joke.

When Nerissa made it to the other side, she called out, "Okay, I'm done! Send the next one!"

"I guess I'll go next," Strefonio said.

"Wait, it's not because of what Nerissa said, is it?" Alizon asked.

Strefonio stared. "I'll just be on my way."

Alizon stood dumbfounded while Strefonio slid against the mountain. "I'm really not that fat. A little overweight, sure, but not fat."

Lance did his best to reassure her. "I know. She didn't mean it. We're just not ourselves."

"Like, I'm done!" Strefonio cried.

Alizon's brow furrowed. "Let me go next." Lance nodded. The mage placed her back against the wall and slowly inched her way through. She made it without any issues.

"See? I made it just fine!"

"Thank the gods for small miracles, or in this case, not so small," Nerissa snickered.

Lance could still hear them bickering as he placed his back against the wall. He didn't want to mention it to the others, but he was worried. The weight of his armor did make it a chore to move laterally, and his visor provided very little peripheral vision.

Inch by inch, he moved, dragging his left foot as he moved his right. The young man did not realize that the path actually got just slightly smaller at a certain part. His four companions had seen that tiny gap and were able to move their feet past it without a second thought. Lance was not.

He felt his right foot fail to make its hold. The knight started to fall. A cold sweat instantly formed on his back and dripped heavily down his legs. His arms and hands flailed in panic. Lance reached, almost out of instinct, for the ledge. His right hand missed.

But his left hand didn't. With just his fingertips, not even his thumb, he managed to catch a small bit of mountain, which prevented a premature death.

His fingers would not have held for long even with his natural strength had it not been for the amulet, which glowed and provided him enough strength to hold himself long enough for his right hand to join. He slid his hands across the foothold to the other side, where the trail expanded once again. His friends displayed varying degrees of horror when he finally appeared.

Alizon ran to the young man and grabbed one of his shoulders in a feeble attempt to pull the man back up onto solid ground.

"Ah, look, there he is," Strefonio said as he sat cross-legged in the middle of the trail.

Sanders continued to flip his dagger as he stood with his bag against the mountain. "Took him long enough."

"Just like him to not do things the easy way," Nerissa snarked as she leaned next to Sanders.

"Why aren't you guys helping me?" Alizon demanded.

"I don't think he needs help," Sanders explained. "He's stronger than the rest of us combined. He can lift himself."

"He's right, don't worry." Lance elevated himself with ease, up, then horizontally, with the flabbergasted Alizon with him, as her arms were still wrapped around his shoulder. She let go when she was sure the two of them were safe. On her knees, she turned her attention toward the rest of her companions.

"What is with you guys lately? You've done nothing but argue with Lance since we left Angenehm!"

"What the hell are you talking about?" Sanders asked. "We escorted that caravan with him, we defeated the terrapin, we followed him everywhere he's gone, and have done everything he's asked us."

"You've been terribly belligerent in the process!"

"So you're policing how we choose to respond to his demands," Nerissa said. "That's rich coming from the queen of snark."

"Lance nearly died, and you refused to help him!"

"We knew he could like handle it just fine," Strefonio said. "And he did, so what's the big deal?"

"It's okay, Alizon," Lance said. "They're correct. I'm fine. This experience has been trying, and the wizard's spell is undoubtedly affecting us all, changing who we are. None of us are to blame for how we act."

"Wizard's spell?" Alizon asked. "Do you believe the wizard's spell is affecting our personalities?"

"I read it in a book in the library. I believe the name was *Apocalypto*. It discussed this very phenomenon in detail."

"I haven't noticed anything," Sanders said.

"Me neither."

"Me three—er, neither have I. Is this like, part of your overly active imagination again, Lance?"

"Have you not noticed the increase in anger and the overall apathy? Adventures used to thrill us, now you all seem perpetually upset."

"I'm upset because I have a wedding to plan, and this prevents us from doing so. Then when I try to improve community relationships in these hick towns, you keep me on a leash. If you ask me, you're the one in the perpetual bad mood."

"I wanted to spend some time with the gals in the tavern and spend some loot, not go off right away. Working for these dirt towns and backwaters has done nothing to increase my coffers, I might add. And right now, all I really want to do is talk to some friends to go over some, let's just say, business opportunities."

"I like, wanted to get some rest too, settle my nerves, and relax a little bit. I'm like, really low on mushrooms right now, and I really would like to replenish my stash. Constantly fighting like this is really bumming me out too, man."

"And you, Alizon?"

"I...I'll do whatever you think is best, Lance."

For a moment, nothing was heard but the slight breeze.

"Let's just go," Sanders said. "We have to defeat the evil wizard regardless."

"If Lance is right," Nerissa mocked, "We'll go back to our bubbly selves immediately afterward. I bet we'll feel so happy we'll sing on our way back down."

"Like, what would we sing?"

The trek continued rather uneventfully for a short while. Lance internally hoped, he prayed, that nothing else would happen. It was obvious that none of them were in the best of moods even before they arrived in Stonewall, and the mountain seemed to only exacerbate these emotions. He did not know what would happen should the party encounter another issue before Al Kahim.

Then the weather changed. Storm clouds moved in. Initially, a few drops fell, to some consternation. Then the deluge began, much to the anger and frustration of all involved. Stronger gusts of wind soon followed. Then the sleet and the hail.

None of them were prepared for this sort of weather. Nerissa perhaps suffered the most from this change in climate, as she was the least dressed of the group, though Sanders was kind enough to offer her his cloak.

"Thank you, Sanders. At least someone knows how to be a gentleman," Nerissa said as she scowled toward Lance.

"But Lance has nothing to offer you," Alizon said. "He wears a suit of armor. Besides, we're all really at fault. We were so eager to get up here that we forgot to prepare."

Nerissa pointed at Lance. "He was eager. The rest of us were not."

"Okay, but the end of the world is nigh. Can you blame him for being in a bit of a hurry?"

"Would you stop defending him? You're always defending him. We all know why, but it's still annoying."

Lance interjected. "This argument is not helping. Whether we should have waited or prepared better is frankly moot. We're here now, and it is too late to turn back. Let us just try and make the best of a bad situation."

No one said anything. They continued to scale the mountain in silence. This was as good as a tacit agreement, though this hardly meant that tensions were quelled. Everything that had come before, all the stress and suffering endured during the climb, was a mere prelude to what awaited them near the peak of the mountain.

There was a gap. A huge gap. Once past there was nothing but an easy walk ahead, as the trail was even wide enough to allow the five of them to walk side by side.

"Now, can we like, turn around?" Strefonio asked.

"Let's just go," Sanders said. In a blink, the man took a short sprint and leaped over the gap with the grace of a gazelle.

"That was an incredible jump!" Nerissa swooned.

"You should go next, Lance," Sanders instructed.

"Sure, but why?"

"To catch the girls, of course, so they land safely. Oh, and Strefonio too."

Lance hesitated. He was sure he had the strength in his legs to make the jump but was not sure whether the armor would hinder his leaping ability. There wasn't enough room to get a good running start.

The knight took a couple of deep breaths. After a couple of warmup swings with his arms, the knight took a couple of steps back, then quickly dashed and leaped over the gap. He made it with room to spare. It was not as far as he had anticipated.

Nerissa was next. Both Lance and Sanders awaited her on the other side. The knight was especially encouraging. "Don't be afraid, my love. I will catch you."

After walking back and forth from the ledge to ensure she knew where she wanted to leap from, the elven maiden ran a few steps and jumped. She cleared the gap with ease and landed in open arms—Sanders's open arms.

"Good catch," she giggled. She turned to Lance. "Sorry. I meant to jump into your arms. Just a slight miscalculation." The young man had no choice but to accept her apology.

"You can go next if you want, Strefonio," Alizon said.

"All right, but I'm certainly not jumping without one of these." The wizard pulled out a large purple mushroom and devoured it. "It's to, uh, enhance my magic ability. Allow me to float a bit after I jump."

"I didn't know you could do that," Lance said.

"Uh, sure, yeah, I know float spells, but it like, only works for me, and only if I eat a mushroom or something, you know? Anyway, here goes nothing." The wizard took a few steps back and took a running start before he leaped.

Strefonio's feet hit the edge of the other side, which caused him to slip and fall back. He cried in fear. Lance reached for his hand. He caught his wrist and pulled him back, narrowly avoiding disaster.

"Don't make me do that again," Strefonio scolded before he started laughing uncontrollably, much to the confusion of his party.

Finally, it was time for Alizon to leap. "Okay, my turn, right. Just let me warm up a little bit." She hopped up and down a bit and then put her arms inside as she moved from side to side with her waist.

"If you can't make that jump," Nerissa teased, "You can just stay there. We promise we'll come back for you."

"No, I can make it. Just watch."

With anger clouding her better judgment, the mage ran and leaped almost without thinking. She missed the other side completely — her feet weren't even close. Alizon screamed loudly as she began her descent. The mage closed her eyes and braced herself for the harsh impact below. Tears welled in her eyes. Knowing it would not hurt for long did not ease her fear and sorrow.

Her plunge was suddenly stopped. Two hands gripped her arms and shoulders tightly. She looked up to see the armor-clad young man staring back at her. He'd dived on his stomach and reached over to catch her before she could plunge into the abyss. Most of his torso and his arms hung over the ledge. He pulled her to safety.

"I knew she couldn't make it," Nerissa mocked. Water poured from Alizon's eyes.

"Nerissa, how could you say something like that?" Lance yelled.

"I was only kidding. Sorry."

Lance glared at his love. Sanders intervened. "You caught her in time, so everything's fine. No need to worry about a dumb joke."

Alizon sobbed. "You should have just let me drop."

"What are you saying?" Lance asked. "If I had, you would have fallen to your—"

"Shut up, just shut up, okay?" There was an awkward silence. "I just need a minute."

"Of course. Take as much time as you need."

Several minutes passed without anyone saying a word.

The mage finally rose and managed to compose herself. She wiped the tears from her eyes. "Okay, let's go."

"Are you sure you are ready—?"

"I said let's go."

Alizon paused to cast a couple of heal spells to ease the physical exertion but could do nothing to help the mental. Each of them was cold and distant. There was a palpable disquiet amongst them. Walking the remainder of this trail proved to be the most difficult part of the ascent.

As they climbed, Lance looked up at the sky. It had turned almost black. How light managed to shine through baffled him. How he managed to still see the cracks, including the new ones that had formed, was equally perplexing. He prayed the madness was soon coming to an end.

They arrived at the apex of the mountain. Under better circumstances, their collective breaths would have been taken away with the view from so high up. The five would have appreciated the amount of effort necessary to reach the top and would have felt a sense of accomplishment.

However, their overwrought minds could do no such thing. Their attention turned immediately to the foreboding black mortar edifice, the lone structure erected at the summit.

Upon seeing it, Lance felt something in the pit of his stomach, something he'd never felt before in his life. Was it fear? No, he dismissed that possibility. He was the Chosen One. It was impossible for him to feel fear.

It must have been something else. A residual effect from one of Alizon's spells causing an imbalance in his humors, perhaps. Or perhaps the evil wizard's spell was having an odd effect on his biorhythm. Perhaps it was simply stress or excitement over the impending encounter. Regardless, he dismissed the possibility of it being anything more than an inconsequential feeling.

They slowly approached the building. A large mahogany door grabbed their attention. It was taller than the knight, much taller — at least a whole head, if not an entire torso. The purpose of having such a large door was lost on Lance. Perhaps its size was meant only for intimidation.

The young man observed it closely. There was no handle. The knight slid his hand over the door. He felt no switch or button. There seemed to be nothing that would allow him entrance. His friends joined in his search and looked all over for a means by which the door would be opened. There was nothing.

Lance drew his sword. His colleagues moved out of his way. They knew his intentions and did not wish to interfere. The young man was ready to strike.

Then the door opened, suddenly, as if by magic.

Lance stood flabbergasted for a moment, unsure of what to do next. He sheathed his blade and then spoke. "He must know we're here."

"That means we're walking into a trap!" Nerissa exclaimed.

"I don't think walking into a trap's like, a good idea," Strefonio said.

"Maybe it isn't too late to turn around," Sanders said.

"We have to go," Lance said. "The fate of the world depends on us."

"I knew you were going to say that."

"I shall lead."

Lance entered, with his companions following closely yet reluctantly behind. None of their nerves were alleviated when the door closed behind them with a thunderous crash.

The five walked a long path down a barren, empty hallway. The walls were black and featureless. A dim ray of light shone from a glass ceiling above. Each step was deliberate. They wanted to avoid traps that may have awaited them.

None did. The walk was shockingly uneventful and led them to the building's lone room.

Much like the hall, the room was empty and unremarkable, save for a light-blue, high-backed chair that was pointed away from the entrance. The party of five did not take more than two steps before a voice emerged from it.

"We meet again." Lance recognized the voice.

"I'm here to end your evil ways and save the world," Lance said. He drew his sword.

The wizard rose from his chair and looked at the five adventurers who were at his door, especially the young man. He stared into his eyes.

"You are beginning to see the truth. The façade is being torn apart. Yet, no, no, you're not ready. You still haven't quite accepted it. You still have much to learn. It is not time."

"What are you talking about? I have Artus's Sword. I am the Chosen One. You shall meet your end today."

"Someday, you will learn of the truth. One day you will see who I truly am."

"You're an evil wizard hell-bent on ending the world. That's all I need to know."

"How long do you intend to hide?"

"I never hide from anyone."

"So you keep lying to yourself."

"I've wasted enough time listening to your inanity. You will never get that final ingredient. I will make sure of it."

"That is what I am afraid of the most."

"Enough talk! To arms!"

Alizon cast her protection spells. Strefonio launched a fireball. Nerissa fired her arrows. Sanders ran to flank. Lance led the charge.

Al Kahim calmly raised his hand. With but a flick of the wrist, Strefonio's flames were snuffed. Nerissa's bolts were broken. Sanders's feet became tangled. Alizon's spells were nullified. Lance's charge was ceased.

Panic ensued.

"I'm freaking out, man, I'm freaking out!" Strefonio screamed. His eyes were transfixed on the smoke that used to be an inferno.

"I can't even get off a shot!" Nerissa screamed as bifurcated arrows landed at her feet.

"M...maybe I can cast a speed spell, or blind him or—"

Alizon was interrupted by Sanders, who was scrambling to his feet to recover the daggers that had flown from his hands. "Do something! And Lance, what the hell are you doing?"

"My arms, they won't move!" he yelled while he remained hunched over, his upper limbs refusing to budge. His amulet glowed but did not assist.

His horrified group looked at Lance, desperate for instruction. He didn't know what to do, but he knew he had to think fast. An idea formed.

"It's time for our 'Haste Plan'!"

"Are you sure?" Alizon asked. "It should only be used in desperate situations."

"Can you think of anything more desperate than this?" Sanders exclaimed.

"It is our only chance," Lance said. The five of them nodded in unison. They were ready.

Alizon cast her spells in succession, first on herself, taking only a second, then to the rest, which took mere fractions of seconds to complete. The spell she cast wouldn't last long, thirty seconds at most. Moreover, the spell's side effects were great. It made the recipient exhausted after its effects had worn off. Yet, the speed increase often made it worthwhile, as it allowed a person to vastly exceed their physical limitations.

Nerissa fired her arrows at a more rapid pace, ten in just one second. Sanders ran at speeds unimaginable. It was as if he wasn't even there. Alizon cast all sorts of protection and augmentation spells to assist her party. They believed they had caught him by surprise.

They were wrong. Al Kahim was able to counter everything.

With his right hand, in one sweeping motion, the wizard made the arrows collide into the wall. With his left, he gently placed the thief who was mere inches from him down behind him. With another flick, his daggers were bent in two. With both hands now free, he nullified Alizon's attempts to conjure spells to increase her party's strength and agility.

Yet this was all part of the plan.

The purpose was to distract Al Kahim, freeing Strefonio to line up his shot. It would only take a second, but it would require everything the wizard had to complete.

Strefonio understood the gravity of the situation. He knew how vital his role was in the plan. His stern expression showed a determination he had never displayed before.

Al Kahim turned towards Strefonio. For just a moment, he saw what was coming. It was too late. The spell hit true. The evil wizard became nothing but a block of ice frozen in place.

Lance felt the weight in his arms evaporate. He managed to lift the blade high over his head once again. Elation overwhelmed his four companions, followed by exhaustion.

Lance was the only one still feeling vigorous, as the spell was not cast on him. For the others, the spell's effects had worn off, but it appeared to no longer matter.

"We did it!" Alizon rasped. Though the words were meek, the joy was not. Everyone, except Lance, let out an exuberant, though anemic, cheer.

"Not quite," Lance said, moving toward the frozen wizard. "I don't think he's quite dead yet. Not until I apply Artus's Sword to him."

Lance moved his blade back, ready to strike.

The ice began to move—first, a few bumps and a couple of cracks. Shortly afterward, it started to move from side to side with increasing rapidity. It stopped for a moment. Then, with the suddenness as the shaking began, ice chunks flew everywhere.

Al Kahim freed himself from his icy prison.

"I suppose that's my fault," he said. "I underestimated you all. I wish I could say that was a particularly clever tactic, but the truth is I just let my disdain for everyone here sully my decision-making capability."

Lance let out a primal shriek and swung his sword hastily at the wizard, clumsily, impulsively, lacking any sort of grace or style or skill. It was as if a lower level primate, a mere beast, had grabbed the sword and started flinging it wildly.

Al Kahim pushed aside every swing using arcane magic even the ancients were likely unaware of. Every attempt caused Lance's arms to sail backward, causing him great pain. It was as if his blade was repelled by a wall. With a couple of waves of the wizard's hands, Lance found himself disarmed. Artus's Sword flew across the room. It was only then that Lance started to realize the hopelessness of it all.

Al Kahim pointed to the ground. Lance was suddenly on his knees, unable to move. The wizard grabbed the amulet from around his neck.

"What's this?" he asked. He looked it over thoroughly and recognized the gold vermeil and black mother of pearl design. "Ah, an amulet of strength. You shouldn't rely on such trinkets. A good warrior, a complete human being, relies only on himself and his friends." He placed the item on the ground and crushed it with his foot.

Lance struggled to talk. His voice was muffled. He could

hardly move his lips.

Al Kahim's hands began to glow. He raised his arms. Words from an ancient tongue escaped his lips. The room was engulfed in light. Strefonio yelled. Sanders struggled to run. Nerissa screamed. Alizon cried, "Lance! No!"

The world began to fade.

Chapter 7

Lance awoke to find himself in an unfamiliar setting. His vision was blurred, and his head felt as if someone had been pounding on it with a hammer. He blinked several times to adjust to the light. The faint smell of timber and animal hides assaulted his olfactory nerves. As his head cleared, the knight became more aware of his environment.

Cold. He definitely felt cold. He had grown accustomed to wearing his armor for so long that it was an unusual sensation being free of that iron torso and steel pants. Now he wore nothing but the long underwear he wore beneath. It did not register that he should think of what happened to his armor.

He lay in a strange bed in the corner of the single-roomed home surrounded by four symmetrical, wooden walls in a tight space, with hardly enough room for the potbelly stove, the bookshelf, the cupboard, and the small table that demarcated the furnishings of this tiny abode. Even the purple and gold chest with a large silver lock next to his bed took up a considerable amount of room. It blocked the entrance slightly, which made it difficult to open the rickety door directly to his left. That door and a small window above his feet were the only portals to the outside world. Outside he could hear the unmistakable sound of running water, steady and loud.

What was he doing before he arrived here? He couldn't quite remember. He did recall being delirious, yet somehow, in that state, he had the sensation of being dragged across the ground. He remembered being placed in front of someone, along with the words, "Protect him...found out what the final ingredient is...word has been sent out...all will know soon...it's a bit more complicated than that...." He couldn't fathom what that meant.

A large creak startled the knight. His limbs flailed under the sheets, and his head immediately jerked towards the door. A head popped in through the portal, and an unfamiliar pair of hazel eyes stared back at him.

"Well, it's about time you woke up," the scraggly grey-bearded man said as he entered the door. "Take a look at this." The old man displayed several fish on a line and beamed. "Not a bad haul. I've had better, but not bad."

Lance tried to speak, but he had difficulty. It was as if his tongue was numb, and his mouth felt like it had been dried with cotton.

"Just a second, I'll get you some water." The old man placed his fish on the table and pulled a cup from the cabinet. Filling it from a jug on the table, he poured and gave the water to Lance. The young man drank greedily. The old man sat and filleted his fish as he talked to the young man. "Now, what did you want to say?"

"Whe...where am I?"

"You're in the forest of Killingford Grove. The nearest city is Stonewall, which I'm guessing is around twenty miles from here. At least a day's trip, anyway. You're in my cabin, but I think you already knew that."

"Who are you?"

The old man looked up for a second. "My name is Guston."

"Guston!" Lance wheezed. "As in the 'Great Guston' of old?"

"So you've heard of me."

"Of course!"

Who hadn't heard of the man who for nearly two decades was King Rudolph's most trusted knight? He was called the slayer of demons, the expeller of dragons, the great foe of orcs and goblins alike. He was offered tracts of lands and titles for his accomplishments but always eschewed such honors. He preferred to live his life obsequiously amongst the people, which made him an even greater hero to the masses.

Then he suddenly disappeared. He announced to the people of Evermore that he was to take his leave and wished to remain alone. No explanation was provided. Some suggested an injury caused his impromptu retirement. Others believed there was foul play. No true verdict was ever reached. This all happened about a decade before Lance became the Chosen One.

Now he appeared before the young knight, though not quite appearing as the man of legend he was purported to be. His shiny pair of armor and chainmail had been replaced by a dirty white tunic and brown stockings, a sheepskin hat, and a pair of leather boots.

"I can't believe it. Why are you here? Why did you go?"

"I'd prefer not to talk about it."

"Then why am I here? The last thing I remember is…." His voice trailed. Images flashed before him. His friends squirming, begging for help. His body feeling inflamed. Moments of brief agony embracing his nerves. His armor torn apart like wet parchment, leaving his body exposed. The solemn stare of Al Kahim when he shone a blinding light that made the world fade.

"I have to go," Lance said. As he rose, for the first time, he became aware of his body. "What happened to me?" he screamed. He looked down, aghast. Not due to injuries or mutilations that were afflicted. His wounds were nothing more than mere superficial bruises, which was a surprise. Certainly, they were nothing that made the knight blanch.

It was the amount of flab that poked through his long underwear that made him wretch.

Instead of the lean figure he had become familiar with, his body was plump and bloated. He lifted the upper part of his underwear. His skin was mottled with odd blemishes. It was far more difficult than it was previously to breathe or even move. He convulsed in panic.

"Easy, relax. You shouldn't move around too much. You're still recovering," Guston said. He tossed his wares on the table and patted the young man on the shoulders.

Lance patted his neck and chest. He was surprised not to find anything. "My amulet? Where is my amulet? That is probably why I look the way I do."

"You mean this?" Guston reached into his pocket and pulled out its shattered remains.

The young man's heart sank. "Then it is hopeless."

"What are you talking about?

The young knight closed his eyes and exhaled a deep sigh. "The body I have, rather, had, is not natural. You see, the amulet morphed my body into the muscular physique that ultimately allowed me to become a knight."

"Where did you find something like that?"

"Just outside the city limits of my home, Angenehm. A man in a black cloak dropped it. I intended to return it to him, but I felt a great energy surge through my body the moment I picked it up." He paused. "I kept it. I know it was wrong, but I kept it. And as the amulet dangled around my neck, I saw, nay felt, my body change. I went from a chubby little boy to a rather muscular one in a week."

Guston scratched his head. "And your friends and family didn't notice?"

"I didn't have any friends at the time other than my cat. And my mother believed I finally lost my baby fat."

"I see. So the amulet became like a crutch?"

"Yes, and without it, I will remain this way for the rest of my life."

Guston waved dismissively. "Nonsense. You don't need an amulet to get yourself in shape. I can help you out with that."

Lance thought for a moment. "What of my friends? Where are they? Have they been brought here as well?"

"You are the only one who was brought to me."

"What? Who brought me here?"

"I promised I wouldn't say. All I can tell you he is a very good man."

"Yet if I were the only one who was brought here, that would mean my friends were...." Lance's voice trailed once again. "Oh, dear gods. Sanders, Strefonio, Alizon, Nerissa...oh my Nerissa, my love! They are all —" The young man began to sob lightly. Guston comforted him as best he could. "How could this have happened? I had Artus's Sword."

"Do you mean this thing?" Guston stood and cracked his neck. His clothes slipped a bit, giving Lance a glimpse of the old man's age-defying muscular frame. He reached under the bed and pulled out the mighty blade with both hands.

"Yes, that thing. Artus's Sword was supposed to be able to defeat any foe, but it failed me."

"No wonder. A blade alone isn't going to do you any good."

"What do you mean?"

"Perhaps your technique was lacking. What sort of style did you implement?"

"Style?"

"With a longsword of this weight, I'd recommend the western schools of Blossfechten and Harnischfechten. I know you'll probably find more use out of the latter since you'll likely be wearing armor as you fight, but I think some unarmored skills would do you well."

"I don't have any idea what you are talking about."

"What sort of technique did you use when you fought with your sword?"

"I just kind of swung it and hoped to connect."

"I see. Then it's no surprise that you failed. A weapon is only as good as the person using it. Don't worry." Guston played with the blade a bit. He displayed a grace Lance had never seen. "I can teach you."

Lance laid down and moved to his side, away from the old man. "What does it matter? It's too late. Al Kahim has already won."

The old man set the blade down and leaned on it with one hand. "It is only too late if you surrender."

"Look at me!" Lance sat up and pointed at his body with both hands. "I couldn't defeat him when my body was normal, and I had my friends. How can I ever hope to defeat him now?"

"I can train you and help you prepare. Not just what you'll encounter with Al Kahim, mind you, but with everything that will follow after. Life's greater trials."

"What could be more harrowing than the world ending?"

"You'd be surprised."

"Will I even have the time?"

"The world will not end before you are done with your training. I cannot say why I am so adamant in this knowledge, so you're going to have to trust me."

"You've been asking me to do that a lot."

"I know. It's a lot to ask of someone."

"Especially when we've just met."

Guston smiled and began playing with the sword once again. "Actually, we met once before."

"When?"

"I'm not surprised you don't remember. You were just a wee lad then. I told your father you were much too young to be hunting, but he was just so excited to have a son that he brought you everywhere."

"You knew my father?"

"We hunted together quite often until I got caught up in knightly duties, and he became domesticated."

"You heard what happened to my father, then?"

Guston paused and set down the sword. "Yes."

"I still cannot believe he left my mother and me two years ago and made us fend for ourselves."

"You shouldn't be so harsh with your father."

"I realize there was a good reason, but I still cannot forgive him, even if that is unfair."

The old man stared at the ceiling for a bit, as if he were looking for something he knew he would not find.

"Is the world not truly on the verge of ending?"

Lance's question interrupted Guston's deep thoughts. He smiled. "I can guarantee it will not end before your training has been completed."

"Then, w…would you be able to teach me how to do all those things you were doing with the sword?"

"Of course. Why don't we try some out now?"

Lance gleefully jumped out of bed and nearly tripped due to the awkwardness of his new body. After regaining his composure, the young man attempted to take the blade from Guston, only to find that his arms let it fall to the floor. He could no longer lift the blade.

Lance was nearly in tears. "It's no use. I cannot do it. I need the amulet's magic."

"Nonsense. Many a knight has gotten big and strong without magic. I know I look like a doddering old man, but I learned a thing or two in my day. I'll teach you some techniques I learned when I was your age. Hell, I'll make you even stronger than before, as long as you're willing to work."

Lance dried his tears. "Can you train me so I will be able to kill the wizard Al Kahim?"

"I can prepare you to defeat all of your enemies."

"Then I'm willing to do anything. When do we start?"

Guston picked up a piece of string from his closet and some parchment paper. "First, I'm going to get your measurements. Then, I'm going to head into town to get you some new clothes while you rest. Tomorrow, we shall begin."

Chapter 8

The sands of time perpetually fall, each grain of sand representing a moment in time that can never be replaced. Some choose to live in the moment and pretend the future shall never come, fearing each moment of the negatives the future represents. Others embrace it, believing each day is an opportunity to learn, to grow, to improve, to strengthen oneself physically or spiritually. After over two years, Lance had become this kind of man, though it had certainly been a slow ascent up that proverbial mountain.

***

His apprehension over the prospect of exercise had quickly turned to exhilaration when Lance first laid eyes on the training course Guston created for himself behind his home. A dirt trail surrounded a grass infield that contained a rock, two rectangular wooden structures that ascended high into the heavens, several stones of varying sizes, and various other unusual, disparate items, including several axes and a hammer. A few stumps were also found amongst the trees that surrounded the dirt track. The babbling river Lance had heard from inside the old man's tiny abode bordered the plot of land to the south. A shack that Lance assumed was meant for no real reason was used to house items that would be used for training but had seen better days as it had fallen into severe disrepair.

A pair of horses were tied to a hitching post next to the main house. Lance nearly went over and petted them before being reprimanded. This did not deter his enthusiasm, though. He had the spirit of a child surrounded by toys.

"All right, Lance, day one," Guston said. "We'll start light today. Do you see that dirt trail? I want you to run around it."

"How many laps?"

"As many as you can muster until sundown."

"Are you kidding?"

"I am not. Pace yourself. No need to run hard or sprint. Just be consistent."

Needless to say, Lance's previous excitement was replaced with anger and loathing. Once he started running, perhaps a bit of nausea was mixed in for good measure. After two laps, the young knight started to wheeze. Running was much more difficult than he remembered. Fatigue set in early, and, believing he'd hit a wall, Lance stopped to take a nap on the grass.

"What are you doing?" Guston asked.

"I cannot run any longer."

"You only managed to complete two laps."

"In this body? Two laps is practically a marathon."

"Get up. Keep going. I refuse to let you be a quitter." Guston forced the young man onto his feet. "Go," Guston demanded.

Lance refused.

"Go now," Guston said more forcefully.

Lance still refused.

"Now! Now! Now!" Guston began to scream, calling him

all sorts of pejoratives that implied he was fat, following it up with harsh expletives strung together with a loose theme that generally meant that Guston meant to do bodily harm to the young man. The venom in his voice and the bile coming from the man's mouth convinced Lance that he should, at the very least, not wait to see whether the old man was going to make good on his threats.

Lance ran around and around. The seemingly gentle man had become a cruel taskmaster, refusing to allow him rest. The old man would bark at him to continue running while he attended the horses, taking care of all their needs, as he did daily.

The young man passed him by with his third lap, then his fourth and fifth. Soon Lance had lost count of how many he had run. After he finished what he assumed must have been his hundredth lap, Lance collapsed in the grass. This time it was involuntary. His legs simply gave out.

"How many laps was that?" Lance wheezed.

"About fifteen or so," Guston said.

"That's it?"

"That's it."

"Forgive me. I don't think I can do anymore."

"Fine. We can start again tomorrow. Now we will spend the rest of the day catching our dinner."

He helped Lance to his feet and into his abode.

"I thought we were going to learn swordplay at some point today," Lance said as they entered.

"You are not ready. You need to hone your body before we can draw swords." He handed a rod to lance and led him to the river in the south.

There they fished for the rest of the day. The young man had done so before, but the old man's pointers did make his fishing more effective, or would have, had the young man been in any mood to listen.

His body ached, and his stomach growled. The knight had experienced excruciating pain before—yes, several times in fact—but he always had the aid of a healer to cool his inflamed nerves, repair torn muscles, and patch up any sores he might have. Now he just had to live with the pain. Any conversation Guston tried to start was quickly brushed aside. The young man was in no mood to chat.

At the end of the day, Lance had only caught one fish, while his mentor had caught several.

"Seeing how it is your first day, I will be charitable and share some of my bounty," Guston said. "I will not be so charitable tomorrow." Lance sarcastically grunted his appreciation.

Compared to the delectable cuisines he had grown accustomed to, his food, which consisted of fish, beans, and rye-grain bread, was remarkably bland. The amount he consumed was also less plentiful.

After they had finished the meal, it was time for bed. "Follow me," Guston said as he rose.

"I'm not sleeping here?" Lance asked.

"No, this is where I sleep. You sleep elsewhere."

Lanced followed him. He was shocked to learn where he would reside.

"You want me to live in this dilapidated shack?"

"It's not so bad. You've camped outside before, haven't you? At least it has a roof."

Lance glanced inside. "You're not even giving me a bed. All that's in there is a cot and a small desk." The young man sniffed the air and then covered his nose. "I think the shack is beginning to rot."

"I know it's not as luxurious as you are used to. I don't have the resources to give you a better place to lay your head for the night. Think of it this way. An austere life with modest sleeping conditions builds character. Trust me. This is the kind of place I lived in when I was your age."

"Is this some sick ploy to torture me? How do I really know you're Guston?"

"Just go to bed," Guston snarled.

The young man stared at him for a moment and, deciding he had no other options, entered the shack. He looked around for a bit, not that there was much to look at, sighed heavily, and lay on the cot. It sunk and nearly hit the floor. It was uncomfortable, but Lance was exhausted and still somewhat hungry. Sleep proved to be the poor man's dinner.

The clashing of pots and a gravelly voice awoke him from his slumber. "Wake up! Wake up! Wake up!"

Lance awakened, rose halfway, and looked out his tiny window. "It's still dark," he protested.

"Weren't you part of the military? Surely you've risen this early before?"

"I was the Chosen One," Lance muttered as he lay back down on the cot. "I could wake up whenever I wanted."

"Not here."

The old man pushed Lance out of his cot. The young man landed with a loud thud. His body ached from the previous day's activities. He literally crawled out the door.

Once outside, Lance noticed that Guston had placed a ladder next to a tree. It wasn't set up very high, only about halfway up the tree's trunk. He wondered the utility of that. It was hardly set up high enough to allow the old man to pick fruit off the tree. Perhaps it had slipped down by mistake, or the old man had simply rested it there. Lance found out the answer after a quick breakfast with the old man in his abode.

"You want me to climb this ladder?"

"From the bottom side, yes, and only use your hands. Don't worry. You won't go up very high. Even at the top, you'll only be about a foot off the ground."

"How long should I do this…?" Lance's voice trailed. He knew the answer.

Up and down he went. Much like the previous day, Lance tried to quit early. Also, much like the previous day, Guston yelled whenever Lance felt the urge to quit.

Eventually, his arms were truly pushed past their limits. Like the day before, the young man thought he'd completed more sets than he did. Also, like the day before, the duo spent the rest of the day fishing. Again, like the day before, Lance only caught one fish while his mentor caught several. Unlike the day before, no mercy was shown, and the young man ate an even more Spartan dinner than the day before.

Another morning arrived. Lance received the same wake-up call and once again struggled to wake up. This time his task was to shimmy up the two tower-like structures. He was not instructed to go very high, only a few inches at most, but it still proved to be a near Herculean task for the young man. After several exchanges between the two implying the young man wanting to quit and the older one adamantly refusing to allow it, using colorful language when necessary, Lance continued until he was truly exhausted.

Then commenced another fishing trip, where Lance's effort proved to somehow be even less successful than before. He caught nothing, so all he ate for dinner was some nuts and fruit. There was no meat in his meal.

"How do you expect me to be able to train when I am given such scanty portions of food?" Lance asked. His complaints fell on deaf ears, though they did continue for the entire night.

A fourth day passed, and it was no better. Guston tasked him with cutting down one of the forest's many trees. The young man could not even cut halfway through the trunk of the smallest one he could find before he had to call it a day. Another unsuccessful fishing trip was followed by yet another paltry dinner. Lance complained once again and was met with silence.

The fifth day was nearly Lance's breaking point. Every fiber in his being wanted to raise the white flag. At an intellectual level, he'd known this wouldn't be an easy undertaking, but he was still unprepared for the training's difficulty, and more importantly, how it'd make him feel.

His mentor had told him to lift the smallest boulder, throw it as far as he could, and to continue to do so until he was no longer able. After the tenth throw, he felt tired. Lance practically passed out on the grass.

"Surrendering already?"

"My limbs ache. I am exhausted. I cannot go on."

"Have you never experienced hardship before?"

"Of course. I have slain many a beast."

"That is not what I asked. Have you never experienced hardship before?"

"Slaying those beasts were hardships."

"Then why is moving a boulder so difficult for you?" Guston picked up the boulder and tossed it a few feet, even further than Lance was capable. "I'm old and enfeebled, but even I can throw this rock around. Why are you having so much trouble?"

"Have you forgotten that I don't have the amulet anymore? My body now gets out of breath easily, and I'm always in pain."

"You've never experienced pain before?"

"Of course I have. But Alizon, a mage friend, would heal me so I wouldn't have to feel it for long. I've never experienced pain for this amount of time."

"So you used your friends as a crutch?"

Lance sat up abruptly. "No! I used them as support, but I did not depend on them. They needed me as much as I needed them."

"And when things got rough, did you just surrender?"

"Of course not. I'd always led my friends through adversity."

"Why did they follow you? Was it just because you were the Chosen One?"

"They were my friends. Of course, they would follow me."

"I've had many friends I wouldn't consider a leader. I ask again, why did they follow you?"

"I saved Alizon, Strefonio, and Sanders. Nerissa loved me."

"So it was gratitude and obligation."

"I came up with plans."

"Were you the only one who could come up with plans?"

"I admit Sanders did come up with some plans that Nerissa especially seemed to like." Lance paused and pondered. "I...I'm not sure why they followed me."

Guston patted him on the shoulder. "It's okay to admit you do not know. I think now it's more important to ask yourself should they have followed you? What makes you inspirational? What kind of leader would you have wanted to follow if you were them?"

Lance looked down at his hands, his arms, his gut, and his feet. He contemplated his past and his future. His palms slowly clenched into fists.

He didn't answer. He did not say a word. Instead, he got up with a suddenness that nearly knocked his mentor over. Lance lifted the boulder over his head and threw it. He repeated the action over and over again.

For the first time, Guston had to conclude the activity. He didn't expect Lance to be working the entire day and expected him to stop at some point. When he didn't, the old man had to intervene and end the activity. It was getting late. They needed some time to fish.

When they were by the river, Lance spoke to his mentor. "Would you mind showing me those fishing tips again? It's a little embarrassing, but I was not paying particular attention the first time." Guston gladly gave the young man advice.

Lance had difficulty but made it a point to implement the old man's techniques. When the day was over, he had only caught a single fish, yet he was thrilled to simply have caught one again.

At dinner, Lance was surprised to find two fish on his plate.

"I believe you have made a mistake. I only caught one fish today."

"Hard work should be rewarded. For your efforts today, you deserve a second fish."

Lance thought for a moment and then placed it back onto Guston's plate.

"Why, Lance?" the old man asked.

"As you said, you eat what you catch. I appreciate it, but I only caught one today."

Guston smiled and said nothing.

The next morning Guston did his usual morning routine. "Good morning!"

"Morning," Lance grumbled as he rolled out of his cot. Combating soreness and pain, he rose to his feet, stretching out as best he could before walking out the door.

"What?" Guston asked. "No argument? No fight? I don't have to kick you this time?"

"Let's just get started," Lance grumbled.

"You're no fun anymore."

Day six involved tossing the ax Lance had previously used to cut down a tree around the yard. Simple enough, though tiring. Once again, Guston had to cut off the training. Then the duo fished the rest of the day. Lance caught double what he had the previous day.

Before bed, Lance was informed that the seventh day would be a recovery day. The old man would not barge into his room to wake him up early, and the young man was free to do what he wanted, which included sleeping or joining him when he went to town to gather supplies.

"I think I'll stay here," Lance said.

"Are you sure? You aren't a prisoner here."

"It's just with my failure to defeat Al Kahim, I'm sure the townsfolk—"

Guston cut him off. "Say no more. You want to preserve your anonymity to both preserve the element of surprise and to be able to train in peace."

Lance stuttered. "R...right. Exactly. Thank you for understanding."

"If you're going to stick around the farm, I'd recommend trying to bond with the horses. Feed them, pet them, groom them, do whatever you need to do, but please don't try and ride them for now."

"Why not? I know how to ride a horse."

"Not to be rude, but they aren't exactly Clydesdales."

Lance looked down at his massive girth. "Ah. I see."

"Don't worry. Continue to work like you did today, and we'll be riding very soon."

Lance did indeed rest the seventh day, spending much of it asleep, though he did take care of the horses too while Guston was away. Or at least one of them, as the old man had taken the bay mare when he rode into town.

As he had seen his mentor do, Lance used the ladder, climbing over it this time as opposed to under, to pick some fruit off a nearby tree. He fed some to the rose gray mare that remained. He used a brush to comb her. Her brown eyes expressed gratitude.

"Your sister's named Bella, so you must be Rosie," Lance said as he patted the horse on the side of her head. "I'm glad you stayed behind. I always preferred the silver-haired horses instead of brown."

The horse neighed her appreciation. When Guston returned, he was pleased to see his apprentice bonding with the horse.

Night fell, and just before bed, Guston did have a request for the young man. He set Artus's Sword on his floor. "Lift this sword."

Lance tried and managed to elevate it a few inches at most. The young man let out an exasperated sigh.

"It's all right. You've just started. It's just a way to measure your progress. This sword isn't too much heavier than the rock you've been throwing around, so I'm sure you'll be able to lift it soon."

The young man nodded. He was a bit demoralized and skeptical, but he was still willing to work.

Day eight began, and the cycle began anew, with only

one activity added. Guston now involved the young man in the gathering of fruits and nuts and other such foods from the land. Though Lance was an experienced hunter, the gathering part was often left to others, so Guston had to ensure that he knew the difference between what was poison and what was fine to eat. The old man once had to slap a berry out of Lance's hands. Then he lectured him on the dangers of eating belladonna.

"A woman once tried to kill me by poisoning my food with it," Guston said. "It's why I only exclusively date elves." He never elaborated on that comment.

Thus, Lance's activities consisted mostly of exercise in the morning until the early afternoon, followed by fishing and food gathering. Otherwise, it was just as it had been the previous week.

Another week passed that was typified by early rising, hard work, pain, and modest meals. Again Lance used his day off to bond with the silver-haired horse, and again Lance was unable to lift the blade particularly high.

Another week flew by. A little more weight, further and faster runs, a little higher climbs, and a little more pain along with the same modest meals. His day off bonding with the horse was enjoyable, but his inability to raise the blade started to instill frustration.

Lance was making incremental progress. His weight shed little by little, and his muscle increased at almost the same rate. Guston's excursion to town often meant another new outfit for Lance, as the weight was beginning to melt off his body.

Yet, doubt started to creep into his mind. What good was it to train if he could not even lift the sword? How much progress was he truly making?

By the end of that week, he was just going through the

motions. The vigor he had earlier was replaced with lethargy. Even playing with the horse, as he was apt to do, had lost some of its charm. When night fell, and Guston asked him to try and lift the sword, Lance refused.

"What's the point?

"We're measuring your progress."

"What progress? I still cannot lift that sword."

"It takes time."

"How much time? The end of the world is near, and I'm no closer to defeating Al Kahim. I cannot even lift Artus's Sword!"

"You need to be patient. There's still a lot more work to do."

"How much more work could I possibly need?"

"I didn't think you were still averse to working hard."

"I'm not! I wake up at the crack of dawn every morning, willingly, and I do the same repetitive tasks over and over again, and for what?"

"You sure do love to complain. Are you really the one who defeated the firedrake and saved the people of Maldonia?"

"Of course I am!"

"I don't believe you. How was somebody like you able to do something like that? You don't have the courage. You don't have the skill. You don't have the will."

"I'll have you know that I took my sword and plunged it into that monster's neck."

He began to regale the old man with the story. He became so engrossed with the tale he lifted the blade when he reached the climax. The sword had reached his head before he fell over backward, landing with a loud crash on the floor. The weight was still a bit too much.

Yet, he had just lifted it higher than he had been able since the training began.

"Are you all right?" Guston asked as he dashed to his pupil.

"I'm fine," Lance said. The sword rested safely on his chest as its blade landed flat.

"It looks like you are making progress after all."

Lance silently agreed.

Rejuvenated, Lance spent the next month training even more diligently than he had the month previous, though not necessarily without incident. Though Guston appreciated his newfound enthusiasm and the fact that not only did he not have to wake him up anymore, he'd often find the young man on the field training before even he had a chance to wake, he did at times find him a bit overzealous.

In the second week of the month, during climbing training, when the young man was shimmying between the two wooden structures as part of an exercise, reaching heights he had never achieved before, Guston could see his pupil's arms and legs shaking and that he was ready to fall. The old man told him he had trained enough. The young man defied his mentor's orders and continued his ascent. Guston chastised him but could not deter his stubborn pupil.

Then it happened. His arms and legs wobbled. They could no longer sustain their tenuous grip. His hands and feet slipped. Lance took a plunge.

By this time, though, Guston had placed himself underneath the young man to catch him, though it would be more accurate to say his body caught him. Not that the old man set himself up incorrectly or that his hands and arms failed him. Lance weighed too much and fell from too great a height to make a clean catch possible.

The old man did not respond when Lance checked to ensure he was okay. Guston rasped meekly and incoherently. He struggled to breathe. The young man pounded on his chest and shook him, unaware that such behavior would not aid his mentor in any such way.

After several attempts, Guston was finally able to wheeze out a phrase loud enough for the young man to hear. "Stop hitting my chest! You knocked the wind out of me, you moron!" The young man was relieved.

There was another incident in the third week of the month, and though less dramatic, this one, along with the one in the aforementioned week, caused a change in the young man's regimen. While the two rode together around the training area, with Lance riding Rosie on an off day, having been cleared to do so earlier that week, the old man regaled his young apprentice with a yarn he'd heard from a traveler back in his youth. He was a bit fuzzy on some of the story's details.

"Do you know why birds trust cats?"

"I wasn't aware that birds trusted cats."

Through gritted teeth, Guston continued. "They do, and do you know why?"

"Their fur is so soft?"

"Because they smile! Their pleasant smile, it disarms birds! Do you get what I'm trying to tell you?"

"I should smile more?"

"Don't trust everyone who smiles!"

"Should I trust those who don't smile? If so, then you would be the most trustworthy person in the world." Guston stormed away from a jubilant Lance.

It was then that his mentor realized he needed to do more to train the young man's mind along with his body. He had great insight into swordplay, training, equestrian, and combat, but perhaps his knowledge of the world was a bit lacking. The books he'd gathered during his travels, though, would perhaps teach what Guston could not. Besides, if Lance thought the method of resuscitation was pounding the chest with fists and was too dim to appreciate the lesson of a well-told anecdote, perhaps some book learning was in order.

Thus, Lance's grueling days were turned into equally grueling nights. Every night he was given stacks of manuscripts to peruse by candlelight. The prospect of reading was met with some light resistance, but not much. He and Guston had such a rapport at this point that he trusted his elder, even if he didn't completely understand his motivations.

Reading his first book about engineering and mathematics showed him how little he knew and how much more he could learn. It shocked him to find out how ignorant he was of the world. He wanted to do whatever he could to rectify the situation.

That is when he began to study everything he could — medicine, literature, philosophy, mathematics, from the east or the west. The young man gathered stacks and stacks of manuscripts on his own. Reading by candlelight was difficult at times, but the lad still managed to devour every single word.

This practice somewhat surprised him. He was often told he was an imaginative individual. He never expected to want to know the technical and more practical aspects of the world.

One book, in particular, fascinated him. It not only explained the kingdom's system of laws, but it discussed some of the philosophical musings about why laws even existed and why it was imperative to not live in a world where merely might made right.

He learned of other topics, such as how to improve his

home. Using the timber he acquired during his training felling trees, he repaired his shack and expanded it, creating a modest home for himself. He built himself better furniture, including a better desk at which to study, as well as a few other modest furnishings.

Another month passed with more intense training, with the weight, distances, and muscular structure of the young man increasing while the amount of fat on his body decreased. Lance had improved much even in this short period of time, in almost every category, even when it came to fishing. By this time, his yields often surpassed his mentor's.

At the end of the month, on the last day of a week, the old man asked the young man to lift Artus's Sword, as was his weekly practice. This time, much to his ebullient delight, Lance was able to lift it comfortably and wield it as he would a much lighter blade. He swung it through the air as if it were a part of him. Granted, his arms tired after minutes of whipping it around like a mad man, which compelled his mentor to holler at him for his carelessness, but he finally managed to do what took months to germinate.

A wave of emotions encompassed the young man as he sheathed the blade. He was almost moved to tears.

Guston sat up and patted his pupil on the shoulder. "Now you are ready to learn how to use that thing."

Lance's skill with the sword was appalling. He knew what end to grip, how to stab, and how to whack people over the head, and to be fair, it had worked for him for several adventures. Yet the fight with Al Kahim showed that he needed to know more.

Guston was sympathetic. "They tell a boy that he's the Chosen One then throw him out into the wilderness, with the only advice given to stab his enemies with the pointy end. No matter, I can teach you."

For several months, interspersed with the exercises and the studying, were fencing lessons. It was a slow process. Lance had to unlearn a lot of the bad habits he had before. His hands, positioning, form, everything had to change for Lance to learn even the fundamentals.

The young man's body often rebelled against his mentor's teachings. Lance had no say in the matter. The bad habits had bored into his subconscious so deeply that it caused him to actively resist, even if that was not his intention.

Guston taught him swordplay from the various eastern and western schools, especially the Blossfechten and Harnischfechten. Artus's Sword was a longsword, so learning from these schools was only natural. The old man used to be a champion fencer in his day, and it was a chief hobby of his. It was no wonder he knew so much about handling the blade.

Eventually, the younger man learned how to hold and swing his sword properly, how to block attacks and evade blows. Artus's blade was used when the young man needed to work on his form. Otherwise, wooden swords manufactured from trees Lance had chopped down were used. Guston won all these early fights. It wasn't even a contest, but the lessons learned in the process were invaluable.

Lance learned the patterns, learned the tells, learned the subtle movements that showed him where a blow was coming from. He learned a vast arsenal of moves to counter every potential blow, as well as many to deliver fierce offensive strikes. Plus, he had skill, quickness, and strength that came naturally. It was only a matter of time before he turned the tables, which he did one summer day.

"You just got lucky," Guston said when Lance first gained

the upper hand, tripped his mentor, and placed the tip of the wooden blade at his throat.

"We can spar again if you really think so," Lance said. Of course, the old man agreed, though he was bested yet again. After a third time, his mentor was convinced.

"All right, all right, you got me. Hell, I suppose I was the lucky one—lucky we weren't using real blades. There's still a lot to learn, and you still need to practice, but you're improving quite a bit. You're becoming quite the swordsman." Lance smiled proudly.

Though the old man taught the knight a lot of combat and swordplay, he also taught him stealth, because as he put it, "Why fight head-on when you can sneak up on them or avoid it altogether?" For a little while, once a week, he would wager a steak dinner should Lance ever sneak up on him and tie a ribbon around any part of his body. Most weeks ended in failure, as Guston would catch the young man, often long before he was near. But sometimes, the young man would be close, and Guston would catch him just before he could seal the tie.

One day, though, Guston was particularly disappointed with Lance's effort.

"You did not even try this time around."

"I figured what's the point? I can never sneak up on you, old man. No one could. It's impossible."

"I thought we were past this, Lance. You always need to try!" The two got into a shouting match, which ended with the two sides leaving for their respective rooms.

Guston slammed his door shut as he entered his hovel. His fists slammed against his table, and he let out a furious curse. That is when he noticed a yellow ribbon tied around his left wrist.

His door opened suddenly. Guston's head turned, and

there was Lance, standing there with a large, smug grin. "I expect to have that steak dinner tomorrow, old man."

After Guston cooked him his steak dinner the next night, he ended the wagering lest he was forced to pay for the young man's steak dinners every week for the remainder of the young man's time there.

This was just one of many examples where, while the process was slow and the learning was gradual, to say the least, Lance's vigilance found him success. The old man found it less necessary to push his pupil, and because of this, he could act more and more as a confidant and a friend than a teacher.

To that end, Lance told him many things. Of how much he missed his friends, especially Nerissa. Of his great adventures and various successes. Of his dubious successes in the three towns, he visited to retrieve the gems needed to attain Artus's Sword. Of how it ultimately did not help his cause.

"Don't worry," his mentor would often say. "In many ways, you are stronger than you were before — not just physically, but mentally too. Better yet, you no longer rely on trinkets or other such things — you've done it all yourself. And you're beginning to learn how to swing that sword too, so it isn't like a feather duster."

Lance would interrupt. "I bested you, did I not?"

"Yes," Guston would sigh. "You did. Anyway, my point is, you'll be ready. You're taller, too, now that I think about it. When did you grow taller than me?" As an old man, he did tend to ramble, but the words comforted Lance.

As the relationship grew, they learned much more about each other. For example, one time when Lance was browsing through Guston's bookshelf of manuscripts while the old man mended his own clothes, one particular book caught the young man's fancy.

"A book about Angenehm and the royal family," Lance said.

"I'm not a big fan of that book."

"Are the pictures badly drawn?"

"I can read, Lance. Perhaps I should do it more often, but I can read, and it just happens that I read that one."

"Is it not well written?"

"Oh, it's written incredibly well. It's just about the best piece of propaganda I've ever read in my life. It discusses an idyllic version of the capital that never really existed. It's a fever dream, an illusion. Having lived there once, it is not the paradise the book claims it to be."

"Is that why you left? You never told me. You never told anyone, as far I know."

Guston paused. "Do you promise to accept my explanation and not pry any further?"

"Of course."

"King Rudolph wanted me to do something I could not do. I parted before he could insist too strongly."

Lance looked quizzically at his mentor. "I don't understand."

"I don't expect you to, but you will find out what I mean in due time. For now, you will just have to accept that I have my reasons."

"Okay, Guston, if you say so. I won't ask you any more about it."

"Thank you for understanding, Lance."

Lance thumbed the spine of the book. "Did you know my mother lives there?"

"In Angenehm."

"Yeah. I miss her. She probably thinks I'm dead. I hope she's all right."

"You may visit her if you'd like. As I have said many times, you are allowed to leave any time. I will be here when you return."

Lance sighed. "No, I'd rather not — at least, not yet. I cannot leave until I'm ready to defeat Al Kahim."

"I worry about you, Lance."

"It's nice to know you care."

"I fear that your hatred for Al Kahim clouds your judgment."

"I disagree. I'm thinking clearly for the first time in my life."

"You mustn't let hatred oppress you. Let serenity and logic be your guide."

"I appreciate everything you have done for me, but I would really rather not discuss this now."

"As you wish. Please consider my words, Lance."

The young man wondered what he meant by that. As much as he wanted to dismiss it as ramblings, he was sure the old man knew something profound. He could not dislodge it from his mind. It remained like a raspberry seed stuck between teeth.

Near the end of the second year, when Lance showed much improvement with his swordplay, the lessons began to set in, and his body was sculpted back to its previous warrior form, if not a superior version of it, Guston began making more frequent trips to town, going almost daily when previously he'd visit at most once a week. When Lance asked the purpose of these more frequent trips, Guston evaded the question and threatened an increase in training if the young man persisted. Not that it was much of a threat at this point, as Lance would not have shied away from extra work, but his mentor's obvious irritation made it clear that the young man should stop his probes.

His question was soon answered anyway.

"I'd like to give you something," Guston told Lance one day after a particularly intense training session where Lance had somersaulted around the track, as even carrying weighted backpacks full of sand proved not to be challenging anymore.

This was suspicious. In the more than two years previous, Guston had never given him a gift. He was led to the side of his home.

Lance was greeted by a horse-driven cart. He looked inside. The young man rubbed his eyes several times to confirm he wasn't dreaming.

There stood a shiny, silver suit of armor. Lance eyed it with wonder. He could not resist trying on the gauntlets and was surprised to find they were a near-perfect fit. Absentmindedly, he put on the boots. He called out to his mentor, "This is for me, right?"

"Of course, who else?"

"Is this your old armor?"

Guston laughed. "Not quite. I got rid of that old thing years ago, and even if I didn't, I'm afraid you are far too big to have been able to fit into it. It is in a similar style, though. The blacksmith in town is a really good friend of mine, having been my weapon and armorsmith during my days as an adventurer. When I told him it was time for me to pass the torch, he gave me an excellent discount on this thing."

"That explains the extra trips to town," Lance said as he put on the boots.

"I had your measurements from all those times I had to go to the tailor to get your clothes. That actually worked out well because I wanted this thing to be a surprise. I hope it fits all right."

It was a bit tight in places but was otherwise a perfect fit.

"Wait," Lance said as he exited the cart. "You said that you are passing the torch."

"Indeed I did."

"To whom?"

"To you, of course."

"To me?"

"I understand that perhaps the wording is wrong because I know you are already the Chosen One, and you wouldn't actually be following in my footsteps, but I had no other way of conveying that I am proud of what you have accomplished. When I first heard of your exploits, from the townsfolk and bards, I thought you were nothing more than a charlatan with excellent connections. I was once considered a hero to the people. I believe you can be the same."

"I'm honored."

Guston laughed. "Considering you're the Chosen One, I'm surprised it means anything to you at all."

"It means the world."

The old man beamed. "Thank you, Lance. I have to admit, though, that I am not just giving you this armor out of benevolence. I'm also giving it to you because I think you're ready." Guston handed Lance Artus's Sword in its scabbard, with a leather belt attached to it. The knight tied the belt around his waist.

"Ready for what?"

"The last part of your training. I want you to go to the towns you visited two years ago. This time you are to succeed where you previously failed. As far as I'm concerned, you did not earn the gems that allowed you to unlock Artus's Sword. You were only given them because of a perceived obligation to the

Chosen One, regardless of whether the keepers wished to admit this. You've been living in a dream world, Lance, where being the Chosen One grants you rewards even when you don't make an effort, or worse, fail. It is time to wake up. Here, take this."

He handed the young man a black domino mask.

"What's this for?" Lance put it on. It covered about three-quarters of his face, leaving the mouth and the bottom of the nose exposed. He placed his visor down. His helmet still fit properly, if not a bit more snugly.

"I want you to go by an alias. You will now be known as Joe Kaime. Never tell them who you really are. Any success you achieve now will be genuine."

"How will you know of my success?"

"Don't worry. Word travels fast for people like me. Good luck, Lance. I'm sure you will succeed."

Lance nodded. He untied his horse and mounted it. The young knight waved at his mentor. His visor was placed down before he left for the first town he'd visited over two years ago, Sheepshead.

As he rode, he looked upward. The sky was somehow brighter than before. Not nearly the azure it once was, but much closer to it than it was to the black it had been before the fight with Al Kahim. True, there were still cracks, perhaps even more than before, but just seeing that the sky's color had lightened, if just slightly, filled him with hope.

Chapter 9

Lance remembered that bridge. The length, the rocking, the waves splashing in his face and against his armor. The sheer unpleasantness of the experience still rattled in his brain.

Rosie wasn't even there on the last trip to Sheepshead, but she somehow knew, whether by intuition or a past experience — it was difficult to tell — that the bridge was unstable. Whenever the knight tried to get her to go across, the mare would stop suddenly, raising her hooves into the air, turn around, and pace along the shore.

Lance sighed and dismounted. "I guess I'm going to have to go across on foot," he thought aloud. He started to walk across the bridge. Rosie followed him until she reached where the bridge began on the edge of the shore and let out a loud bray.

"If you want to follow, you're going to have to cross this bridge. Otherwise, I'm going to leave you on this side." The mare shook her head and whinnied softly. "Okay, so I guess we agree. I'll ride you over there."

The knight hopped onto his steed. He patted her softly a

couple of times on the head. "I know it's going to be rough, girl, but we'll get through it. Just go slowly, and we'll be fine."

Rosie paused again when she reached the bridge. She stuck a hoof out and tentatively placed it on the bridge. Gradually, she applied her full weight. Satisfied the bridge wasn't going to collapse immediately, she carefully placed another foot. A few steps were taken with her front legs on the bridge and her back legs on the grass. Eventually, her back legs joined the front, and she suddenly found herself walking on those precarious pieces of wood.

Every step she took was deliberate. Her rhythmic hoof steps were replaced by a single beat every two or three seconds. The waves of water in her face were annoying, but the shaking really seemed to bother her.

It was not a particularly breezy day. The waves hit the occasional crest at around the horse's knees but were hardly fierce. Though it was beginning to approach autumn, the temperature was moderate, neither hot nor cold.

Each stride, though, caused the bridge to quake and the horse's legs to wobble. The wet wood made her footing even more unsteady. Several times the horse stopped and refused to move. If not for the soft words and cajoling of her master, she would have quit and become an immobile object. Her brays were loud and constant. She wanted to make it very clear she did not enjoy her walk.

For a moment, Lance pondered whether it would have been better to take the long route around the Ewe River. He saved himself at least two months' worth of travel, travel that he was woefully unprepared for, but crossing the bridge was such a struggle and seemed to take so long that he wondered whether he made a mistake.

When they neared the other side, Lance gripped Rosie's reins hard to prevent her from going into a full stride. It didn't work. The horse was too excited to finally be done to listen. She slipped. Lance's heart stopped. For a moment, he worried that her legs would be caught under her, likely breaking one. He let loose a vexed cry. Luckily for him and her, she maintained her balance, though she still gave a frightful shout.

The sounds of hooves against the wood and the braying did attract some interest from the populace, especially as the duo got closer to town. Yet, it was the shrieks of the horse and her rider that truly caught their attention. Seeing the horse stay on her feet and make it into town in one piece caused an excited yet relieved cheer from the onlookers.

Mayor Brown exited the building when he heard the commotion. His hair was a little bit grayer, and his skin was a bit more wrinkled, but otherwise, he was the same man as he had been two years prior. He wore a smile until he saw the armored figure atop the horse.

"Oh great," he said. "Another knight. We had such good luck with that the first time around."

"What do you mean?" Lance asked as he trotted his horse closer to the man.

"I apologize, stranger. I'm Jebediah Brown, the mayor of Sheepshead. I know it's unfair, but the last time we had a knight come around, things didn't quite go as planned." Mayor Brown unwittingly explained to Lance events from two years ago that the young man already knew, being one of its central figures.

"I cannot help but feel if he had protected that caravan better, Stonewall would not have been discouraged from trading with us." Jebediah paused and sighed. "That's unfair, though. The bridge we have at the entrance of the town is a joke, yet sadly it's the best one we have. Even your trusty steed could attest to its inadequacy." Rosie snorted in confirmation.

"This may be a foolish thing to ask, but why not just build a better bridge?"

"Because we are farmers, not engineers!" the mayor screamed. He paused to adjust his clothes that had become ruffled. "I apologize again, stranger. We are experts in forestry, agriculture, and even animal husbandry, but when it comes to physics and engineering, our skills are lacking."

"Why not send for some in the capital? I've heard that it is home to some of the greatest engineers in the land."

"We have. Our initial plan was to attract engineers from Angenehm to Sheepshead by providing work with the brick and ore we traded for, only obviously those plans didn't come to fruition. Still, we explained the situation to King Rudolph and asked for engineers, but he refused to provide them." The mayor turned red.

"Did he say why?"

Mayor Brown growled. "He said he did not wish to risk his engineers by moving them through hostile orc territory. I could not believe it. The man signed a treaty with them, effectively banning our people from engaging in conflict, even going so far as proclaiming that the threat of orc attacks is over, only to cite their danger as the reason we cannot get support."

Lance silently and internally scrutinized the situation. He took a long look at the rickety bridge. His eyes surveyed the stout men that inhabited the town. The knight was lost for a moment in deep thought. Mayor Brown's inquiry as to whether something was the matter was ignored as Lance maintained his deep contemplation.

This must be the task I can help the townsfolk with, Lance thought to himself. *This must be Guston's test.*

"I suppose I could help you out," Lance said, breaking his silence.

"How so?" the mayor asked. "Have you some sway in the capital?"

Lance thought to himself that he perhaps did, as the Chosen One, but chose not to bring it up. For one, he'd promised Guston that he'd remain incognito and figured that exposing himself and going to the king for assistance defeated the purpose of the tests. Second, he wanted to remain incognito for now to preserve the element of surprise with Al Kahim.

"Not quite," Lance said. "I studied some engineering and mathematics over the last two years or so. I won't claim to be an expert, but I might be able to provide some assistance to make your bridge much sturdier if I could use some of the villagers for help. I came up with some crude ideas as I crossed the bridge just a moment ago."

The young man proceeded to explain the rudimentary concepts of a suspension bridge and how using certain properties in physics could allow large wagons to cross with ease, which would ultimately allow for trade.

Mayor Brown put his palms out, a large smile plastered on his face. "Whoa, slow down. What you're talking about is a little bit over my head, and I'm sure it would be over the heads of most people that live here, but I am thoroughly convinced you can help us. What is your name, stranger?"

"L…. Er, Joe Kaime."

"Well met, Joe. Shall we go discuss our agreement in more detail?"

Lance followed the man to the town hall, where they discussed the specifics of the arrangement. The mayor agreed to pay for his room and board at the inn in exchange for his engineering expertise.

This suited the young man just fine. He mostly wanted to help out the town, and besides, though the tavern was a bit musty, the food a bit overcooked, the ale a bit weak, and the beds a little lumpy, compared to the Spartan living conditions he was used to it was paradise.

The mayor gathered the town's strongest men and told them to work for Lance in constructing the bridge that would change the fate of the town forever. Despite Mayor Brown's endorsement, the men were initially reluctant to take orders from Lance. They stared at him with dead eyes after he completed his instructions, leaving the young man confused. He made a poor effort to come up with a joke and laughed awkwardly alone when he recited it. No matter how much he tried and cajoled, the men refused to budge

That is, until the gray-bearded Phil Carter bellowed, "Come on, you heard the man! Time to get to work!" The other workers immediately did just that, and they no longer seemed to have an issue following Lance's orders.

Lance thanked the man for his assistance and for getting the others involved. Phil grunted his acknowledgment. Unlike any of his previous encounters with townspeople, Lance found himself getting to know and like the people he was bound to work with, including the reticent Phil.

Phil didn't speak very often, and when he did, he preferred to communicate with grumbles instead of regular speech. Outside of a few cursory details Lance practically had to pull out of him, the young man knew very little about him.

Not that it mattered much to Lance. Phil dutifully did his job and commanded a lot of respect and did a fantastic job leading by example. The knight wouldn't have cared had the grey-bearded man never spoken.

About the only thing Phil enjoyed talking about for any particular length was his family, and even then, he often did not talk to Lance about them for very long. It did not help that the young man was mostly uninterested in the subject. The topic of fathers and sons, for some reason, grated on his nerves.

In contrast, derby-wearing Maximilian Williamson was a talker. He'd often involve himself in sesquipedalian discussions even when he had to actively seek an audience. "Let me tell you about what my daughter did yesterday," he'd say. Other times he'd go at length about, "Something that reminds me of my childhood." Lance lost count of how many times he discussed how he met his wife Emily, which actually only amounted to a glorified schoolyard crush.

His loquacious nature would sometimes get him in trouble because he'd concentrate so much on his stories that he'd forget the purpose of why he was there. When caught, though, he'd sheepishly apologize and immediately get back to work. His heart was always in the right place, even if his head wasn't.

"I'm proud to be part of something bigger than myself," he once told Lance. "I was kind of drifting through life. Now I'm helping build the future of this town. I'm proud of what we're doing." Lance reciprocated the emotion.

Rodney admired Lance. He was called Young Rodney by the other men, as he was a full decade younger than the next oldest of the workers, though he was only about a year younger than Lance. Young Rodney was rail-thin, with scruffy auburn hair, which made him appear even younger than he really was. Conversely, the knight's large physique and habit of covering his face hid his age, making him seem much older. Young

Rodney somehow figured out Lance's true age, though, and this knowledge helped build a bit of a bond.

"Yer so smart," Rodney said one morning when Lance attempted to discuss a particularly complex mathematical equation. "I's don't know 'alf of whot yer sayin', or any of it really."

"It's not that I'm smart. I didn't know any of this until I read up on it. I'm sure you would know just as much if you read a bit about it."

"Makes sense. Course, I reckon'd it help if I's knew how to read."

"You don't know how to read?"

"Never learned."

Lance promised to teach him as soon as the work was done, to which Young Rodney was incredibly appreciative. He'd often ask Lance for advice, and though Lance often questioned the effectiveness of his words of wisdom, Young Rodney seemed to enjoy them.

"There's this gal named Gwen. Right pretty thin' with pretty black 'air. I want 'er to know how I feel, but I'm not sure I can. I'm too nervous." Lance gave him advice that amounted to basically "tell her how you feel." If she didn't feel the same way, at least he'd know. Rodney was incredibly thankful for the trite advice, and doubly so the next day when he announced the two were engaged.

His friendships with these three increased the morale of the rest. It made the problems the other workers may have had taking orders from an outsider evaporate.

The project took several months to complete. Lance served as the foreman, providing instruction on where to lay the logs and where to tie the papyrus ropes to get the best leverage. He showed how to connect the wooden structure such that it could support a large amount of weight.

He demonstrated where to put the struts, he described where to put the brace, and he sketched where to put the floor beams, the stingers, and the deck. The young man did his best carpentry work to illustrate how to create the aforementioned parts. To his delight, he found some of the men, both young and old, were able to make products that surpassed his creations.

Lance taught them that connecting elements to form triangular units could be used to help resistance from swaying due to traffic on the bridge or the wind and to support more weight. Whether they comprehended the specifics of tension and compression with dynamic loads was immaterial. Most of them had never even heard of a truss, nevertheless understand its intricacies. As long as the young man could show them where to place the wood, the beams, and the rope, they were satisfied. He sounded like he knew what he was talking about and, when they found that even the part of the bridge they worked on could hold significantly more weight than before, they were satisfied.

That is not to say that Lance was reluctant to get involved with the heavy lifting, whether literally or figuratively. He had no qualms about chopping a tree from the abundant woods and carrying the log to its destination. Lance often jumped in to help people tie a loose rope or to relieve a tired worker.

The only thing he refused was to allow Rosie to get involved in the grunt work. Other horses could be used as pack animals, but not his dear Rosie. Her only exercise was the daily rides through town. Not only were the townsfolk accepting of this practice, it was cheered. Much of the town even fed the mare whatever fruit they could spare as she passed by. Indeed, the knight and his horse were a popular attraction.

About the only thing that made his behavior suspect was his insistence that he kept his face covered with his mask. He told everyone not to touch it because he never wanted it removed. Rumor had it that he even wore it to bed. How they knew this was a mystery Lance never solved.

He claimed it was due to the scars he received in battle. Most people were satisfied with the explanation, but Mayor Brown's wife Eleanor had grown incredibly curious about what the young man looked like. His physique had enraptured her, and there was a certain charm with the way he commanded people. The young man's intelligence far exceeded any other townsperson's, so he was, in her estimation, the perfect combination of brains and brawn.

The woman was perhaps a bit long in the tooth and very much married to realistically think she'd have a chance of running away with Lance, though a past encounter with another young man a couple of years ago may have given her a bit more confidence than was her due. Regardless, she was desperate to see what he looked like under that mask.

She made him feel at ease with some casual conversation. The woman feigned interest in the bridge. Her eyes glazed as Lance went into in-depth explanations into the minutiae of mathematics. As he went into a third boring rambling mathematical lecture, as she considered it, she saw an opportunity.

"I know you say you're horrifically scarred," she whispered, "But how bad could it really be?" She reached for the mask slowly. Eleanor believed she was being sneaky and playful. She did not realize the potential ramifications of her actions.

Her hand was slapped away. Hard. Much harder than Lance intended. Often it is said that one does not know his own strength. This time, it was absolutely true. He only wished to remain incognito. Even he was surprised by how violently he swung his arm.

Eleanor's hand was a deep purple. She screamed in agony. Men quickly gathered to attend to her wound. Lance profusely apologized and hastily excused himself.

Under cover of night, Lance attempted to leave with Rosie. He unhooked her from the tavern's barn and gave her a couple of pats to the head before mounting her. "All I meant to do was remain in disguise," he whispered in her ear. "I took it way too far."

He made his way to the rickety bridge. Lance paused when he arrived, looked to his right, and sighed. The bridge he and his men were working on was only about half-completed at the time. It was going to replace the one he'd crossed to get into town, but it looked like he was not going to be around to oversee its completion. Lance prayed that he'd taught them enough to complete the bridge. He wondered how Guston would handle his failure. Would he still assist in his training so that he could defeat Al Kahim?

He wondered but did not have a chance to wonder for long. His supposed failure was never reported.

"Going somewhere?"

Lance turned around to see Mayor Brown leading a group of men, the same men who had been working under him. Next to him was his wife, Eleanor. She smiled, though she clutched her wrapped bruised hand.

"Eleanor! I'm so sorry for what I did to you."

"What, this?" she asked. "It was an accident. You told people not to remove your mask. I should apologize to you for trying to invade your privacy."

"That does not excuse my violent behavior."

"Everyone makes mistakes. Learn and move on."

"Besides," the mayor said with a wink, "We had a deal. You're stuck here until you complete the bridge."

"That's right!" a townsperson yelled out. "We had a deal!"

"You can't leave us now," another one said. "We love you!"

"You've become part of our town!"

A chorus of voices concurred. More villagers joined the crowd, each lending their support. Lance was overwhelmed.

"Thank you. Thank you all. It means a lot to me." He rubbed the back of his head. "Of course I'm staying. Though I must admit, I'm a little embarrassed now." Everyone laughed at his admission.

He returned to bed and resumed his post in the morning. The rest of the construction went as planned. Days were spent working or spending time with Rosie, while nights were spent at the tavern with his newfound friends. Every morning Lance would visit the mayor's home to check on Eleanor.

"I know I'm not the young woman I once was," she said during one of his visits as she sat on a plush couch while Lance remained standing. "When I was young, though, I was so thin and beautiful."

"You still are."

"You don't have to flatter me. Sometimes I just wish I could go back to those days when I had so many male admirers." She looked out the window and sighed. "Sometimes, I just wish I could go back to when I had friends. People don't talk to me that often."

"Why not? You're a wonderful person."

"Thank you, but again there is no need to flatter me. Did you know I'm not originally from Sheepshead?"

"I did not."

"Although I suppose my doughy physique, not suited for farm work, is a bit of a giveaway. I was once a young girl from Angenehm. I was thin and oh so beautiful. I had many admirers at the time. Then I met a handsome but nervous chap named Jebediah. Oh, he was tall and strong, his glasses made him look smart, and I suppose in some ways he is, though not as smart as you. He's certainly no genius. He told me how he was going to make Sheepshead into a major metro-something or the other, like Angenehm. His confidence and his determination, as well as his charm and looks, made me fall in love and hard. I married him and followed him here.

"Now, I don't regret marrying him. If that thought even enters your head, I want you to kick it out immediately. Yet, I could never quite connect with anyone here. Shortly after we arrived, Jebediah got involved with politics and became the mayor, so my life was pretty pampered, and it has been pretty nice. However, most of these women are farm girls. I'm a city gal. I could never quite connect with them. Oh, Emily Williamson is nice enough, and Rebekah Carter is a doll, and there are several more women like that around town, but we never really connected. You're from the city, aren't you?"

Lance confirmed that he was.

"I think that's why we get along so well. You do think we get along well, don't you?"

"Of course. I wouldn't be here every day if I didn't."

"To be honest, I think you're here mostly out of guilt, so I'd like you to make a promise."

"What's that?"

"Promise me that from now on, if you decide to visit, it's not out of guilt but out of a genuine desire for friendship.

Otherwise, don't visit me at all."

Lance agreed, and he visited every day afterward.

"I'm so happy you decided to help us out," the mayor said one night, sitting with Lance at one of the tavern's large round tables when the bridge was near completion. "I've been wary of knights. My past experience with one was shaky, but this has surpassed all expectations. I thank you for all you have done."

"I'm just trying to make amends for a past mistake."

"Is tonight the night you're going to tell me what you mean by that?"

"Unfortunately, no, it will have to remain a secret."

The mayor smiled. "There's so much we don't know about you still, yet I cannot will myself to get upset about it. You've become a member of our community. I am so happy now that the king refused to send one of his engineers."

"What do you mean?"

"You've treated us far better than anyone from the capital would have. I've visited a few times. I've noticed city folk tend to look down on farming communities like ours. Eleanor being one of the exceptions, of course. They think we're a bunch of hicks that don't know their ass from their elbows." He took a large swig of his beer. "You treated us like equals, even going so far as trying to teach us even when we didn't understand a lick of what you were saying. It means so much that you didn't treat us like we're idiots."

"It'd be hypocritical of me to act otherwise. I was once like you."

"It's amazing to find someone like you in these trying times. So many people are willing to take advantage of other people. Take Maldonia, for instance."

"What happened in Maldonia?"

"A group offered protection in exchange for coin. Sounds good, right? Except the town didn't have a choice. Pay them, or they would torch the town."

"That's extortion!"

"It's certainly a threat disguised as an offer."

"It's terrible that those kinds of things happen."

"This is why we appreciate you so much. Hey barkeep! Next round is also on me!" Lance thanked him for the drinks and the kind words.

When the bridge was finally completed, the mayor held a ceremony to commemorate the occasion and to venerate the hard work of everyone involved. It was a humble affair. There were no minstrels. There were no dancers. There wasn't any sort of formal entertainment. No lavish feast was available. The attendees were forced to stand, as seats were not provided. They could hardly even afford the podium, the blue ribbon, or the giant pair of scissors that were to be used in the cutting ceremony.

The attendance was modest, mostly consisting of the workers, their friends, and their families. There were some random farmers present. These were mostly passersbys who decided to stick around just to see what the commotion was about. Some still had the rope of the livestock they were transporting in their hands.

Phil Carter was there, along with his wife Rebekah and their son Jeremiah. Lance was happy to see them but could not help but reflexively groan when he saw the child hug his father. As to why the young man didn't quite know. Maximilian was also there with his wife Emily and their daughter Rose. That family's hugging bothered him far less for whatever reason. Lance was pleased to see Young Rodney in attendance with his fiancée Gwen.

Mayor Brown stood at the podium. To his left was his beloved wife Eleanor, and to his right was Lance. They each stood on the grass just in front of the bridge.

"Today is a marquee day," he told his audience, "Not just for you or me, but for the entire town of Sheepshead. This bridge is more than just a bridge. It is a symbol of growth. It is a symbol of change. It is a symbol of this town's advancement toward the future. It opens up so many opportunities for trade that we did not previously have. This leads me to some incredible news. I sent word to Stonewall, and our messengers have just returned. They told me that our new bridge 'intrigues' them. They are willing to try trading with us once again!"

A low but enthusiastic cheer erupted amongst the crowd. Mayor Brown raised his hand to hush the crowd and then motioned toward the workers. "Truly, we have all of you to thank." He motioned toward Lance. "I'd be remiss if I didn't thank you specifically. You've become a fixture of this town. We couldn't have done it without you. I think I speak for everyone in town when I say, as sincerely as possible, that I — rather, we — thank you for everything you have done."

Another rousing cheer erupted. A few of the townsfolk went to Lance to shake his hand or pat him on the back.

"Now, without further ado, it is my great pleasure to open this bridge which will be known henceforth as...." He made a dramatic pause. "The Eleanor Brown Bridge!"

"What?" his wife asked as the mayor handed her the giant pair of scissors. "After me?"

"Who else, my love?" He winked at his wife.

"But I thought you said.... I mean, I was under the impression...." She paused and smiled. "Thank you so much, my dear sweet Jebediah." The woman gave her husband a warm hug and a kiss, which elicited more than a few catcalls from the more unsavory members of the crowd.

The mayor moved aside to allow his wife access to the ribbon tied to both sides of the bridge. He whispered to Lance. "I'm sorry, but she comes first no matter how much you've helped."

The young man laughed. He nodded and patted the mayor's back, signifying he understood.

Eleanor was about to cut the ribbon when she paused. Her eyes widened. The scissors fell limply out of her hands. A look of horror washed across her face, and she turned pale. Her jaw slowly dropped.

Her reaction initially baffled the crowd. Then they heard the clattering of hoof steps against the wood. They saw the reinforced bridge shake. They heard the battle cries. Then they saw them. Sickly green creatures with pearl white fangs clad in plated armor atop stallions were approaching. The orcs were about to arrive.

The killing began before anyone could react. What happened next was a blur. A vague memory of men falling by the orc's blades. A faint recollection of a woman's scream. The distant sound of a little boy's cries. A little girl's sobs. A young woman's shrieks.

Lance's vision turned red. He drew his sword and attacked. His armor sat at home, yet he still charged with reckless abandon. There was only one thing on his mind, death. They killed several of his friends. It was time to exact vengeance on a biblical scale.

When his vision cleared, the knight found himself in a field with a dozen dead orcs. The ground acted as a sick menagerie of their various amputated limbs. A pair of orcs arrived late and, upon seeing the carnage, immediately fled. Lance murmured he would find them soon.

Coming to his senses, Lance sheathed his sword and gazed at the devastation. He was grief-stricken. Emily cried over her dead husband. Poor Max. Lance had found him to be a true friend. He would now remain silent for eternity.

Gwen mourned over her fiancée's corpse. Alas, Young Rodney. He had so much to look forward to. A wedding, a life, a future. Those reading lessons would never come. No words of wisdom could ever help him now.

Lance continued to scan the grounds. There were several more dead. Even more were attending their wounds, hastily patching up large gashes and mending, as best as possible, their fractured limbs. The young man assisted whenever possible, providing whatever rudimentary medical service he could provide.

As he moved through the field, he saw it, the scene that struck him the hardest. Sorrow reared its ugly head every square inch, but one, in particular, hurt Lance the most.

Jeremiah shook his father's body, begging him to wake up. His mother tried in vain to move her son, but she found herself lacking the strength and the will to do so.

Tears began to well up. Lance did everything he could not to completely break down. He found it odd that of all his new friends, Phil's death was the one he seemed to lament the most.

He then saw Mayor Brown. The man was on his knees, hovering over his dead wife. A trickle of blood flowed from his head. The lenses of his glasses were shattered, their bent frame resting awkwardly on his nose. His face was expressionless, yet Lance still could feel his sorrow.

Lance wiped his tears and headed to the tavern in silence. He shed the formal wear he wore for the occasion and put on his armor and vowed never to take it off again, as unrealistic as such an aspiration may have been.

The young man went to the barn. Rosie was clearly agitated due to the events that had proceeded. She moved anxiously, trying to free herself from the rope. Lance gave her a couple of reassuring words and a couple of pats on the side of her head. She calmed down and neighed appreciatively. He then unhooked his horse and mounted her.

He rode back to the bridge, back to the mayor who had not moved a fraction of an inch since Lance's brief departure.

"I will get revenge."

"But what of the treaty?" the mayor asked without averting his eyes from his beloved. It was more out of obligation than a genuine concern.

Lance placed his visor down. "If anyone asks, I was never here. The killing was done by a random stranger. You never saw me."

The mayor nodded. Lance rode his mare toward the bridge. They were headed to the orc's lair.

Rosie had already taken a couple of steps on the bridge when Mayor Brown called out to Lance. He turned and faced him. Their eyes met. A look of acrimonious fury was plastered on the mayor's face. "The leader calls himself Knaugh. He's the supposed king of the orcs. Bring me his head."

Lance did not reply. He rode off, his objective clear.

He traveled for no more than a mile when he bumped into a familiar face.

"Hey, Lance, where are you going? Aren't you even going to say hello?"

Lance stopped and turned toward the old man. "Sorry, Guston, I didn't notice you. Hey, wait, what are you doing here?"

"I heard that the bridge was finished. It looks like you've helped out quite a bit."

"But I didn't help. There were unforeseen consequences. The orcs used the bridge to attack. People were killed because of it. The mayor's wife and the rest were my friends!"

"Dear gods, Lance. That's horrid. Were you able to fend off the attackers?"

"They are no more."

"You've done well, Lance. You've done enough. Your test, as far as I'm concerned, has been passed. You can go home now."

"No. I must make amends."

"Your mission is done. The mayor asked you to help him build a bridge and nothing more."

"That bridge caused the deaths of townspeople."

"You mustn't blame yourself. These things happen."

"This isn't about blame. I can't bring the dead back, but I can make the rest of them safe."

"What about Al Kahim? Have you forgotten about the end of the world?"

"Have you not assured me the world will not end until I have passed my tests?"

"Did you not say that you are still worried about time?"

"I cannot just walk on by. The end of the world is a looming threat, but the orcs are the more immediate one to the people of Sheepshead."

"You don't have to do this."

"I know." Lance rode off without saying another word to his mentor.

The old man muttered, just quietly enough it was out of earshot of the young man, "I'm proud of you, kid." Guston then continued toward Sheepshead.

For several days Lance tracked them. Horse prints and other animal-like activity, foliage displacement, and frankly, the careless manner in which the orcs rode were dead giveaways as to where they were and where they were headed. Lance had to utilize very little of Guston's teachings to track these men, though he did put his ability to hide to good use whenever he was reckless and got a little too close to his prey. When they ate, he ate. When they hunted, he hunted. When they slept, he slept. When they moved, he moved. He was their shadow.

Eventually, they arrived at a cave in the middle of a random patch of woods far off the beaten path. They approached to speak to their allies who guarded this cave. Perhaps they discussed what had happened to their allies at Sheepshead. Perhaps they spoke of something else. Lance didn't know. He wasn't paying attention. His mind was preoccupied with eliminating every single one.

At first, he thought of just taking the fool's approach and attacking them head-on. He was not one for subtlety, and his skills surpassed any of them, perhaps even all of them combined. Yet he was vastly outnumbered, he was fighting in unfamiliar territory, and he would likely be fighting in close quarters as opposed to an open field.

There was always the chance that a direct approach would notify their leader King Knaugh of the attack and give him a chance to escape. Lance wanted to eliminate the possibility, so he opted for a more stealthy approach.

He hid Rosie behind some trees and told her to wait, promising her a lot of apples when he got home should she stay put. She grunted in agreement.

Lance debated whether he should take off his armor to augment movement and agility but decided against it. If anything went wrong, armored combat was a better fallback plan than the non-armored one. His training also allowed him to move nimbly in armor. Did he move as well with it as without? Hardly, but even with it on, it would have been folly not to call the young man deft.

He hid behind some rocks and studied the orc's movements carefully. One by one, he singled them out, putting his sword through them and hiding their bodies before the guards were completely aware of what was happening.

By the time the remainder of the eight guards realized their numbers had dwindled to two, it was too late. Even when Lance exposed himself, it didn't matter. He was able to cut them down before they had a chance to alert their allies.

The cave was cold and musty. What little illumination there was came from the torches bolted on the wall. Lance mostly improvised while there. He hid in corners, tossed pebbles down halls, he walked slowly and carefully to sneak up on them from behind, a task that required extra care due to the armor. The young man was very careful to minimize the clanging.

As he approached deeper into the cavern, he continued to single them out one by one and run his cold steel through their warm throats. On more than one occasion, he was caught, though his quick hands and even quicker blade ensured that the orc did not live to tell anyone else.

Near the end of the cave, there was a fork. Lance had a choice to make, whether to take the left path or the right. He looked one way, then the other. Then he looked the other way, then back again. After doing this several more times, he decided to walk toward the right. Just a hunch.

Lance was greeted by a dozen fanged faces, several of whom were sharpening their blades. All had weapons at the ready. His hunch was wrong.

The knight drew his sword. Several clawed fingers pointed at him. Infuriated shouts rose from the bile of their throats as the orcs charged.

King Knaugh was on the other side. He heard the sounds of clanging swords and steel going through flesh. He heard the anguished screams of his men. He rushed to his feet and scurried to grab his weapon. His sword had barely been pulled off the wall when Lance arrived.

"Men! He's here! Help me!"

"Sorry," Lance growled. "They're all dead."

A look of disdain and sorrow washed over King Knaugh's face. He screamed, "You will pay for this!"

Lance held his sword to his side. He was ready. The orc drew his sword and raised it high into the air. Its blade shone in the torchlight.

The other orcs may have been, but fodder to the knight, but Knaugh had more skill than the rest of them put together. He was motivated. His only desire was vengeance. He attacked fearlessly.

The clash did not last for very long.

***

"Here's his head," Lance said. He dropped Knaugh's head on Mayor Brown's table.

The stench of decomposition filled the air. Mayor Brown covered his nose. He felt nauseous.

"Did you have to do that?" The knight looked to his left to see a familiar old man who was also covering his face as he sat across from the mayor. "Why can't you say hello like a normal person, especially after, what, not seeing each other in about a fortnight?"

"Guston, what are you doing here?"

"I was having a pleasant conversation with the mayor until you arrived. Get that thing out of here!"

"He asked for his head."

"So you decided that he meant that literally and wanted you to drop it on his desk. Lovely. Just get rid of it. The sight alone makes me gag."

"I agree with Guston. Please get rid of that thing."

Lance left with the head, and as he did, he overheard his mentor say, "Sorry about the kid. Sometimes he acts strangely. I tried to drill it out of him, but he can be pretty stubborn at times."

The young man paused, looked over his shoulder, and glowered. He wanted to say something but instead chose to ignore the disparaging comment. He carried the head to the edge of town and discarded it in a shallow grave. Afterward, he returned to the town hall.

"What are you doing here, anyway?" he asked his mentor.

"It's really that hard for you to say hello," Guston admonished. "Anyway, while you were out delivering justice, I've been helping around town. I told Mayor Brown here how the two of us are old friends and how I taught you everything you knew."

"He also told me the real reason why you won't expose your face," the mayor interjected. "I'm sorry about your skin condition."

"Thank you so much for telling him that, Guston," Lance sneered.

"Anyway, I stuck around to train some of their men and form a militia of sorts. I've been doing it for the last two weeks or so, and I'm planning on continuing until the end of the month. They won't become knights or anything, but at least they'll manage to defend themselves."

"The bridge opened up new opportunities, but it also opened more threats," the mayor said. "We must be prepared in the future." Tears began to well in his eyes. "We cannot let that happen again."

"I am so sorry, Mayor Brown," Lance said.

He put up a conciliatory hand. "I should have been the one who thought it out. The orcs had never traveled that far to attack. They must have caught wind of the new bridge and decided to take us by surprise."

"Perhaps someone caught wind that you were building a bridge and told the orcs to watch you guys and get ready," Guston wondered aloud.

"That was merely idle speculation on my part, Guston. I have no proof of this. Besides, it is pointless to cast blame now. We can only prepare for the future. Regardless of what happened, I still feel we have a bright future. Trade with Stonewall is still happening. We will expand." He wiped away a few of his tears. "I will make sure her death was not in vain."

"It won't be," Guston assured. "And we will make sure you guys are ready if another attack happens. This kid may have gotten rid of the orc threat, but surely others will come in time. Speaking of which, would you like to help me get the men up to speed?"

"Of course," Lance answered. "I will be happy to assist however I can. Do we start tomorrow?"

"The day after," the mayor explained. "After the service."

"What do you mean?" Lance asked but immediately followed with, "Oh yeah, right. The service."

A beautiful funeral was held the next day. Mourners clad in black arrived to cry for the dead. The priest and the priestess provided words of hope and comfort for the souls of the lost. The families of the fallen were given a chance to say their final words.

Lance seemed especially moved by the words of Jeremiah. He could hardly contain his tears, though his mask prevented the others from noticing.

The following day, Guston, along with Lance, resumed training the volunteers. They taught them the basics of combat, how to use their village to their advantage against invaders, and, if all else should fail, how to fend off attackers long enough so their families could escape.

In truth, the men probably wouldn't last very long against a formal army. Their training was woefully inadequate for that, but they knew just enough to hold their own against marauders. It was enough for them to feel confident in the future. Lance and Guston still recommended that Mayor Brown reach out to the capital for troops. The mayor said he would consider it.

Then it was time for them to leave. A group of townsfolk gathered to say their goodbyes. Amongst them were Emily and her daughter Rose.

"Thank you for everything," Emily said as she hugged the young man.

"I'm so sorry about your husband."

"I'll miss him, but he wouldn't want me to mourn forever. I'm sure he'd want you to move on as well. He'd still be proud of what he accomplished."

Lance commended her for being so strong. Rose gave him a little wave, which he reciprocated.

Gwen was also there to say farewell. "Rodney told me that you were the one who gave him the courage to tell me how he felt."

"I merely gave him some advice."

"Still, he appreciated it. I appreciated it. I only knew him a short time, but I loved every moment."

"I'm so sorry for your loss."

"As am I, but I will be strong. For him and his memory."

Rebekah was the last one to see the young man off. "I miss Phil so much, so much."

"I know. I'm so sorry."

"It must be tough for you as well. You and Phil must have been very close."

Lance looked at her quizzically. "Did Phil say that?"

"Phil didn't talk much, so he never said anything specifically, but on that dreaded day, I saw you break down when you saw what had happened to him. You did your best to hide the tears, but I noticed, and it was appreciated." Lance did not have the heart to tell her the truth.

"You're very popular, it seems," Guston whispered. "And this time, it's not because you're the Chosen One." The young man beamed.

"Are you sure you cannot stay longer?" the mayor asked.

"I'm sorry. I've stayed too long as it is. I have pressing business to attend to elsewhere."

"I won't pry. Instead, I will thank you once again, my friend. I hope you return to us soon."

Lance promised he would. He waved goodbye with his mentor, and the two began to exit town atop their steeds.

The young man paused for a moment in the middle of the bridge. He had crossed several times previously, but now he had time to savor the moment and take it all in.

Waves no longer reached his face. The boards were dry except for the edges. It was much wider. The swaying was almost non-existent, as it easily carried the weight of multiple horses and their riders. A man and his goat even passed as Guston and Lance crossed, and it still felt like their horses were walking over level ground.

Lance thought about all the effort that was put in to make this happen. So much had gone into this, so much love and trust. Lives were ultimately lost for it, but all with the hope that one day it would lead to better things for the town. He hoped and prayed it would. A single tear fell down his face.

"Everything all right?" Guston asked.

"Yeah," Lance said. "Everything's fine." He patted Rosie on the head, and they continued on their way.

Lance looked toward the sky. More cracks had formed, which was disconcerting, but on the positive side, the sky was once again blue—or at least, more recognizable as blue than black. He could not explain why, but it made him feel somehow optimistic.

"So, what did we learn?" Guston asked after they were about a mile out of town.

"Building bridges is tough but ultimately satisfying work."

"And?"

"Doing good deeds sometimes has unintended consequences," Lance said.

"What else?"

"The mayor didn't seem to like King Rudolph very much because he didn't send engineers to help him out. That was a little surprising."

"Anything else?"

"Outside of how to make friends and influence others, not really. To tell the truth, I'm not quite sure what this had to do with Al Kahim or how this will help me prevent the end of the world."

"Did you regret helping them?"

"Not at all."

"Did it feel good to help others?"

"Absolutely."

"What about the treaty? Why did you violate the treaty?"

Lance hesitated. "I guess because I felt it was more important to protect the people than it was to abide by a sheet of paper."

"Even if it meant violating King Rudolph's word?"

Lance paused. The revelation hit him like a ton of bricks. His blood grew cold. "Yes," he said gravely. "You're right. Even if it meant violating the king's word."

Guston rode over to him and gave the young man a friendly shove. "Ah, don't think about it that way. Just think of it as doing the right thing under hard circumstances. And I know you're confused now, but believe me, my lessons will become quite clear as we go on. You'll find out what this is leading to. For now, let's go home, rest for a while, and then we'll make our way to the next town."

"You're going with me this time?"

"Yes, but only to get you to our next destination. I'll let you figure out the rest from there."

"Where are we headed?"

"Why, to Ylaserine, of course."

Chapter 10

It was all so familiar to Lance. The rocks and the trees. The flowers and the grass. The rivers and the soil. Even that little robin looked strikingly familiar, though he knew the odds of it being the same bird from before were astronomical, and frankly, most robins looked the same.

Various scents flooded Lance's nose and instantly sent his mind into a wave of recollection, where memories of past adventures, both good and bad, flooded his mind. He remembered the first journey to the village, where he first met Nerissa and saved her people from the goblin menace. He remembered failing to rescue King Kymil. The look of sorrow on Prince Nasir's and Queen Axilya's faces haunted him.

He had many memories of Ylaserine, yet the one thing that eluded him was how to actually reach the place. Familiarity, in fact, served as a detriment. Nothing was noteworthy enough to stand out. It was easy for the young man to conflate memories of other forests, ones that had more distinct features, with the one he currently traversed.

Luckily, he had a guide.

"You know, Guston, you are much harder on the eyes than my last guide."

"To you, maybe," the old man growled. "I'll have you know women still find me remarkably attractive, so shut your mouth."

"You know what's sad? You still have a much better attitude about this than my last guide."

"I thought your fiancée guided you last time."

"She did, but she seemed upset that I did not remember the way."

"Did you go there often?"

"Hardly. It had been about a year since I visited."

"A year? This place is confounding. You can't be expected to remember after a year."

"How are you able to remember so well? Has it not been ten years?"

"No, I visit more often."

"Really? What for?"

"Personal reasons. Let's just leave it at that for now."

"If you say so." The young man decided not to delve further. He had other things occupying his mind.

He paused for a moment. The young man took some time to carefully etch his surroundings by noting every landmark, every nook and cranny, every little detail on the map he was creating.

Rosie shook a bit as he did this. Lance's arm moved erratically, causing him to make a mistake. The young man scolded his horse. She apologized with her eyes. His ire evaporated. He gave his horse a few pats on the side of her neck.

"Planning on coming here often?" his mentor teased when

he noticed the young man doing this.

"You never know," he answered. "It's possible I'll need to return someday. I don't want to have to rely on you for everything."

His mentor smiled. "Good answer. Exactly the right attitude to have."

Lance would need to pause a few more times, and each time Guston waited patiently for him to complete his markings.

Eventually, they arrived at the entrance of town. They were greeted by the same royal courtier Lance had met before. Of course, the man did not recognize him as Lance since the young man was two years older, donned a new set of armor, and wore a mask. The duo could feel the eyes of apprehensive elves upon them. It seemed throughout the intervening years that Ylaserine retained a feeling of discomfort toward visitors.

"Welcome to the humble village of Ylaserine. I am the royal courtier, Eldaerenth. Might I ask the purpose of your visit?"

"Just a couple of do-gooders that wanted to see if anyone needed help with anything," Guston answered.

The courtier suspiciously glared. "Thank you for the offer, but we are in no need of such services. I do not wish to be rude, but if you aren't here for any specific reason, I would like to ask you to leave. We are not in the habit of allowing just anyone in."

"Would it be too much to seek an audience with the king?"

"Of course, you cannot do such a thing. It's unheard of for just a random stranger to have an audience with the king. Who are you to make such a request?"

He paused. His eyes focused on the older of the two men.

"Wait, is that you Guston?"

"Guston?" a passing elf asked, pausing mid-walk.

Another examined the old man closely. "By the gods

above, it is Guston!"

The village went into a frenzy.

"Guston! It's Guston!"

"The Great Guston has returned!"

"Lupi will certainly be happy to hear that."

"Our hero has returned!"

Many elves surrounded Guston. The old man's befuddled face and Bella's erratic movements exuded their discomfort over receiving such attention. However, the elves were too busy praising him and literally patting him on the back to notice.

"We are so happy to see you, Guston. It has been years."

"Eldaerenth, I must say, it is good to see you all."

"A lot has happened since you've been away. Most of it has been unfortunate, I'm afraid." The elves hung their heads sadly. "King Kymil has passed."

"So I've heard."

"Indeed. His son, King Nasir, has taken the throne and has done an exemplary job as his successor." The man frowned. "We've been mired in a war. It has been terrible, to say the least." His expression softened. "But that may be at an end. I will let him explain when he arrives. I'm sure he will be elated to see you again." He then flashed the old man a wry and knowing smile. "As will Lupi, I'm sure."

Guston laughed softly. "Unfortunately, as much as I want to, I don't have time to see her."

"What about your audience with the king?"

"I wasn't asking for myself. I was asking for my friend here, Joe Kaime." He patted Lance on the shoulder.

"For your friend?" The courtier looked over Lance carefully. "Can we trust him?"

"Absolutely. He's the most trustworthy young man I've

ever met."

"Won't you show us your face, young man? Take off the mask."

"I'm afraid he can't do that. He's incredibly ugly." Guston laughed uproariously.

Lance's eyes were ablaze as he glared at the old man but were also obscured by the mask, so the old man failed to notice.

"I'm kidding," Guston said. "His face was deeply scarred from a terrible battle."

"I see," the courtier said. "That is quite unfortunate. Regardless, any friend of yours is a friend to the village. The king is not here right now, but he will return soon. For now, I would like to direct you to Queen Aleesia, Guston. Axilya abdicated when Nasir ascended to the throne."

"Ah. Anyway, I believe this is where I will take my leave. Good luck. I will see you soon." After taking a minute to separate himself from his adoring admirers, Guston departed.

The courtier led Lance to the royal estate. He went inside to introduce the young man, discuss Guston's visit, and explain why he wore a mask. Through the thin walls, Lance heard that the queen understood and would not pry into the matter. Lance thanked her internally.

When the courtier returned, he reminded Lance to take off his helmet before he answered. He did as instructed and carried it with him inside.

"Joe Kaime, Your Highness," the courtier said. The two men bowed.

A tall, beautiful elven woman with auburn hair and wearing daisies that served as a crown greeted the young man.

"I'd like to welcome you to the village of Ylaserine," she said. Lance could not help but be transfixed by the young woman's rosy lips and her soft voice. Her flowing white gown accentuated her thin frame. It reminded him of someone. "Might I ask what brings you to our humble village?"

"I suppose Guston believed I could assist you in a certain way."

"Yes, I was told that Guston brought you here, and I must admit I am not sure why. Perhaps his timing was just a little off. The last year has been a struggle. It started well with my marriage to Nasir. Unfortunately, not long after that, our village was invaded, and suddenly we were in a war with the goblins. Old hostilities returned. Many good men and women were lost." Her face brightened a bit. "Fortunately, the conflict has ended. My husband went to the neutral village of Middleton to sign a peace treaty with King Trekz. He is due to arrive any minute now. He can fill you in on the details."

Lance nodded, and the two discussed trivialities while they waited. The young man did have to think of some answers on the fly to hide his true identity when sensitive questions were asked, and he did it with the aplomb of a hippo. Luckily, though sociable, the queen wasn't particularly interested in what the young man said and nodded with whatever answer he provided. She was, after all, growing increasingly concerned about her husband.

Morning gradually turned to afternoon. Afternoon gradually turned to evening. He was expected to arrive hours ago, and the king had a reputation for punctuality. Had something delayed him, he would have made an effort to send a messenger to notify his beloved of his extended absence. This was not like him at all. It was not as if the trip from Middleton was a particularly long ride—a day's worth at most. The queen became increasingly vexed with every passing minute.

"I wonder where he is," the young woman thought aloud.

"I could go looking for him," Lance volunteered.

"I couldn't ask you to do such a thing. We've only just met."

"Nonsense, it's fine. I'm used to doing such things. I live for it. It's why Guston likes me so much."

"Thank you. Please take Eldaerenth with you. He shall be your guide."

Lance thanked her and left the village with the royal courtier.

Eldaerenth did know the way to Middleton, and Lance followed him closely. Finding the main road from the village was the difficult part, but once there, it was a simple ride to the town.

The dirt road contrasted sharply with the green grass, making it an easy trail to follow. A few boulders lay here or there, mostly to serve as landmarks on the trail, but hardly marred the beauty of the pastoral landscape. The young man took some time to mark it all on his map, explaining "Just in case" when the courtier asked him the purpose.

The trip was a bit uncomfortable. Eldaerenth was naturally suspicious of strangers, and the fact that Lance insisted on wearing a mask did not help matters. He could not resist peppering the young man with questions that Lance had difficulty answering while hiding his true identity.

"I'm glad the war is over," Lance said, shifting the conversation away from himself.

"As am I. Not just for my village, but for myself. My son, Vaeril, fought in the conflict."

"He must be very brave."

"He is. He was truly dedicated to protecting our village. Not a day went by that I did not worry. He's an excellent marksman and soldier, but so too are the goblins."

"That must have been very tough."

"Incredibly. Vaeril never worried. He has the courage I never needed to possess. I suppose I am fortunate in some ways. I was too young for the battles thirty years ago, and I am too old for the battles of today. My father wasn't so lucky."

"What do you mean?"

"He was killed in the goblin wars thirty years ago. I think I was twelve years old at the time."

The revelation hit Lance like a stone. "It is very difficult to lose a father, isn't it?"

"Not as difficult as it is to lose a son, I assume."

"Still, it's not like losing a father is easy."

Eldaerenth paused and slowed his steed to a stop. He looked at Lance with paternal concern. "Young man, did you lose your father?"

The courtier never had a chance to hear the answer. An arrow passed right through his head. He was dead instantly. His horse bucked and threw him off his back. The courtier landed with a sickening crunch.

The young man looked on in horror. He cried out, knowing full well it was in vain. He was almost in tears.

Arrows fell from the sky. Rosie deftly managed to dodge every one, protecting her rider in the process. The courtier's horse was not as lucky.

There was no time to mourn. He was under attack. Lance guided his mare to a nearby boulder and told her to duck down as low as she could. The young man dismounted and joined her on the ground. It was hardly a permanent solution, but it provided a temporary reprieve.

Lance's eyes searched frantically. His mind raced to make

sense of the current situation. Someone was attacking, but why? Then he found his answer.

Though the scene was hidden at the bottom of a sudden downward slope, the view from behind the rock gave Lance the perfect vantage point. About four hundred feet away lay the red and gold royal carriage. It was flipped over and completely off the dirt road. Its wheels were completely broken off and shattered. Wooden splinters were spread everywhere.

Almost a dozen dead elves bedecked the grass. Several were missing limbs. Others appeared to be used as makeshift pincushions for arrows. Some still twitched. Their corpses were so fresh. Blood was everywhere.

So too were the goblins. A great number of them were descending upon the carriage. Several more pointed their arrows in the direction of the young man as they slowly crept toward the rock.

There was no time to think. There was only time to react. Lance prayed that the elven king was still alive. He patted Rosie on the side of her head and whispered to her. It was time to ride like the wind.

She nodded in agreement. She was ready.

They sprung from behind the boulder. Lance drew his sword and held it at his side. Rosie raced toward the closest goblin. Artus's Sword ran through him before he could even string his bow. His partner could only manage a stunned expression before receiving a blade through his head.

Rosie dashed toward another pair who was approaching, a cavalcade of arrows narrowly missing her head and rear. A few went whizzing by Lance's head and torso. A few downward strikes made short work of these archers, the last ones remaining. Lance dismounted and commanded his horse to hide. He'd take care of the rest on foot.

The goblins drew their swords and clubs and charged in unison. None of them were any match for Lance's superior skill. With a few quick swings, their parts were strewn all over the field. Ten sets of arms, legs, and torsos lay at Lance's feet. Very few heads were still connected. It happened faster than the goblins' frail minds could comprehend.

There was no time to celebrate. Lance sheathed his sword and ran to the overturned carriage. He pried open what remained of the door and looked inside.

Nasir was there, blood dripping from his pants. Lance inspected the man closely. There was a nasty gash on his right leg, starting from the hip and ending around the ankle. Someone had applied bandages to slow the bleeding, but the wound still gushed.

The pallid elven king attempted to speak. The knight placed his head near the king's dry lips. "We were betrayed," he murmured.

Lance took off his gauntlet momentarily and felt the king's skin, then his forehead. It was hot and clammy. King Nasir had a fever. His heart was beating rapidly, and he began to shake.

The knight put his gauntlet back on and carefully peeled the man from the carriage. Once free of his wooden prison, he lifted the elven king over his shoulder and whistled for his horse.

"I overheard them talking," the king wheezed as Rosie galloped to the men.

"Try not to speak."

"No, you must listen. This was a trap. They are going to attack early tomorrow morning."

"What happened here?"

"They ambushed us. The healers were the first ones killed.

My most loyal guard bandaged my leg as best he could before he was killed."

"Don't worry," Lance said, placing him on the horse. "I will get you home."

Lance mounted his horse. King Nasir grabbed him with his free hand. "Tell them. Warn my village. They must know."

Lance felt the grip suddenly loosen. King Nasir was unconscious.

The knight rode Rosie as hard as the horse could run to the village. His map proved vital, as he was able to make his way back to the forest and then through it using what he had etched out. There were moments where he had to pause and regroup, but for the most part, he was able to navigate to the hidden village without any issues. He silently thanked Guston for providing him all those books about cartography.

Lance ignored the horrified faces of elven villagers as he rushed through town and made his way to the entrance of the royal estate.

Hearing the raucous commotion, Queen Aleesia ran from her home. "Dear gods!" she screamed. "What happened to my husband?"

"Get your best healers over here now," Lance commanded as he took the young elf off his horse and carried him into the royal estate. He placed the elven king in his bed and removed his blood-soaked clothes.

Three elves, two males and one female, arrived. They asked Lance to leave so they could apply their craft in private. The young man did as they requested.

Queen Aleesia and an older woman Lance recognized as Queen Axilya, though he could not admit he knew her, ran over to Lance. Both begged him to tell them what had happened.

Others joined, hoping to learn the same. Among them was a particularly concerned young man with gold hair and blue eyes. He wore a green and white tunic along with long green stockings and brown boots.

"The queen informed me that my father went with you," he said. "Where is he?"

A shiver went down Lance's spine. "You must be Vaeril. I have terrible news."

He explained to the horrified crowd what happened. Queen Aleesia, Axilya, and Vaeril were especially distraught. Lance did his best to comfort them. His efforts were mostly in vain.

An uncomfortable silence encompassed the land. The only sounds that were heard were the wailing of a man and two women, along with the sounds of children playing, oblivious of what had occurred. Though their parents did their best to hush them, they were mostly unsuccessful. The children's laughter cut through the adults like knives.

A healer emerged. "We did all that we could," he said as he wiped his hands with a rag.

Lance gulped. "How is he doing?"

"He'll survive for now. We managed to close the wound, but our spells don't seem to have much effect otherwise. His cuts remain infected, and he seems to have some sort of ague."

"What's that?"

"It's a kind of sickness that even magic cannot cure."

"Your spells do nothing?"

"I have not seen anything like this before, though I have heard of such things. It seems to happen when our healers are not able to cast their spells quickly enough."

"What can we do?" the queen screeched. She grabbed the

healer's shirt and fell to her knees, literally begging him to cure her husband. She quite obviously did not care how unbecoming it was for a queen to act in such a manner.

"I don't know. I wish I could say otherwise, but I simply do not know what to do."

Queen Aleesia was inconsolable. She cried, she bawled, she screamed, and she hollered. The young woman did not respond to any of Lance's or the healer's attempts to calm her.

Axilya remained strong. She whispered a few soft words in Aleesia's ear and helped her to her feet. Together, they walked to a nearby house that Lance assumed was the former queen's new abode.

Lance's head suddenly jerked. Something he read before suddenly appeared in his mind. Before he managed to express his epiphany aloud, though, someone else spoke.

"This is terrible," Vaeril said as he wiped the tears from his eyes. "King Kymil died not long ago, and now it looks like King Nasir is not long for this world. There is no heir. If he dies, then the whole kingdom will be in disarray. And of course, my father...." His voice drifted for a moment. "Still, we have much more pressing issues to focus on."

"The impending invasion!" one of the villagers cried.

"You're right," Lance said, gears still turning in his head.

"They will arrive in the morning."

"I'm a little baffled by that. Finding this village is no easy task. How do they know where you are?"

"They've known our location for many generations. We were not always the secretive village we are now. The goblins changed all of that. They were the last ones we ever welcomed to our home."

"I understand. Do you have enough fighting men?"

"I can gather all the soldiers we have, along with our young men and women of fighting age," Vaeril said.

"Good, thank you. Now, we need a plan," Lance observed.

"I might have one."

"Go ahead."

"There's a beach not far from here."

"Are you referring to Death's Alcove?"

Vaeril looked at him quizzically. "Death's Alcove? I haven't heard that name in two years, not since another knight and his companions cleared it of monsters. How did you know its old nickname? Have you been here before?"

Lance started to sweat. "Guston might have mentioned something about it before."

"That's odd. I'm not sure how he'd know about it. It's actually named Orianna's Grotto after our great queen of yesteryear, but we started nicknaming it Death's Grotto three years ago after the monster invasion. I thought Guston had been gone longer than that. Maybe I'm wrong, or maybe he heard it from someone. He's good at gathering information."

"The plan?" Lance asked, desperate to change the topic.

"Ah, of course, sorry. Goblins aren't the brightest bunch as far as I can tell. They are excellent fighters, of course, good at hiding, good at ambushing, but when they think they have the advantage, they tend to get overaggressive and not think things through. I suggest we use that to our advantage."

"How so?"

"We need to funnel them into Orianna's Grotto. Our men and women know that beach well and can set up places to ambush them if they are all gathered in one place. Our arrows should make short work of them. We'll hide the king and queen, mothers, children, and the elderly in the cave."

"That's an excellent idea. Just one question — how are we going to get them there?"

"Well, that's the only problem. We'll need bait."

"I'll be the bait."

"What? Why you? I was actually thinking of using myself."

"My horse Rosie is incredibly strong and fast. She'll stay one step in front of them. You are incredibly vital to this town. I don't know what your exact position is, but you're obviously a leader in some respect — whether it is official or not is moot. I'm just a stranger passing by. What happens to me is immaterial. Be with your men and provide moral support."

Besides, he had to make sure the son of Eldaerenth survived. He owed it to the royal courtier. He believed he should have protected him.

"Thank you. That is incredibly noble. Here, take this." He handed Lance a map. "It will show you the way to Orianna's Grotto. I'd suggest you going over it tonight and getting a feel for where it is before tomorrow morning."

"I appreciate it, and I will."

The queen emerged from Axilya's home. She did her best to wear a resolute smile as tears continued to flow down her cheeks.

"I apologize for my unflattering display moments ago," she said, voice wavering. "As your queen, I must be strong in such trying times. Vaeril, I overheard your plan, and I approve. I will be by my husband's side as we move to the cave along with the others. I trust you will be able to handle the military endeavors." She looked over toward Lance. "Stranger — "

"Joe."

"Joe, thank you. Thank you so much for your help. It means so much to us that you're willing to fight for a cause that is not yours."

Lance did his best to be modest. "Well, you're Guston's friends. That's good enough for me." He did an all right job.

The elves moved their noncombatants into the cave. Several men carefully carried the infirm king in a makeshift stretcher. Queen Aleesia held her husband's hand as they walked. Axilya walked with them on the other side. Vaeril positioned his soldiers and young militia in the appropriate spots on the beach.

Lance spent much of the night exploring the town. Several of the more restless elves abandoned their posts momentarily to see what the young man was doing. His behavior seemed odd.

One explained to his friends that Lance was merely learning the town's geography, and for a little while, this was true. The knight did indeed study the map Vaeril gave him closely and used it to chart the path he needed to ride to herd the goblins to the beach. He also made several edits to the map as he found some parts lacking.

Yet this explanation only went so far. As another one pointed out, he seemed to be spending a lot of time in the town's compost heaps. None of them had any idea why. One sarcastically suggested he must not have gotten enough to eat.

At some point, though, Lance excitedly grabbed an item from one of the heaps. The elven onlookers could not make out the details, and Lance ran away from them before they could ask any questions.

He rushed to Orianna's Grotto and made his way to the cave, seeking an audience with Queen Aleesia. He was, of course, granted access. She and her husband, along with Axilya, were in the deepest recesses where the terrapin used to reside, him using the stretcher as a makeshift bed. The queen and her mother-in-law sat on the floor next to him on a pair of small mats.

"Tell me, stranger," the queen said upon his arrival, "Have you heard the rumors involving the end of the world?"

"Yes, I've heard that the evil wizard Al Kahim is behind that threat."

"I see. So word has spread throughout the land; I presume if even a random knight has heard the rumor. I must confess, though, that I do not believe it to be true."

"What do you mean?"

"My husband told me about it. An evil wizard was threatening the world, and the so-called Chosen One was supposedly fated to stop him. I've heard no word that he did, yet the world remains intact. It's been over two years. I wonder why the world hasn't ended yet."

"I really could not say."

The queen shrugged. "Perhaps the Chosen One was successful, and we simply did not receive word. Or perhaps there is another possibility."

"What do you mean?"

"Perhaps King Rudolph was lying to us. It would not have been the first time he's done so. If my husband could speak, he'd concur with what I am saying. Most of the villagers here would feel the same. None of us particularly like the man. Personally, I blame him for what has happened to my husband."

"We blame him," Axilya corrected.

"How is he to blame?"

"Do you remember what transpired a year and a half ago?"

"How could I forget? It may have been one of the most harrowing experiences of my life, but it is how I met my beloved Nerissa."

"Do you know what happened after the conflict?"

"I'm afraid not. My party and I had already left on another adventure before I found out exactly what occurred."

"Your victory did not end the war in and of itself. This should serve as no surprise if you are familiar with the goblin credo."

"'If not at war, then drowning in gold.'"

"Like his father, King Trekz embodies that credo. During our negotiations toward peace with your King Rudolph—"

"He was there?"

"Yes. He told us that goblins are no less a threat to him than they are to us, even if the latest conflicts have been centered on this village. 'Gods forbid,' he said, 'Should they ever attain victory, they would no doubt go after my kingdom next. I'd rather deal with it by pen now than by sword later.'"

"Or so he said." Axilya scowled.

"What do you mean?"

The queen raised her index finger. "Her judgment may be harsh, but I believe I can explain why her feelings are not baseless. Let us start with the negotiations themselves. During them, the goblin king made it clear he refused any sort of armistice unless someone provided him what he wanted."

"Gold."

"Mountains of it in exchange for peace. And remember, gold is a resource we elves typically do not have."

"Because your economy is mostly centered on bartering."

"Correct. Naturally, my husband was going to refuse those terms when King took him aside. He offered a trade—his gold for our wood. My husband was hesitant at first, but ultimately his skepticism gave way to trust. It is in his nature to believe in others."

Axilya spoke through clenched teeth. "He is a fool! He

trusted that dastardly man at face value! He even let him write the treaty, which he didn't even read! And I can't believe he let him and his people carry off a king's coffers' worth of wood before payment!"

Lance expected a harsh reprimand but only found the queen to be sympathetic. "I understand your anger. I will not defend my husband's actions other than to say he was desperate for peace. And King Rudolph had up, until recently, always seemed like a trustworthy man. Similarly, when he offered to write the treaty, it wasn't suspicious. After all, the king of Evermore has traditionally penned those sorts of things."

"Now, because of the wording of that treaty, we're being blamed for what King Rudolph failed to provide!" said Axilya.

"Wait," said Lance. "King Rudolph never paid you for the wood?"

Axilya sneered. "What do you think? And guess what? The treaty says we were responsible for the gold, not him! It's worded very carefully to make sure he bore no part of the blame. He, it says, was only a third party to ensure the deal was legally binding."

"Why would he do such a thing?"

The queen shook her head. "We have our suspicions."

"Suspicions?" Axilya sneered. "He tricked King Nassir to steal our wood!"

"On the surface, it's hard to deny. We have sent several envoys to King Rudolph to beseech him to explain, but he's refused to see every single one of them. Of course, we stopped our investigations shortly after the goblin horde attacked." She sighed. "Perhaps there is a reasonable explanation for everything, but I simply cannot fathom what."

"I'd like to hear it too," Axilya muttered. "I love fairytales."

"Knowing this, why did King Nasir go to see King Trekz?"

The queen's face hardened. "The goblin king lied. He told my husband he wanted to clear things up. That King Rudolph confessed to a mistake in the wording, just as Nasir had said. Little did we know at the time that King Trekz was leading him into a trap."

Lance sighed. "I confess I'm not sure whether I can believe my king would do such malicious things without a reason. However, while I can't do much for you politically, I believe I can help your husband." Lance handed her a slip of paper and what he'd found in the garbage.

"What's this?" she asked, quite perplexed.

"They're instructions. It's something I read about in one of Guston's texts. I'd do it myself, but I need to get as much sleep as I can before morning, so I don't have the time. Think of it as a spell, the miracle you're looking for."

"What's your game here, stranger?" Axilya asked.

"What do you mean?"

Queen Aleesia interjected. "She's right. It's odd that you are so kind to us."

"Is it? I just happened to be passing by with my mentor Guston when this was placed upon my lap. I could not just walk on by, especially after what had happened to Eldaerenth."

"That's right. Guston, of course." Aleesia looked at Axilya, and the two nodded. "Forgive us. As I said, my mind is not in a good place, and after what happened to Stagvale, you must excuse our cynicism toward unsolicited kindness."

"What happened in Stagvale?"

"A group of criminals extorted them under the guise of protection in exchange for coin."

"I heard the same thing happened in Maldonia."

"Then you understand. Injustice seems to be spreading."

"I do, but you must trust me. That note holds the key to your husband's survival as well. Read it. What do you have to lose?"

Aleesia looked bewilderedly at the item Lance handed her. "Does this hold the key to my husband's survival? Really?"

"I know it's hard to believe, but yes, I believe it does. You're going to have to trust me."

She was skeptical, but she nodded and thanked him, as did the former queen. Aleesia's skepticism wasn't assuaged when she opened the folds of the piece of paper and read its contents.

Lance did one last cursory check of the town before he decided he had scouted enough. A kindly old man allowed him to use his stable, his home, and his bed for the night.

He tied Rosie to one of the posts. "Try to get some sleep now," he whispered. "We have a big morning ahead of us."

He entered the home. He was alone that night. The old man was in the cave.

The young man snuffed the lone candle and slept for as long as he could afford to the remainder of the night. It was not the fanciest bed he'd ever slept in—a bit dusty, with a faint musty smell, equitable to the tavern of Sheepshead. But he reminded himself, compared to the dirty cot he'd slept on for the past couple of years, it was like sleeping in the goddess's arms.

Lance awoke before daylight. He knew they would be arriving soon. He prepared his horse, and after giving her a few strokes and a few comforting words, he guided her to the entrance.

He waited for the sun to arrive and did his best to distract his mind from the impending danger. Lance amused himself momentarily by thinking the worst thing that could happen now was the goblins deciding to cancel the invasion and go home. It would mean this entire hullabaloo was for nothing.

Dawn broke. Lance could see the light from the world's radiant sphere shine through the myriad of trees. The sky seemed to glow. It was breathtaking.

That was when he heard it and felt it—the low rumble of hoof steps against the ground. They were rapidly approaching. They would be here soon. There were many.

"Calm yourself, girl." Lance patted his horse along the side of her head. The anticipation was killing her. She raised her hooves a couple of times, eager to turn around. It was not necessarily in her nature to flee, but it was also not in her nature to be a sitting duck.

A horse's head poked through the edge of the woods, emerging as if it came out of the ether. Several more joined, flanking him on both sides. Step-by-excruciating-step they entered. Soon, what appeared to be an entire squadron of troops descended upon the village. Some carried bows, while others carried clubs or swords, axes or knives, all sorts of weaponry. Their fanged teeth glowed in the sunlight. Their diminutive yet muscular frames bulged from their bronze armor that was turned black from lack of care and showed very little of their jaundiced skin. Their pointed ears poked through the holes of their head coverings.

The goblins searched for signs of life, riding through town, toppling over whatever was in their way. Several houses were rummaged through and ransacked during these escapades. Lance waited patiently. He needed to wait for the exact time to ride, even if it meant sacrificing a bit of crops and property.

They were perplexed. The goblins expected some activity. They knew the failed ambush had probably alerted the populace of their betrayal, but to find the town completely abandoned? That was unexpected.

Yet, there was no hint they were about to turn around. Quite the opposite. If anything, it made their efforts even more resolute.

One of the goblins separated himself from the rest during this search. It was the opportunity that Lance was waiting for. As the goblin investigated what was, unbeknownst to him, an abandoned alley, Lance gave Rosie a few pats on the back of her head and told her, "Okay, girl, now is the time." She strode toward the wayward goblin.

The goblin's head darted up, and his back straightened. Hearing the gallops of an unknown horse confounded him. Others of his cadre also noticed the sounds and started looking in his direction.

He turned around just in time for his face to meet the end of Artus's Sword.

The goblin's horse fled as his head flew from his body. Rosie was positioned sideways as Lance stared at the mass of goblins from between two homes. He raised the sword over his head and commanded his mare to raise her legs. She did so with a hearty bray toward the heavens.

A skeletal finger jutted out from the one who appeared to be the leader of the horde. He motioned to the others and shouted orders in an indecipherable language. He led the charge as his allies followed. It was time for Lance to run.

Rosie turned around, and the duo raced toward the heart of the village, with a battalion of goblins nipping at their heels. Several arrows zoomed by his head. Several more landed at his mare's feet. Despite the danger, Lance urged his horse to press on.

She did so. Not just because stopping would have meant certain death. Rosie trusted her master. She loved him. She would always try to ensure nothing bad ever happened to him.

They were about halfway through when he noticed a couple of figures emerging from atop two of the houses. To his chagrin, he quickly realized who they were. There stood two elven archers. They fired their bows into the crowd of goblins, killing two of them. Each reloaded and fired again, killing two more.

Lance motioned for them to hide. It was dangerous for them to be there. He wanted to do this alone.

They refused and continued firing. An arrow went through one of their heads. The other quickly met the same fate. That was all they received for their courage. Lance winced as they were struck.

The knight continued to ride. He had no other choice. Rosie galloped fast enough to stay ahead of the goblins but slowly enough to ensure they stayed on her heels.

He had ridden even further into the village when two more archers emerged from the top of two other homes. This time Lance screamed at them to hide. They, too, refused and fired into the crowd. They, too, were killed for their efforts.

Deeper and deeper, he rode until he was almost at the edge of the village, where the roads turned into forest paths that led to Orianna's Grotto. There, on top of two more homes, another pair of archers emerged. Lance recognized one of them instantly. His heart sank. It was Vaeril. The young elf fired his bow several times into the crowd, slaying many goblins in the process, more than any other archer was able to do. His partner did well but paled immensely in comparison.

An arrow went through Vaeril's partner's arm and chest.

His lifeless body fell like a stone.

Vaeril received an arrow through the leg and shoulder. The momentum carried him off the roof, and he plunged below.

Lance looked over his shoulder, deeply concerned for his new companion, expecting the worst. However, as the goblin horde closed in, he noticed that Vaeril, though wounded, was very much alive. The young elf was doing his best to position his bow toward his attackers with his quaking arms.

"Rosie, turn around!" Lance commanded. The mare did just as she was instructed and strode over to where Vaeril lay.

"I'm not worth it!" Vaeril screamed when he noticed Lance approaching. "You mustn't deviate from the plan!"

His words fell on deaf ears. Lance continued to ride.

Several goblins had reached the injured elf. A few of them had their bows drawn and aimed. Vaeril closed his eyes. He was ready for the end.

They never got the chance to fire. Lance had arrived.

With a few swings, their limbs were bifurcated. With a few more, their torsos were removed. With the imminent threat momentarily abated, the young man dismounted his horse.

"Forget about me!" Vaeril begged. "I'm not worth it!"

Lance said nothing. He picked up the young elf. Despite the shaking and struggling, Lance managed a tight grip and threw him onto his horse, then mounted behind him. With a couple of quick pats, he commanded his horse to turn around and continue.

"You should have left me there," Vaeril admonished. "Now, you put the plan at risk!"

"I couldn't leave you," Lance said. "You are still alive. I leave no man, woman, or child behind."

Vaeril would normally admire such valor, but under these

circumstances, he felt it was foolish.

Then Lance growled. "What were you guys doing there anyway? I thought I was doing this alone!"

The young elf smiled. "I couldn't let you hog all the glory." Lance scowled. "Actually," Vaeril said. "I was afraid the goblins would catch on if it was just you. I needed to make sure they thought they were headed to the heart of our army, not to an ambush. I wanted to make them think we were fools, not them."

"I guess that makes sense. I mean, you certainly were fools, that's for sure."

Vaeril laughed a bit, but the pain prevented him from doing it for long.

The horde managed to close in quite a bit during the delay. Arrows flew even closer and seemed to be more numerous. Lance used his sword to swat away the ones that did not bounce harmlessly off his steel armor. A few managed to find their way through to soft flesh. His mare whinnied loudly when a couple glanced off her rear and side. Lance's breath nearly left him when he saw it happen. Blood began to pour.

Lance petted her and apologized. He begged her to continue running despite the pain, promising her that he'd make things up to her and feed her extra apples. He promised he would fix her wounds. *Just keep running, girl.*

Not that he had to say anything. Of course, she continued to stride. Rosie would not let a little pain keep her from their goal.

Rosie continued to run through the forest with the goblin horde right on their heels. They ducked tree branches. She leaped over rocks and fallen oaks. She ran through rivers and dirt and mud and grime to get her master to where he wanted to be.

The goblins continued to close in. The pain was starting to get to her and slow her down. They came closer and closer.

The grotto seemed so far away. It seemed for every step the mare took, the horde was able to take two.

Yet she continued to run, with full confidence she would get there, with full confidence she would arrive at the grotto with her master atop of her. He would be proud of her. She thought about the fruit she'd receive and the praise she'd get when she made it. It comforted her and eased the pain. She had no doubt she'd arrive on time.

Luckily, she was right.

They arrived at the beach, which seemed quiet and tranquil and even appeared lifeless. For a moment, Lance wondered whether the elves were really there, but he had no time to think about it too closely and put his trust into Vaeril and the rest of his elves.

The knight dismounted his steed and told her to run to the cave with the young elf on top of her, and she did as she was told. As loyal as she was, she had been through enough and was more than a little enthusiastic to free herself from danger.

Lance then turned to face the horde. His sword was at the ready. He prepared himself for the upcoming fight.

The mob of goblins gathered on the beach. Their leader looked around a bit, perplexed, expecting to have run into the elven military at this point. He turned to discuss the matter briefly with the others. He was sure the elves would be there. For a moment, it went dark. Though Lance could not understand him, one of the goblins told his companions that it was an odd time to have a solar eclipse. Little did he realize it was not the moon that covered the sun. It was arrows. They were about to learn this the hard way.

The arrows rained from the heavens. Goblins were falling in vast numbers, sending them into a panic. Baffled, their horses bucked many of them off their backs, causing their riders to hit the ground with a nauseating crunch. Those that did not perish upon impact were cut down by yet another wave of arrows.

Those that were somehow still alive had the good sense to turn and run. Unfortunately for them, Lance had used the cover of arrows to intercept any possible escape. Some goblins attempted to fight, only to quickly realize their skills were no match for the superior warrior.

One goblin remained, the one Lance presumed to be the leader. He ran around in a panic until he realized there was no escape. The fear drove him mad. He took off his helmet, pulled his dagger, and stabbed himself through the head. Lance did not know what to make of this scene.

No matter. The goblins were routed. The day was won.

Lance's jaw dropped as the men and women showed themselves from their hiding places. He had no idea where they were before and was glad that he was on their side.

"We have won!" Lance shouted. The elves let out a triumphant cheer.

Shortly after, the queen emerged from the cave. With her was Vaeril, riding on top of Rosie. Both had recovered from their wounds. The young elf dismounted and let the mare run excitedly to her master.

"We met a healer in the cave," Vaeril explained. "Our wounds weren't that bad."

The mare nudged Lance's face with her nose. He laughed as he patted her. "Good girl. You are such a good girl, Rosie. You are getting so many apples when we get home." She neighed in delight. "Queen Aleesia," Lance shouted. "I have good news! We have won!" Then he said sheepishly, "Though I suppose the goblin bodies were a dead giveaway." He laughed awkwardly at his unintentional pun.

"I have incredible news as well!" she announced. "My husband's fever has broken. The swelling has subsided considerably. One of our healers told me he is going to be okay!"

Vaeril gave Lance a half-smile. "The same healer that helped me and Rosie out."

Another jubilant cheer emerged from the elves.

"I have a question, though," she said to Lance. "How did you know that eating baked moldy bread would heal my husband's disease?"

"One of Guston's books described a land in the north where certain tribes do not have healers and must rely on medicine men. They described a disease that had similar symptoms. I believe they called it 'blood poisoning.' Moldy bread was one of their remedies. I figured it was worth a chance."

She walked over to him and gave him a soft kiss on the cheek. "I thank you so much. You saved my husband's life. You are a hero. Our children will tell the story of Joe Kaime."

Lance blushed. "You are too kind."

Yet another cheer emerged from the relieved elves.

Over the next few days, the elves regrouped. They returned to their homes, and upon doing so, took some time to remember the fallen and the deceased. Vaeril, too took time to grieve for his late father.

Lance broke down again. He managed to hide his tears, but it still momentarily destroyed him. The knight could not fathom why. He did not know the courtier for that long. Sadness made some sense, but despair? It was unusual, to say the least.

On a more positive note, King Nasir gradually recovered. When he did, he thanked Lance for all his help and continued to do so when it was time for Lance to leave.

King Nasir, flanked by Queen Aleesia and his mother Axilya, stood at the entrance while Lance was on top of Rosie, ready to depart.

"Thank you once again for saving my life, for saving everyone," he said, shaking the young man's hand.

"You are too kind. Everyone here deserves credit for saving the town, however. Vaeril especially. It was certainly not just me."

"Regardless, you have done an amazing thing for my people. I sincerely thank you for all you have done."

"I'd like to thank you once again, as well," Queen Aleesia said. She motioned to Lance, who leaned over to hug her.

The former queen Axilya spoke. "You saved my son's life. I can never properly repay you." She gave the young man a maternal embrace.

The elven king continued. "Now I know that King Trekz cannot be trusted. I will work with the intellectuals of my village to come up with a viable plan to end the goblin menace."

"I'm sure you will, but please be careful. Your kingdom needs you." He smiled at Aleesia. "Your wife needs you." She smiled back.

"Hey, you're going to leave without saying goodbye to me?" A familiar voice rang through the air.

"Vaeril!" Lance shouted and waved at the approaching young elf.

Vaeril approached and firmly shook Lance's hand. "Thank you again for everything you've done for us. Thank you too for saving my life."

"It was the least I could do, considering I failed to protect your father."

"Are you going on about that again? Like I told you, I've

been in many battles. If I've learned nothing else, war is awful. Good people die because of it. My father was just one of its much too many victims. Do not blame yourself. I certainly don't." He smiled. "Thanks again, and take care."

"You too. Your village needs you."

Lance waved and began to depart. Before he quite could, though, another familiar face arrived.

"Guston, what are you doing here?" Lance asked. The same buzz as before emerged in the town.

"You hadn't come back in a few days, so I was checking up on you," Guston explained. "Did I miss anything?"

Lance laughed and explained the events of the last few days.

"You had quite the adventure, it seems, but you handled things about as well as possible. Hell, what am I saying? You exceeded all expectations. Congratulations, kid, I'm proud of you. It looks like you're ready for the final test. Time to visit Tortuil."

Lance pulled his mentor over to the side, away from prying eyes. "Guston, I'm pleased with what I did but must admit that I'm not sure what this accomplished in the grand scheme of things. Al Kahim still looms as a threat. I'm not sure what this had to do with the end of the world."

"Let me ask you something, Lance. Why did you help them?"

"It's not as if I could abandon them. They needed my help."

"It seems to me that you were more concerned about helping these people than using them to accomplish a goal."

"Of course. What kind of person would I be if I did otherwise?"

"Fascinating." Guston flashed a knowing grin. "The point

of these lessons, the truth, will become more apparent soon, I promise. Right now, you have to trust me when I tell you that all of this is leading to something, and will help you solve the enigma that is Al Kahim."

"If you say so, Guston."

An elf female with jet black hair and a particularly large chest, which clothes did not quite cover, exited one of the homes and ran toward the old man. "You're not leaving without saying hello this time, Guston!"

The old man smiled and dismounted Bella. "Looks like Lupi caught me this time around."

"Should I go home and wait for you there?"

"Yeah, you do that."

Lance left his mentor to his vices. He placed his visor down to obscure an unsavory smile.

Lance took another look at the sky. The cracks had become so severe that it looked like broken glass. For a moment, he questioned whether his mentor was correct and that the world's doom was much closer than Guston predicted. Yet seeing the fluffy white clouds in a sky that had almost returned to its original color made him feel at ease and tempered such uneasiness. It made him feel that everything, though dire, would be all right. Somehow, he still felt good.

Rosie brayed loudly. Lance patted the side of her head. "Don't worry, girl, I haven't forgotten. When we get home, I'll give you all the apples you could possibly eat." The mare whinnied in delight.

Chapter 11

A common expression amongst the other towns of the kingdom was there were only three guarantees in life—death, taxes, and Tortuil being the same farming community as it ever was.

This was not literally true, of course. In the two years separating his visits, Lance noticed many changes amongst the population. The young Carver son was now able to walk and form simple sentences on his own. Miller's son, the older one, who had displayed a proclivity and expertise in swordplay and the equestrian arts, now was a squire for a knight in the capital. Alan, who had been courting Catherine, was now married to Elizabeth, a villager who had moved with her parents mere months before.

There were many other differences, subtle perhaps, virtually imperceptible to an outsider, and nothing significant enough that would belie the town's conservative reputation, but there were definitely changes.

Not where it mattered the most, though. It was not what

people meant, but there was truth in that expression. The hearts of the people did not change. This was not something unique to the people of Tortuil.

"Have you seen Megan?" a patron at the bar asked the man seated next to him.

"Another row with her husband Roger, I assume," the friend answered.

"Not so much a row as it was a beating."

"Claims she fell again."

"Doesn't she always?"

"We should do something about it."

"What can we do? We have no proof."

"Combined with the extortionists in Oldtown, this world really is going to hell, isn't it?"

"Not to mention the world's impending doom."

"You still believe that nonsense? Just another one of King Rudolph's tricks to raise taxes. Unless the Chosen One already saved the world."

"I suppose you're right."

Lance silently set down his drink and rose from the table. He plunked a few coins down and exited the tavern. The young man still remembered where Megan lived from his previous expedition.

"Hello?" The middle-aged woman stared at Lance from a slit in the slightly ajar door. She didn't want to answer, but the incessant, thunderous knocking made it impossible for her to ignore. Lance's heart shattered upon seeing the large discoloration around her right eye and the cut above her lip.

He handed her a handkerchief. "When you need to cry," he explained.

The woman began to weep. Her handkerchief became

useless, so quick was it dampened with tears. She opened the door more widely. "Who are you?" she asked between the sobs.

"Joe Kaime," he answered. "I thought you might need a friend." She let him into her home. "Why don't you just leave him?" he asked. A light shined onto him from a lone window. The scent of rosemary pleased his olfactory nerves. He tapped his fingers against the oak table as he sat, waiting for her reply.

Lance looked around the home. It was sparsely decorated. There was one large bed, a large mahogany closet that he was sure was a luxury given the sparse furnishings—perhaps an inheritance or a gift. It was large enough to fit two people, though Lance doubted it contained that many clothes, if any. On the shelves were a bunch of wooden cat figures that were like toys one might give a child.

The kettle's howl pierced the awkward silence. Wordlessly she set two cups on the table and poured tea into each of them. Megan picked up her tea and sat next to the young knight. She took a couple of sips. The other cup remained on the table.

"It's not that easy."

"Don't you have family elsewhere?"

"I don't. I am an only child. My parents died many years ago."

"Perhaps you could stay with a friend?"

"I don't have any friends outside the town. He'd find me, and I'd go back to him."

"Your friends would betray you?"

"They wouldn't, but I love him, despite what he's done to me. We grew up together. We've always been together. I can't imagine life without him."

"Does he love you?"

"Of course he does."

"He's got a funny way of showing it."

"You don't know him as I do. In tender moments, he can be very sweet. He tells me how much he loves me, how much I mean to him, how much it hurts when he sees me with other men, how I'm the only one for him, how much it'd kill him if I ever left, that he might kill himself if I did."

She paused to take another sip and stared aimlessly. "He doesn't mean to hurt me. He just has issues with jealousy, not to mention his job is just very stressful. He works all day at the tavern stocking shelves, moving barrels, that sort of thing. It's not what he wanted to do in life, you know. He wanted to be an adventurer."

Megan took another sip. "Of course, the drinking doesn't help. He becomes a different man when he drinks. I've tried talking to him about it, but he tells me drinking is the only thing that gets him through the day. It doesn't help that he works at a tavern, and his boss can get away with paying part of his salary with booze."

"None of this excuses his behavior," Lance said.

"I know," Megan said, the tears beginning to well up again. "I know."

"Megan, how about this? Find somewhere safe to go, for now. It doesn't necessarily have to be a permanent arrangement. Just go somewhere to clear your head."

Megan sipped her tea in silence. She finished and poured herself another cup and continued to drink. Her next cup was nearly empty before she found the strength to answer. "Where would I go?"

Lance thought for a moment. "My mother's house."

"Your mother?"

"She lives in the capital."

"The capital? That's so far away. How can I get there?"

"I've made long journeys like that a countless number of times. I could take you there. I will make sure you get there safely."

"Would your mother be all right with this?"

"Of course. She's been alone since my aunt died. She'd appreciate the company."

"I don't know."

Lance smiled. "She has a cat."

Megan perked up. "Really?"

"His name is Albert. He's kind of standoffish, to be honest, but once he gets to know you, he's incredibly friendly."

"Isn't that true of all cats?" She paused. "Let me think about it, all right?"

"All right, that's fair. Please think about it."

Internally, Lance questioned the wisdom of taking a strange woman to live with his mother. Not that she would mind, but he was supposed to be incognito. His mind poured through ideas to come up with an explanation while keeping his identity a secret. He failed to think of one.

No matter. The circumstances required him to get this woman out of her terrible living arrangement. He could figure out exactly how to explain this to his mother on the way there.

Night fell. Megan's husband Roger was finally coming home from the tavern. His breath reeked of alcohol. Had the couple owned any plants, they would have wilted upon his arrival.

"Where's my dinner, woman?" he growled as he sat at his table.

"I'm sorry. A friend came to visit, and we had a long conversation, and I lost track of time. I can get started now." She went to grab a frying pan and some other cooking utensils.

"I work all day, and she doesn't even provide me dinner," he muttered. "What the hell were the two of you talking about that was so damn important you forgot dinner?"

"It's difficult to say."

"Tell me, now," he commanded.

"But—"

"Now!"

The ferocity in his voice caused her to drop the utensils on the stove. They landed with a loud crashing noise. She wanted to come up with a lie but had difficulty thinking of one, especially since she was under duress. The truth escaped her lips as if she were an automaton.

"He invited me to visit his mother, so I could have some time to think."

The man leaped up from the table. His chair flew behind him and hit a wall, causing the woman to jump backward and fall to the floor. "He invited you to his home? He? A friend? More like a lover, wench."

"No, it was nothing like that."

"Who was it? Was it Tom Miller? I've seen the way he's looked at you. I'm sure he's unsatisfied with that sow wife of his!"

"It wasn't Tom! It wasn't anyone you know. He's...he's from out of town."

"So some exotic stranger comes in and wants to take you away! Did the two of you cohabitate my bed?"

"What? How dare you accuse me of something like that? I am your wife!"

"A wife does not leave her husband to lie in her lover's home! A wife does not do these things to a man that loves her so much! You know how much it would kill me for you to leave! I refuse to let it happen!"

"You cannot stop me!"

"Like hell, I cannot!"

His fist reared back. It started forward with full intention to strike.

It never reached its mark. A hand had snatched his arm—Lance's hand.

The young man had spent the rest of his day at the tavern. When he noticed Roger leaving the establishment, he followed him, worried something like this would happen. Luckily, Roger did not recognize the young man thanks to the mask.

Lance had snuck inside. Roger did not hear him due to the row he was having with his wife. Not that it would have made much of a difference had he heard him come in, as Roger quickly learned when Lance threw him out the door. It was as if Lance was flinging a ragdoll.

Megan followed Lance as he stepped outside. Homes were beginning to clear as people made their way onto the streets.

Roger fumed while he rose from the ground. "Who the hell are you?"

"I'm a friend of your wife. I'm here to ensure that the beatings stop."

"A friend? Just a friend? The devil you are. You're the one she's cuckolding me with."

"Watch your tongue."

Roger ran and took a few drunken swipes at the young man. His punches were easily caught. Lance applied pressure to the man's fists, which caused him to shriek in pain. The knight then threw his opponent to the ground once again.

Almost everyone in town, except for the children, was on

the streets by this time. All were gathered and formed a circle around the pair. A few cheered Lance on, even though they did not know him. All of them, at least internally, were on his side.

A few more anemic strikes were attempted but to no avail. Lance eventually grew tired of the charade. He tossed the man onto his stomach and placed a foot on top of his head.

"One false step, and I will crush you," Lance threatened.

"No! Don't hurt him!" Megan screamed. She rushed over to the knight. Both of her frail hands grabbed his elbow as she feebly tried to pull Lance away from her husband.

Gently, the knight removed her. An elderly woman came and took Megan away and back into the crowd.

"You truly don't deserve a woman like that," Lance said to the man resting under his foot.

"Go to hell," Roger growled.

The knight was momentarily distracted. From a distance, he could see a familiar-looking spec, but he wasn't sure. It was tough to tell in the darkness. Only a few torches at the entrance of town, along with the ones a couple of members of the town were holding, served as illumination.

As it moved closer, he realized who it was and waved. It was Guston. He rode Bella next to Lance.

"Is everything okay?"

Lance explained why he had a foot on top of a man's head.

"What are you planning on doing next, Lance?"

"As loathe as I am to say it, I think the best course of action would be for me to take him to the capital so he may face justice for his crimes."

"I agree. That would be the best course of action. He needs to have a trial."

"Excuse me," a nearby townsperson interrupted the

conversation. "Would it not be more prudent for you just to kill him? You witnessed the abuse, as have others. Why put him through a trial when we all know he is guilty?"

Lance explained. "Trials do not exist solely to ensure justice has been met. They also exist to provide the populace comfort in knowing that the accused has been given a chance to have his say in court and that a verdict has been reached fairly. If I killed him now, those who have witnessed the abuse may believe justice was served, but non-witnesses would fret that I am unjustly acting as judge, jury, and executioner, or even tyrannically."

"Good luck with that!" the man on the ground shouted sarcastically. "Other than her word and yours, what evidence do you have of my crime?"

"Your confession."

"My confession?" The man chortled. "What makes you think I'm going to confess?"

Lance increased the amount of pressure he applied to the man's head. "Because I'm going to give you a choice. I can take you to the capital where you can confess, or I can crush your head."

"What about all that talk about fair trials and shit like that?"

"What can I say? It sounded good, right? Truth is, it's just something I read. I'm not sure I even really believe it myself. And besides, what can I say? I'm very amenable."

"Personally, I'd encourage him to crush your head," Guston said. "It's what human filth like you deserves."

The man growled. "All right, I'll go with you. Willingly. And I'll confess. Just let me up."

Lance removed his foot, bound the man's hands with rope while giving himself something to hold onto, and helped the criminal get on top of Rosie.

"I'm proud of you, kid. You did really well. I think by now you should know why I sent you on these trials."

"To test me."

"Of course, but what have you learned from all these tests?"

"To be honest, I'm not sure."

"So saving that woman, bringing this man to justice, what does that have to do with Al Kahim?"

"As far as I know, nothing."

"Actually, in many ways, it has everything. Tell me, and be honest with yourself, why did you help these villages before?"

"So they would give me the gems I needed to unlock Artus's Sword."

"And why did you help them now?"

"Because you told me too?"

"Is that really it? Is that why you've gone through so much extra effort to help them? I never provided you any instructions. You could have quit several times, yet you kept going. You didn't have to listen to the directives of a rambling old man, yet you did. So you only did it because I said?"

Lance paused. "No, that's not the only reason. I helped these people because they needed me."

"Exactly. When you went off to save the world before, you did not do it because you wanted to help the people of the world. You did it for yourself to accomplish a goal. You lost sight of what mattered. I think you know better now and are ready to face Al Kahim."

"Thank you so much, Guston. Your lessons have been invaluable. Yet, I'm not quite done. I do have one more task to complete. I must get this guy to Angenehm so he can face his punishment."

"Of course. Will you be visiting the king while you are there?" Guston seemed noticeably somber when he asked this question.

"Is everything all right?"

"Ah, no, just tired, that's all. Old age, you know."

He did not seem particularly tired. Lance wanted to say something further but couldn't quite find the words. "If you say so, Guston. Anyway, I do not wish to see the king until I have slain Al Kahim."

"Indeed, I believe it would be wise to first pay Al Kahim a visit."

"Will you be accompanying me?"

"Not yet. I must gather something from home. I shall join you in Angenehm. Farewell for now."

Lance turned toward Megan. "There's been a change of plans. It looks like you're going to stay home while I take this piece of human excrement to the capital." He looked toward the crowd. "Would someone here please look after her?"

A pair of old ladies chimed in. Lance recognized them from his initial visit to this town. "We will gladly stay with her."

"Make sure she doesn't try and leave, won't you?"

Another elderly lady chimed in. He recognized her too. "Don't worry. I'll make sure she doesn't leave."

"Thank you, ladies," Lance said. "Now I am off."

As he mounted the horse, he took a look upward. The sky had returned to its original hue. Had it not been for the multiple cracks, it would have been a beautiful scene. Lance still bathed in the radiance that was the sun's magnificence.

The trip to the capital was long but mostly uneventful. There were instances where the knight had to unbind the hands of the man to allow him to eat, drink, and take care of other needs. The knight's stern eye and threats of violence kept his attempts to escape mostly in check.

That is not to say the prisoner made no attempt to escape early in the expedition, but he quickly realized that both the knight's steed and the knight himself were much quicker than he, and frankly, both were more intelligent, so all escape attempts were quickly snuffed.

As they headed further into the wilderness, the environment itself became a deterrent. Lance knew the territory from his years of experience traveling through it, but the man lacked such proclivity to travel and found himself out of his element. Even when the knight had to search for extra food by hunting, he knew his prisoner would wait for him patiently lest he had to face the harsh forest he was unprepared to take on by himself.

After almost a week of travel, Lance arrived at the capital he'd once called home. The sun was setting, and a mist had descended. Even though not much had changed in the intervening years, it was surreal. Through the fog, he could make out familiar edifices and homes, but for some reason, they felt distant to him. Odors felt a little less pungent. Noises sounded a bit more hollow. Colors seemed a little more faded. It was almost as if the town he had pictured before was merely a vision or a dream, and he was just now experiencing the reality.

"What the hell is going on? Why have we stopped?" His prisoner's coarse inquiries woke him from this stupor. Lance led the man to the prison.

The constable was a bit perplexed over why Lance had brought the man to him. He explained that the man's hometown didn't have a prison, and the man must be incarcerated for his heinous crimes.

A citizen's arrest of sorts was highly unusual, especially without any evidence or eyewitnesses. Lance said this would not be an issue, as his prisoner planned to confess. At first, the prisoner tried to weasel out of it. He hemmed and hawed and tried to convince the constable that the knight was insane and had imprisoned him unjustly.

"If you do not confess," Lance whispered, "Then be prepared to face my alternative plan of distributing justice, of which you know I am more than capable."

Sweat dripped down the prisoner's brow. He promptly confessed.

The constable shrugged. He had no reason not to imprison him now. As Lance headed toward the exit, he patted the prisoner on the shoulder and whispered that he'd return to check on him and make sure the trial went as planned.

Lance turned to leave when he was quickly interrupted by a strange sound. It was akin to hair rubbing on steel.

He looked down and saw a familiar pair of green eyes stare right back at him, along with a pink nose, pointed ears, orange, black, and white fur, and a long tail. The knight reached down to give the cat a quick stroke, as was his habit.

"Albert?" If his mother's calico cat was there, that could mean only one thing.

"Albert? Where are you, Albert?" A familiar voice pierced the fog.

"I better get going," Lance muttered.

"Lance? Is that you?" It was too late.

"I don't know who you are talking about," Lance said, trying desperately hard to disguise his voice. "My name is Joe Kaime."

"Do you really think I wouldn't recognize my own son? Where have you been? I thought you were dead. All of us thought you were dead!" She hugged her son tightly. Tears streamed down her cheeks.

"I can explain, Mother." Before he could, though, he was interrupted by a couple of passersby.

"What did she say?" a man asked another.

"That's Lance! The Chosen One has returned!"

The pair of them shouted and knocked on doors to alert the rest of the townsfolk, who, in turn, emptied their homes to hail their prodigal son.

"He's returned!"

"I thought he was dead!"

"At least that would be an excuse."

"Can't believe he abandoned us."

"Now 'e thinks 'e can com' back, and we'll all be lovey-dovey."

"I'm sure he has his reasons."

"Boozin' and whorin', I'm sure."

"He must see the king!"

"Yes, the king! The king!"

"My brother has already headed to the castle to alert him of Lance's arrival."

"King Rudolph will be flabbergasted to hear he's alive!"

"He was pretty sure Al Kahim killed him."

"He hasn't seemed too distraught, though, has he?"

"Plus, he didn't seem too concerned about the world ending after that for some reason."

"That's because he wanted to be strong for all of us, you dolts! Lance was like a son. Of course, he was heartbroken."

"I heard a rumor that after he heard the news, he was

actually relieved!"

"Lies and propaganda!"

Lance's ears perked, but his mother interjected before he could ask any questions. "Yes, Lance, you should see the king. He thinks you are dead. I know he'll be beyond thrilled to see you once again."

"Mother, I cannot see him now," Lance said. "My fight with Al Kahim was an abject failure. I've been training, though, and my trainer says I am nearly ready to defeat him."

"You've been training? With whom?"

"It may be difficult to believe, but I have been training with the great Guston."

The crowd was stirred.

"Guston? Did he say Guston?"

"He's been training with the great Guston?"

"I thought he was dead."

"I thought he was just a legend."

"Why would the Chosen One need to train?"

"I suppose even the so-called Chosen One knew there were limits to what he could do."

"Then this is the perfect time to see the king," his mother said. "You may have failed, but you have trained. This time you will succeed. I'm sure he'll be very pleased to hear that." His mother flashed a comforting smile. "Don't worry. I'm sure he's still proud of you. I am."

Lance eventually relented. He was skeptical, but his mother's warmth eased his apprehensions and convinced him that seeing the king would do no harm.

He made his way to the castle. Some townsfolk followed, but they were hardly the reveling escorts they were but two years prior. Cynicism ran rampant. Even amongst the few supporters he had remaining, there was, at most, a tenuous and mild optimism, born more out of Lance representing their only hope from the metaphorical Sword of Damocles hanging above them in the manifestation of Al Kahim than it was genuine confidence.

"Will you be joining me this time, Mother?" Lance asked when he reached the castle's gates.

"No. Albert still needs to be fed, and I still don't feel comfortable visiting royalty. You'll still visit me before you go, won't you, Lance?" The knight nodded his head.

The reception within the castle walls was not nearly as frigid as the one he received outside. Having only moments ago heard the news of his return from a citizen, there was no time for King Rudolph to prepare an elaborate celebration or even gather anyone for even a crude facsimile. Still, the royal knights that were there welcomed him with a pat on the back and a few kind words. Some even complimented his new armor.

The chamberlain led him to the throne room. Seeing the familiar plush red carpet brought back memories. "Your Majesty, the Chosen One, Lance, has returned!"

The king practically sprang off his seat to greet the young man. "Lance! You have returned! Words cannot express how happy I am to see you again!"

Again the king's physique seemed to have changed. His wrinkles appeared to have deepened, his face was wider, his shoulders were a bit broader, his torso had narrowed, and his legs, oddly, seemed a bit longer.

These changes were subtle. Only someone who knew the king incredibly well would notice. Even then, the young man had been away for many years. He dismissed the changes as his imagination.

Yet, there was something odd about his expression. It

seemed more, dare he think, crazed and manic.

Lance dismissed these thoughts. More pressing matters were on hand. He bowed before the king. "I apologize humbly for not seeing you sooner."

King Rudolph asked the young man to rise. "Please, do not fret over such trivial matters. My heart is filled to the brim with excitement over your return!"

"I have bad news for you, sire. My battle with Al Kahim ended in abject failure."

"Do you think I am concerned with that? After all these years? Do you know how much I've missed you, Lance? Every day I sent men out to search for you. I wanted so badly to see you again!"

Lance looked at him quizzically. "The townsfolk seemed convinced that you thought I was dead."

"Just a façade so my citizens wouldn't panic. Remember, you may be my favorite, Lance, but I consider all of them my children."

"I see."

"Is something bothering you?"

Indeed, there was. Something the king said moments ago vexed the young man. "Forgive me, sire, but your reach extends pretty far. I'm having difficulty believing your men couldn't have found me in two years."

"The world is large, and searching for you was like trying to find a needle in a haystack. Let's forget about that for now. It is time to celebrate." King Rudolph clapped his hands.

Out from the kitchen came three beautiful, exotic women wearing veils, silk pants, and shirts that covered some of their tops and none of their stomachs. It reminded Lance of some of the Eastern women he read about in Guston's books.

They danced in a manner unfamiliar to the young man. Their performance captivated him, so much so that he did not even notice the chef until he bumped into his feet with his tray. On it was a roast duck dripping with a mysterious sauce.

After the women finished, they gathered around the young man. One rubbed his shoulders while the other two got on either side and began massaging his arms and hands. He didn't feel much physically through the armor, but their actions still had an effect. Lance sweated profusely.

"Lovely, aren't they?" the king said. "They are ambassadors on a goodwill tour. Let me just say, the way they spread goodwill is rather pleasant." The three women giggled in response.

"As much of a pleasure as it is to be in these women's company, I must remind you that we have more urgent matters to be concerned with."

"Such as?"

"Al Kahim, Your Majesty. Don't you remember? The end of the world is still nigh. I failed."

Sweat started to amass on the king's brow.

Lance paused for a moment. "If you'll forgive me again, Your Majesty, I must confess I am surprised to see your lack of urgency. For two years, the world has been in peril. Guston assured me the world would not end before my training had been completed. His exploits are legendary, so I trusted his judgment, and his words were true. You did not have such assurance, however. As far as you know, the threat is immediate, yet you seem untroubled. Putting on a brave face is one thing, but you seem unconcerned."

The king flashed an unnerving grin. "It's because the evil wizard is no longer a threat. We can rejoice."

"What do you mean? Is Al Kahim dead?"

"As I said before, now is not the time to discuss such matters. We must have our priorities. Please take a bite of that roast duck before it gets cold. It is delicious. Why even the smell is captivating. You must remember the culinary skill of my chef. You haven't had a bite of his food in two years. Surely you must crave a bite."

Lance sniffed the air. The smell was a treat for his olfactory nerves. He lost himself in the pleasant aroma.

That is until he noticed something. It was faint and mostly hidden. Lance initially thought it came from the women, but though they did have a nice fragrance, they were not the ones giving off that sweet and subtly floral smell. A little bitter, too, reminiscent of unripened tomatoes.

It was the duck.

Lance pushed aside the women and approached the king.

"Belladonna! That sauce is belladonna, and the duck is covered in it! Why are you trying to poison me?"

King Rudolph grew stern. "I wanted this to be quick and relatively easy, but you always have to make things complicated, don't you, Lance?"

Tears welled in Lance's eyes. "How? Why? I thought I was your favorite. Why do you want to kill me?"

"I did not want it to come to this. Knights, come in here now!"

Dozens of King Rudolph's best and most loyal knights flooded the room. They drew their swords upon entrance and pointed them at Lance. The women fled.

"Al Kahim already has the final ingredient. The final stages of his plan are already in motion."

"No. That can't be true!"

"It is. Yet there is a way to prevent it."

"What? What can stop it?"

"Your blood."

"What did you say?" Lance paused for a moment. "My blood?"

"Yes. As the Chosen One, your blood is the only cure for the crumbling world."

Chapter 12

Lance was speechless. He searched for the words to say. Several times he attempted but was only able to make a few incoherent sounds barely above a whisper before abandoning the thought. The king's knights, in the meantime, continued to close in.

"How long have you known this?" Lance rasped, finally able to speak but just barely.

"For about a year."

"A year?"

"Shortly after you left to fight Al Kahim, a messenger arrived. He told me that the wizard had already discovered the final ingredient to end the world. The final stages of his plan had been set in motion. When you didn't return, we feared the worst. We thought you had died and the world was doomed."

"That was two years ago."

"Indeed. However, the world didn't end, at least not after a year. Our scholars searched the world for answers. They discovered missing parts of the prophecy written in the language of the ancients. Orbo translated it for us. It foretold that when the world entered its nadir, the blood of the Chosen One could be used to counteract the spell. When the world didn't end, I thought you'd died in that fight. Obviously, I was wrong. I'm not sure why the world hasn't ended yet. I can only assume the spell takes longer than we had anticipated. I suppose in that way, we are fortunate."

Lance could only stutter.

"I'm so sorry, Lance. You know what you must do."

A bevy of images flashed into the young man's head. Of the adventures he'd gone on. Of the friends he'd met, along with the enemies. Of the creatures he'd slain. Of the people he ultimately helped after having failed them. Of the training he'd completed. Of Al Kahim. Of Guston. Of Strefonio. Of Sanders. Of Alizon. Of Nerissa.

He asked himself what sort of leader he would want to follow.

His experiences taught him the answer. One who would sacrifice his own needs for the needs of others. There was no nobler cause.

"I...I surrender." Lance placed his blade upon the ground.

"I knew you'd make the right decision."

With a couple of careless flicks of the wrist, King Rudolph ordered his knights to attack. The men slowly closed in on him. Lance knelt, placed his palms against the back of his head, and closed his eyes.

Suddenly, a large bang was heard at the entrance, interrupting the knights from running their swords through the young man. The eyes of Lance, the knights, and the king turned towards the door. An elderly man dashed through and rushed toward the young man who knelt in the middle of the circle of knights. A pair of them lunged at the old man. He drew his sword. With a couple of quick blows, they were dispatched.

Several knights left formation to avenge their fallen comrades. Before they could even take a swing, though, one of the others stepped in front of them.

"Wait!" he shouted. He turned to the old man. "Are you not Guston?"

"What?" a knight from the circle asked. "Do you mean The Great Guston?"

"Guston is here?" Lance asked.

"What is Guston doing here?" King Rudolph demanded. "No matter. Knights, attack him as well!"

The knights refused.

"Sire," one of them protested. "That's the Great Guston. He's a legendary knight. How could we even consider attacking that man?" A murmur amongst the rest of the knights confirmed they agreed with his protest.

"I am your king, and this is an order. Attack."

The knights' argument with their lord allowed Guston to push his way through the crowd and get to Lance.

"Pick up that sword," Guston commanded when he arrived. He stood next to the young man with his sword drawn in a defensive position

Lance did as he was instructed.

"I'm sorry I didn't get here sooner. What sort of lies has this man been telling you?"

"He said my blood is the only thing that will prevent the world from ending."

"Why would you tell him that?"

"It was foretold in the prophecy!" the king screamed.

"Then the prophecy is wrong."

"So it's not true?" Lance asked.

"The truth is far more complicated. You need to see the wizard and hear it from him. He can tell you the truth."

"What?"

"I've known him for years. He's a good man. He brought you to me. He asked me to protect you from the king."

Lance was at a loss for words.

"Don't listen to the words of a senile old man," King Rudolph said.

"I knew you were misguided, but to think you were capable of something like this. You're mad."

"I am trying to save this world. I would do anything to protect this kingdom, even if it means sacrificing its greatest warrior."

"Run, Lance. Quickly. Let me handle this."

"I'm sorry, Guston. I'm not sure I should. What if my blood is the only thing that can save the world?"

"It's not. Trust me, it's not. If it was true, why is King Rudolph so hell-bent on killing you here? Al Kahim could do the job just as easily, couldn't he?"

"As if he would do it," the king growled. "That wizard knows as well as I that his blood is the only thing that could prevent the end of the world. That's why he didn't finish him before. I should have figured it out sooner. He won't kill him now."

"If that's the case, why did the king try to deceive you?" Guston asked. "Have I ever tried to deceive you? Have I ever lied to you, Lance?"

"No, you have not," Lance admitted.

"If nothing else, of the two of us here now, who seems to have your best interest in mind?"

Lance was lost in thought for a moment before he mustered an answer. "I can't leave you here to face them alone. These are the kingdom's best knights."

Guston smiled and winked at the young man. "I know I'm old, but I'm still strong, and my skills haven't eroded. If anything, they've improved with age. I'll meet you at Stonewall. But first, take this."

He handed Lance a vial with a clear liquid inside. The young man placed it in his small pouch connected to his belt.

"What is this?"

"It's the reason I was late. I had to get it from home. Remember that chest next to my bed?"

"Vaguely."

"It held this. King Rudolph wanted me to give it to him, but I refused. That is why I had to leave. It's Alathea's Enchantment."

"I've never heard of such a thing."

"I'm not surprised. Not a lot of people like to talk about the entire story. They'd prefer the idea that Artus worked alone. Perhaps there's romanticism in the notion of a lone hero. Perhaps it's because the enchantment needed to be a secret. Perhaps it's because of something more, I don't know. I'm just rambling at this point.

"Alathea was not a mere supporter. She played a vital role in Artus's adventures by producing the vial necessary to enchant the sword that allowed him to slay his enemies. The two worked side by side. I know this because I am a descendant of Alathea. I am the current guardian of her enchantment. I left the king and the kingdom to protect this secret.

"It was foretold that a knight worthy of the spell would come to me someday. He would be the one that would see the light when darkness fell and end the nightmare. Lance, I have every reason to believe it is you. You passed my tests. You've grown so much in the past two years. You proved that you are worthy."

"What do I do with it?"

"You'll know when the time is right. Time's a-wasting. Now go."

Lance sheathed his sword and took two steps back, his eyes never leaving his mentor. After a moment's pause, he turned to run. A couple of the knights that surrounded the men made their way towards him, but a couple of quick swipes of Guston's blade made quick work of those foes.

"Sorry, lads," the old man said to the ones still standing. "I can't let you do that."

"You don't understand," one said. "We have to kill him to prevent the end of the world!"

"I wish I could convince you boys of the truth. Let's go."

The sounds of sword strikes became more muted until they were but a memory as Lance dashed through the entrance door, into the great hall, and out the castle into the streets of Angenehm. Somewhere amongst the multitude of voices, the clashing of swords, the yells, and the cries, Lance could have sworn he heard something quite distinctive. Quite notable. Something terrible. A nightmare come to life.

He dismissed it as his imagination, but the more he tried to ignore it, the more prominent the thought crept into his head. The voice crescendoed and reverberated until it was unmistakable what caused his ears to perk. He heard the anguished screams of an old man. A friend. A mentor. A legendary warrior. The great Guston.

Lance dismissed the notion as foolishness. He told himself a more pleasant and, he tried to convince himself, more likely and more logical outcome. He repeated it over and over again until it became a mantra. He said it more and more loudly until it became a shout.

There were no screams. It was only his imagination. Guston would join him at Stonewall. Of course, he would. He promised.

Lance mounted Rosie and rode like the wind to Stonewall. Time had no meaning for the young man, as his singular focus was returning to the city where his life was turned upside down.

Chapter 13

The world became a blur. Phantasmagorias within his memory indicate at some point, he ate and slept during this journey, allowing a bit of rest for him and his steed as they raced those hundreds of miles toward their destination. There was a mental image of him hunting to resupply his waning stock of food somewhere along the way.

He seemed to recall vaguely fighting some creatures through hazy memories and displayed in a sea of crimson. He could sort of recall feeling sorrowful for not visiting his mother when he promised he would.

Eventually, Lance arrived at the city of Stonewall. A fog had set in, and the sun was beginning to fall.

The town seemed abandoned. Not a soul appeared to be on the streets. There was a quiet to the town, an absurd quiet, almost as if Lance had gone deaf. Even Rosie's hoof steps registered little more than light tapping noises against the pavement.

Evidence of devastation was all around. Fire was everywhere. It was hard to differentiate between the smoke and the fog. Several buildings were toppled. Very little remained standing. Lance was appalled.

He looked to his left on the ground near the entrance. There were only charred remains and a sign that read "LIRAY." Lance's heart nearly shattered. So much history lost.

Worse were the bodies. They were fresh. Human and dwarf lie all over in what appeared to have been a battle of some sort. Their tools lay next to them and appeared to have been used as makeshift weapons. Their bodies were skewered. The streets ran red with blood, making it difficult to tell that these streets were once brown. The young man did his best to ignore these terrible sights and continued riding, wondering what kind of monster would do this to these poor, innocent people.

Rosie did her best to tiptoe around the corpses but still nearly tripped over one. Her front legs bucked slightly, and she moved backward a couple of steps. Lance leaned over to take a look at the body that lay next to his horse's feet.

It was Old Pete. The deceased prospector lay on his stomach, and his head was off to the side. A pickaxe was lodged in his back.

Before Lance could fully comprehend what had happened, a figure suddenly appeared. It was a man dressed in a white cloak. Several men appeared next to him as if they were hiding in the fog. It became apparent that the young man and his horse were surrounded.

They were of many different races. Humans, elves, dwarves. It looked like there were even some orcs and goblins in the mix, and based on the color scheme of their armor, they were once part of either King Knaugh's or King Trekz's army, respectively.

From the haze just beyond the row of men came a familiar

voice. "Long time, no see, 'dear friend.'"

A figure in a black cloak pushed through the crowd and stood in front of the silver-haired steed. Lance's horse instinctively took a few steps back.

"Sanders?"

"In the flesh."

Lance excitedly sprung off the horse and dashed to his companion. "I thought you were dead!"

"I thought the same thing of you."

"There are so many questions to ask. Where have you been?"

"I've been in Swindon, a town about ten miles from here. I've been involved with various activities."

"You live there?"

"Absolutely. Nerissa and Strefonio live nearby as well, though not in Swindon. I don't know where Alizon is, though I don't really care. Between you and me, I never really liked her. She certainly was a stick in the mud. She really didn't seem to like any of us, did she? Except for you, I suppose."

"She was always kind to me."

"Of course she was, you dense moron." Sanders laughed uproariously.

"What the hell happened here?"

"Now that's an interesting story. Do you know what I've been up to the last few years?"

"No, and I hate to say it, but I don't think this is the time to reminisce."

"Well, I feel like reminiscing, so I will. I've been very busy recently. I run a business protecting the people. As I've always said, my primary goal is helping people. It is almost as much fun as collecting loot. Almost. To that end, my protection does come at a moderate cost, but it's worth it. Some people, unfortunately, do not realize how much they need me until after disaster has already struck."

This talk evoked a few memories of what Lance had learned. He remembered overhearing a conversation amongst the townsfolk about this very thing happening to nearby towns.

"You're the extortionist!" Lance exclaimed.

"That is a baseless accusation. We warn people something bad might happen if they don't pay for our services, and yet when something bad happens, and we aren't there to protect them, we get the blame. We're businessmen. We were just offering our services. Everything else is just a coincidence."

Lance gripped the hilt of his sword. "Did these people refuse to pay you?"

"Actually, the people here did pay their protection money, and true to my word, I made sure nothing unfortunate happened to them. It made trading with their fair town a bit more expensive, but such is the cost of security."

"So what happened?"

"A little birdie told me something interesting—almost literally, I might add." Sanders pulled out a slip of paper from his pocket. "Care of King Rudolph's messenger pigeon. I won't read the note, but the upshot is he wants me to kill you. Something about preventing the end of the world."

Sanders crumpled out the letter and tossed it aside.

"Frankly, I don't believe in this whole ending the world nonsense. I never really did, if I'm being honest. It was just something to do and a way to get in touch with some business contacts of mine. But since the king is offering quite the reward for your death, I figured, why not?"

Sanders took a quick scan of the corpses. "Of course, word

travels fast. Once this guy over here caught wind of what we were doing, he rallied the town to try and fight us off. The old guy was very fond of you. He gave his life to protect you. Such altruism is rare in these trying times, don't you think?" He paused to give Old Pete's corpse a quick kick.

"How dare you do that to Old Pete?"

"Was that his name?"

"I never thought you'd do something like this," Lance said. "Betrayal and murder. You've changed."

Sanders glowered. "I didn't change. I've always been the same. You just saw what you wanted to see."

"I should have let you go to jail. I should have never sworn on your behalf."

"At least we agree on that. All right, men. Attack!"

The men in white cloaks drew their daggers and attacked all at once. Rosie barely managed to escape.

They had the advantage in numbers, but he had the advantage in strength, skill, and weaponry. Lance easily managed to evade their attacks and displayed unexpected amounts of agility. They had never seen such deftness before, especially from one who was armored.

Since they outnumbered him by twenty and were used to having the advantage in speed, they expected at least one of them to be able to land a blow before the knight could respond. They were wrong. Instead, Lance made quick work of them.

Several sweeping swings of his blade cut through many of the men. Their bifurcated upper bodies flew into the air as their legs tumbled to the ground. Each of their eyes were wide and panicked-stricken. Their limbs flailed, unsure what to do with the remnants of their rapidly shortened lives. A few downward cuts and several more men were split in two other directions.

Lance chased and caught up to the men who attempted to flee. He was no more merciful to them than he was to the rest.

Soon all that was left was Lance and Sanders. The thief ran toward Rosie, who was standing by a nearby, burnt-down home. He mounted her and struck both feet down on the horse to make her run. As he didn't know her, he didn't realize that she obeyed only one man. She neighed angrily and bucked him off.

Sanders landed hard on the ground with a sickening cracking noise. He used his hands to try and catch himself, and now his left wrist bent in an awkward direction. His right ankle was in no better shape. He could do nothing but lie there and beg for mercy.

"Lance, we were friends before. You once saw that I was a good guy deep down, just misguided. I relapsed without you, but I can recover. I'll help you find Nerissa and Strefonio and even Alizon. She can fix my arm and leg. It'll be just like old times." The thief subtly drew his blade with his right hand and placed it behind him.

"You're right, Sanders," Lance said as he stepped towards his former friend.

"I'm glad you see things my way. Would you mind reaching down and helping me up?"

Lance leaned over. Sanders gripped the blade tighter, ready for the opportunity to pounce.

"You haven't changed," Lance said. "I'm the one who's changed."

The knight lifted Artus's Sword high into the air. Sanders begged. He tried to remind him of the good times they'd had together, to remember they were friends.

It was to no avail. Lance plunged the blade into his chest. Sanders died slowly and painfully.

Lance dislodged the blade, wiped the blood, sheathed the sword, and sighed. A single tear rolled down his cheek. He silently returned to his steed. The two of them headed deeper into town.

Rosie stepped gingerly. The fog was becoming increasingly thick. Each step felt deliberate and weighty. Breathing was difficult.

A familiar figure emerged on the path like an apparition. It appeared to be a wizard, though he could have been a wandering vagrant if one were to judge strictly by looks. Regardless, the man was in terrible shape, emaciated, and enfeebled too. And itchy. Very, very itchy. His long nails on craggy hands seemed to be constantly scratching all over. The head, the arms, the legs, even the feet. His scratching was incredibly frantic.

He was dirty, filthy even, as if he had been dipped in the mud for several years and only recently been allowed to leave. Even his beard was hardly distinguishable as white, looking closer to brown and yellow. His robe was so discolored with dirty brown patches it made it difficult to discern that its original color was blue. A blue that was familiar to the young man.

The wizard had an atrocious and repugnant smell that acted as something of a barrier. Lance had difficulty approaching, as even a whiff of that repugnant smell made him nauseous.

In one of the wizard's hands was a mushroom. When he wasn't scratching, the wizard was sucking on the cap. Lance gently descended from Rosie and commanded her to hide. Once she was hidden, he approached the wizard cautiously. "Strefonio, what the hell happened to you?"

"I'm like, fine, dude," Strefonio said. His eyes darted everywhere but never landed on Lance. "I guess that's not really true, I mean, I could be better, but you know, not too bad." The wizard coughed profusely. Trickles of blood dribbled from his mouth onto his beard. "Maybe I ain't doing so good." He began licking the cap of his mushroom once again. "These mushrooms, man, they're like really good stuff, I mean like, really good stuff. Really enhance your spells and your mind, make you see things, man, like you would never see without using them. Good stuff. Real good stuff."

"We need to get you help." Lance reached out.

Strefonio slapped Lance's hand away. "I told you I'm good, man. I don't need any help!" Strefonio screamed. "Sorry, man, sorry. I think it's just the nerves or something, I don't know. Plus all these insects on me, man. It's driving me nuts."

Lance inspected the man. Nothing was crawling on him.

More men emerged from the fog and stood next to the wizard as the two men spoke. They donned similarly sullied robes, had a similar foul smell and had a similar level of hygiene as each of them scratched themselves heavily. Some even drew blood. All of them carried a mushroom in one hand.

"Who are these men?"

"Just some friends of mine. Met them at Pollyanna, a small little town only about twenty miles from here, so small the kingdom doesn't even believe we're a town. I think they called it a shelter, a den, a hovel, squalor, a camp of some sort, I don't know. They're good guys, though, good guys. All of us have the same interests and do the same kinds of things together. All of us like to party. Good friends of mine. Always willing to help. I would do anything for them. My friends are the most important thing to me."

"This is all wrong, Strefonio."

"Wrong? You dare say I'm wrong, we're wrong? What the hell are you talking about, man? Something's wrong with you!

It's the end of the world! And you're not even trying to stop it anymore!"

"Of course I am. I'm on my way to confront the wizard to prevent the world's end."

"Not according to this, man, not according to this." Strefonio reached into his robe and pulled out a slip of paper. Lance noticed the wizard wore nothing underneath. He also noticed the sores all over his skin. "The king says I need to kill you. He says he had the solution to save the world, but you refused."

"Strefonio, the solution was my death."

"Yeah, and? Aren't you supposed to be the Chosen One? The hero who'd protect the world no matter what? What happened to that?"

"If I truly believed my death would save the world, I would gladly sacrifice myself. I just don't believe that's the answer."

"It's funny. You guys always looked down on me. 'Strefonio is the goofy wizard. Always getting hurt. Never really helping us out. Not someone we have to respect.'"

"We never said that."

"You all thought it. Everyone's always judging me. I'll show them, though. When I save the world, I'll show them all."

Strefonio made motions with his hands. His companions joined. Lance recognized the gestures and knew better than to just stand there.

Beams of flames nipped at his heels and narrowly missed his feet as the young man ran and dove behind the remnants of a nearby home. His mind raced as he tried desperately to come up with a plan, knowing that hiding behind what was essentially a tinder box was a poor strategy against men who could summon flames with their hands.

His hunters spread out. Lance knew he would be discovered sooner rather than later. Constant movement was a smart idea, but the fog made it difficult to navigate. The young man crawled from place to place to find different hiding spots.

A rock helped him ambush two pursuant wizards. He ran them through with his blade before they knew what hit them. The remains of an old mill allowed him to take out a third, fourth, and fifth.

Panic ensued.

"He's dead!" one of the wizards screamed after he tripped over the body of a fallen comrade.

Another screamed. "I can't even see him!"

"This isn't what we signed up for!" cried a third.

"No reward is worth this!"

"Don't freak out, and find him," Strefonio said between coughing fits.

Things became easier for Lance. The wizards were so preoccupied with their fear that they often failed to notice the man who had snuck up right next to them. He was able to take each of them out, one by one, efficiently and coldly. Soon there was only one wizard left.

"It's between you and me now, Strefonio," Lance muttered. He searched and found his prey.

The wizard was standing out in the open down the long dusty road. His back was completely turned. His head darted everywhere except for where Lance was facing.

The young man moved closer to him, closer, and ever closer. Gradually, he inched his way forward until he was practically on top of him. He drew his blade back and was about to strike.

Then the wizard turned around. Strefonio cast his spell.

Lance had no time to avoid it. He was only a few feet from the wizard at most. Had the wizard waited but a second more, Lance would have been able to kill him.

The young man closed his eyes and braced for impact.

He felt nothing. No pain, no burns. Nothing at all. Maybe he felt a little warmer, but that was it.

Did the armor protect him? No, that couldn't have been it. He was encompassed by flame. Strefonio was an incredible wizard. The armor certainly protected him, but he still should have been scalded, at least.

The armor wasn't enchanted. It didn't possess any sort of magical abilities. No spell existed that could permanently or indefinitely protect a man from flame. A flame spell from a wizard of Strefonio's ability should have been devastating at this range, armor or no.

That's when it hit him. Lance realized what had happened. Strefonio had been an incredible wizard. Not anymore.

Lance sheathed his blade. He looked at his friend with compassion and sorrow.

"You're making fun of me, aren't you?" the wizard gasped. "How d...dare y...you—"

Strefonio started hacking and gagging as if he were trying to cough out a lung. He started to fall. Lance caught him and held him in his arms.

"Years ago, you could see I had a problem," the wizard wheezed. Tears welled in his eyes. "Why didn't you help me?"

"I'm sorry, Strefonio. I'm so sorry."

The wizard said nothing. Convulsions had already begun. Strefonio screamed in agony. His pain was excruciating but mercifully ephemeral. He was dead not long after the spasms began.

Strefonio's lifeless body stared at the young man with cold, accusing eyes. Lance gently shut them and placed the wizard on the ground. A few tears fell from the young man's face.

His loyal steed came running to him. She nudged her master up to his feet with her nose. He rose and patted her on the side of her head. With a heavy sigh, he hopped on her back and continued the dismal journey.

The fog was oppressive. Every breath caused grievous discomfort. It was as if the air itself invaded their lungs and pushed against them as they attempted to breathe.

It took great willpower to press on. Only a resolve that Lance did not previously know he had, along with the loyalty of Rosie, kept the two moving forward despite the seemingly vindictive atmosphere.

"Hello, 'dear.'" A sultry voice pierced the fog, stopping the duo in their tracks.

"Nerissa?"

The elven woman entered through the mist, riding atop a litter. Two large, muscular, shirtless men wearing pants that extended only to the knees and large brown boots carried her from below. They set the contraption on the ground to allow her to dismount.

She was dressed similarly to the dancing women in the castle, but somehow she wore even less clothing, and the style looked somehow more provocative. It was both stimulating and discomforting to the young man.

As the pair of men stood cross-armed, the elven woman playfully pawed their chests. She placed her hands on one of the men's biceps as she spoke.

"Yes, Lance, it's me."

Lance practically soared off his horse. His feet had hardly

hit the ground when he started running toward the elven maiden. "I missed you so much! It is so good to see you again!"

The man Nerissa held pushed Lance aside with one hand.

"Nerissa, what's going on?" Lance asked.

The elven woman moved her hand behind her, and thirty men appeared as if from thin air. Each carried large curved swords. "Quite nice, aren't they? Found them in Sandstrom. Not too far from here, only about thirty miles. They treat me as their queen. Some say I treat them as my slaves. It's not true at all. I would do anything for my beloveds. In return, they do anything for me. It works well for us."

"I don't understand."

"Of course you don't. You were always a fool, at least when it came to matters of the heart." Nerissa sighed as she placed her hand over her chest. "Forgive me. I'm not here to give you a lecture. I'm not here on a social visit at all." She pulled a slip of paper from a secret compartment in what could generously be called her shirt. "Order of the king, yadda yadda yadda. Point is, we kill you. We save the world. More importantly, we'll also get a huge reward. Then I can get back home and live the life I've grown accustomed to."

"How could you kill me?" Lance demanded. "I love you!"

Nerissa sneered. "You don't love me. You never loved me. You don't even know me."

"Of course I do."

"Really? Then tell me something about me, anything at all."

"You're incredibly beautiful."

Nerissa ran her hand through her hair. "True. What else?"

"You're incredible with the bow."

"And?"

"You enjoy studying in the library."

"Not at all. I like to have fun, especially at the tavern."

"You have a sardonic sense of humor?"

"I don't even know what that word 'sardonic' means."

"You have a strong sense of justice."

"Not even that is true. I'm only concerned with justice if it benefits myself."

"You're always willing to fight by my side."

"Again, only when it benefits me."

"I...I'm not sure what else. I know I love you."

"Frankly, I don't believe even that's true. You don't know me at all. I am just a prize for you to flaunt."

"That's not true at all."

"Really? Think about it. Who did you describe just now? It certainly wasn't me. It seems like you described that fat little ugly mage whore who used to follow us around."

"Don't you dare call her that!" Lance barked. "Alizon is an incredible person! She doesn't deserve to be insulted like that! She's kind and sweet. She's the nicest person I have ever met. Why she was always the first...." The young man's voice softened to a near whisper. "She was always the first to volunteer to go with me on my adventures. She was always the first to check on me. She knew more about me than anyone else I adventured with. Oh, Gods, why didn't I see it?"

Nerissa waved her hand and shook her hips to bring attention to her face and body. "You wanted the pretty face. You wanted the perfect body. You wanted the fantasy. You wanted the one you always dreamed of but could never have. You didn't care about anything else, or anybody else for that matter."

"I...I...."

Nerissa loosened her grip on the man. "No matter. Your

time is at an end. Slaves, dispose of this fool."

Lance told Rosie to go and hide. The horse hesitated for a moment before turning around and running off. The knight closed his visor and drew his sword, preparing for the attack.

His foes showed agility and grace he had never seen before. Their lack of heavy armor allowed them to move freely, and their constant movement made them difficult for Lance to hit. Each swing from these men was only narrowly avoided. Lance dodged and weaved below circular swings and downward blows and sprung over swipes that intended to amputate his legs from his ankles or his knees. He did not wish to test whether his armor was resilient enough to deflect those blades. Those swords seemed especially sharp.

There was little room to maneuver. The blows came fast and fierce. Lance acted mostly out of habit and instinct. Yet as nimble as those men were, they did not have Lance's endurance or his skill. They did not have the years of training behind a master swordsman, nor were they conditioned as well. Their blades may have been sharp and strong, but they paled in comparison to Artus's Sword.

As they grew fatigued, they became sloppy. They allowed opportunities for Lance to strike. A misstep while avoiding a blow caused one of the men to not leap as far as he had desired. He wound up getting a sword through his chest for his mistake. Another miscalculated his swing, providing a small opening for Lance that he did not fail to take advantage of.

A deflection led to a counterblow. Fatigue forced one to rest. It was only for a moment, but that was enough to spell doom. One was simply outmuscled. His sword flew from his hand before his head flew from his body.

One by one, Lance slew his foes. With each death, there

was more room for the knight to maneuver, which made the skill disparity even more pronounced. A single slain opponent quickly led to two, then three, then eight....

Soon thirty men lay at Lance's feet. Blood and body parts decorated the ground. Lance turned his attention to the petrified elven maiden. She backed away slowly. Lance pursued her with venom in his eyes. A corpse tripped the elven maiden. She fell backward. Her back was on the ground as she stared into the sky.

Lance sat on top of her and straddled her stomach. His weight made it difficult for her to breathe. He lifted the sword over his head.

"Please, Lance," Nerissa gasped, tears falling. "Don't kill me. It's me, Nerissa. Remember?"

Lance loosened his grip on the sword. His arms lowered. A melancholy feeling washed over him. He couldn't kill her. Despite everything, she still held a very special place in his heart. He placed the blade next to the two of them.

"I want to see your face, Lance."

The young man lifted his visor.

"No, it still covers too much. Take off your helmet."

The young man did as instructed.

"Please, give me a kiss."

"A kiss farewell," Lance said as he lowered his head toward the maiden.

"You fool," she sneered.

The elven maiden pulled a dagger she kept in a leather sheath in the back of her silk pants and plunged it near the base of the young man's neck and shoulder. She barely missed a vital artery but still managed to inflict a major wound on the young man.

Lance fell off her limply, his hands reaching for his neck.

Blood poured in a crimson cascade. He gurgled grotesquely and struggled to breathe. He knew that if he did not receive care soon, he would die.

Nerissa loomed above him. She pulled her knife from his neck and readied herself to make a second blow. The elven maiden wore a sinister smile. Lance believed this would be the last thing he'd ever see.

"Illumination!" The voice was familiar. It sounded distant, though somehow Lance knew she was near.

A giant ball of light shined in Nerissa's eyes, which blinded her and forced her to drop the dagger as she did her best to cover her eyes. She let out an almost feral shriek from the pain and the realization that all she could see were large purple spots burned into her retinas.

Though grievously wounded, Lance managed to grab his sword and ran it through the elven maiden. A tortured cry escaped her lips. Nerissa's body trembled as she struggled in vain to free herself from the blade and escape. A few moments later, her body went limp. She had perished.

This proved to be too much for Lance. He passed out.

The world went from light to darkness several times as Lance faded in and out of consciousness. When his head finally cleared, he looked upward and noticed that the fog had disappeared, and his breathing was no longer labored. In its place was a bright azure sky with a few puffy clouds and clean air to breathe. There were several more cracks than before. Yet, for some reason, Lance was not fazed. Somehow, the scene was still comforting. It was serene. It was nice.

He looked to his right, only to be greeted with his trusty steed's nose pressed against him. He gently pushed her head aside so he could look to his left.

Crouching down next to him was the relieved woman who had saved him. She hugged him before he even had a chance to get a good look at her face.

"Oh, Lance, it's so good to see you again!"

"Hi, Alizon," Lance rasped. The young woman had leaped upon him so hard the wind had been knocked out of him. "I'm so happy to see you too."

She gingerly moved off him slightly to give him a chance to breathe. As she did so, he was able to get a good look at her concerned yet smiling face. She was now the most beautiful girl Lance had ever seen, even though her face and body had not changed at all from the last time the two had seen each other.

"I thought you were dead."

"I would have been if it weren't for you."

"I arrived in the nick of time."

"Yes, in another second, I imagine Nerissa would have applied the coup de grace."

"This is why you must never forget to be careful, Lance! That healing spell I cast wouldn't have worked if I waited just another minute. You would have been...." Alizon sighed. "Enough unpleasantness. Where have you been?"

Lance explained what happened after the battle with Al Kahim, how he believed that she, Nerissa, Sanders, and Strefonio were dead, his training with Guston, and the incident at the castle with King Rudolph that had occurred after his return home and the grave encounters he just had with his former friends.

"I don't know exactly what happened," Alizon explained. "After the battle, we suddenly found ourselves at the bottom of the mountain. We had no idea how. We supposed the wizard must have teleported us down. We didn't see you and assumed the worst. We went to the king to report on what happened. I was pretty shaken up, but nobody else seemed too concerned, not even King Rudolph. He told us it was unfortunate, but our services were no longer needed. I wasn't sure why.

"Then he let us go and do whatever we wanted. He kept tabs on us, though. He said he wanted to make sure he knew where we were at all times. He called us a contingency plan. I had no idea what he meant by that. Then we all went our separate ways. I had no idea where the rest of them went, but I returned to the academy. I had nowhere else to go." She paused. "I...I couldn't concentrate on my studies. Not really. I just couldn't get the thought of your death out of my mind. Then all of a sudden, I got this." She pulled a slip of paper from her robe. "It was from the king. He instructed me to go after you, to...to kill you, to save the world. I was so happy to learn you were alive, but at the same time, I knew you were in danger, so I came here as quickly as I could. I didn't know what was going on, but I wanted to help you, to protect you if I could."

"Even if it meant the end of the world?"

"I didn't believe that nonsense. And even if it were true, I don't care. If killing you is the only way to prevent the world's end, then so be it, let the world end."

Lance rose suddenly. He placed his lips upon hers and gave her a passionate kiss. The wide-eyed Alizon first babbled in muffled surprise before wrapping her arms around the young man she loved so deeply, as he did her.

After a short while, Rosie began nudging their arms to separate them. The couple let out a gregarious laugh.

"She's sure the jealous one," Alizon said.

"She must be in love with me," Lance said.

"It's easy to see why."

They shared a little more romance before deciding it was

time to go. There was still a job to be done. Lance helped Alizon onto Rosie, then mounted her and took the reins. Alizon gripped the young man tightly as the pair made their way to Mount Posledna.

The final conflict with Al Kahim lie ahead. They were ready, and whatever happened, they would face it together.

Chapter 14

"I think Guston lied to me about how much this horse can carry," Lance said. "I think he said it just to motivate me."

"What makes you say that?" Alizon asked.

"When I was obese, Guston claimed this horse wouldn't be able to carry my weight. Look at her now. She's able to carry both of us with ease."

Alizon glared. "Are you calling me fat?"

Lance stuttered. "Not at all. I just meant if this horse can carry two people, surely I wasn't large enough to threaten her well-being."

"Especially when one of those two people is a whale like me."

"That's not what I was saying at all."

"The lying only makes it worse." Alizon closed her eyes, crossed her arms, and turned from him in disgust.

The young man bit his tongue. He didn't know what to say. Lance stuttered. "I...I was only trying to lighten the mood."

The young woman peeked at him with one of her eyes

and stuck out her tongue. "I was too." She giggled while Lance feigned anger.

They arrived at the base of the mountain. Lance dismounted his steed and carefully helped the young woman off the horse. He gave his animal friend a couple of pats on the side of her head.

"This is where we part, girl," he said. "At least for now. It's dangerous to go up there." The young man removed her bridle, saddle, and reins. "Don't wait for us, girl. Neither Alizon nor I are sure what's going to happen when we get up that mountain. The last thing I want to have happen is you waiting for us forever. So go, be free."

Lance moved his arms and hands to get Rosie to move. She remained steadfast.

Hoping she understood, the two began to climb the final leg of their journey. As the two went up the mountain trail to ascend the mountain though, Rosie attempted to follow.

"I'm sorry, Rosie. The trail is too dangerous. Horses can't navigate the narrow path — even humans have trouble."

After a few more strokes and a few more soft words from the young man, the steed finally understood and did not attempt to follow. She remained at the base of the mountain, awaiting her master's return.

***

The same narrow trails and precarious paths as before awaited them, as did the crags and buttresses and other like impediments. Again the knight assisted the mage whenever they reached parts she had difficulty ascending on her own.

Lance's training augmented his climbing ability. It made certain parts of the climb easier and also meant he no longer needed assistance carrying his beloved through the more difficult parts of the ascent.

The anxiety of before was drastically reduced. Experience eased some of the worries, but their determination proved to be the key contributor. They found strength in each other. With everything they had gone through, they shared an indescribable bond. Everything they experienced, all the adventures they had gone on separately and together, these experiences only made them stronger, able to handle anything.

The rain fell upon their heads again at some point, as did the wind, the sleet, and the hail. The duo remained undeterred, silently making their way up that mountain focused solely on what lie for them ahead. Neither of them spoke much during the journey. Not that they did not have much to say. There were so many emotions the two of them wanted to share, especially Alizon.

She wished to describe the pain and suffering she'd endured. How much it hurt when he was to be wed to another. How she still resigned herself to lend her aid despite how much it may have killed her inside. How much it pained her thinking he was dead, especially when her friends were so callous. That though she still loved him, there was still a bit of anger and resentment she had to overcome. However, she was certain she eventually would.

Alizon would keep silent for now. It was not the time to discuss such matters. It was time for them to meet Al Kahim once again and determine the fate of the world.

Then they returned to that final gap.

Alizon was paralyzed. She had fooled herself into thinking that knowing about the gap ahead of time would reduce her anxiety. When she saw that giant hole, a flood of unpleasant memories returned. The mage clung to the knight's arm.

"I cannot do this," she whispered to Lance.

"Of course you can. You did it before."

"No, I nearly fell. I nearly died. I can't do this."

"I will catch you as I did last time."

"That was luck. You may not be able to catch me again. I may not be able to even make the jump."

"Of course you will be able to." Lance gave her a warm embrace. "You are much stronger than I am. You have always have been. You can do it. And I need you. I've always needed you. I just never realized it until now. I cannot do this alone."

"Okay, I'll do it, but only because you need me."

Lance whispered his appreciation. After several failed attempts from the knight to get her to loosen her grip, the mage finally let him go.

After a couple of warmup swings with his arms, the knight took a couple of steps back, then quickly dashed. He leaped over the gap with ease.

It was now Alizon's turn.

"You can do it, my love."

"Are you sure?"

"I've never been more sure of anything in my life. I will catch you as I did before. As I always will."

With a few more words of encouragement, the mage imitated the motions of the knight and took a running start. Anxiety flooded her brain despite the short run. She reached the edge and leaped as high and as hard as she could. She closed her eyes the entire time.

Her body soared in the air briefly. Then it fell. It was sudden and with great haste. She began to scream as she made her descent.

Lance caught her as he did before. It was, in fact, a much easier catch. She had cleared a far greater distance. The knight remained on his feet.

When Lance placed Alizon on solid ground, she fell to her knees and practically kissed it, so relieved that she made it.

Still on her knees, while Lance sat awkwardly next to her on his posterior, Alizon stuck a finger in his face and ordered, "Don't ever make me do that again."

***

They arrived at the apex of the mountain. The wizard's abode had changed very little in the past couple of years, if at all. It was still the same foreboding black mortar edifice. Yet it was somehow less intimidating. The fear that Lance had felt before in the pit of his stomach was notably absent.

Yes, it was fear. Lance could admit that now. He asked his mage companion whether she felt the same. She confirmed that she, too, felt strangely calm.

Lance looked at the sky one last time. It resembled a hardboiled egg that had been dropped. The knight gasped. He pointed to a part of the sky. Alizon looked to where he was pointing but could not see what the knight observed.

Off in the far distance, a piece was loosening. Parts of the heavens fell as if it were sawdust as the piece shook. After a couple more shakes, the entire thing rapidly fell. Shockwaves were sent throughout the kingdom when it landed. The couple held each other, using each other as support as the mountain shook.

Eventually, the quake ended. Though it only lasted a few seconds, it felt like minutes.

"I hesitate to ask, but did you see the sky fall?" Lance asked.

"I'm sorry," Alizon answered. "I did not. I only felt the shaking."

"No matter. I think the end of the world truly is nigh, and

we've arrived in the nick of time. It is time to confront Al Kahim once again." Alizon agreed, and the two made their way to his home.

When Lance and Alizon approached, the mahogany door once again opened automatically. The duo walked down the long and barren hallway into the lone room. Sitting in his light-blue, high-back chair with white trim was Al Kahim.

"So you've returned," the wizard said. He rose from his chair and turned to the couple.

Lance drew his sword. "I'm ready this time."

Alizon stood next to him. "We're ready this time."

"Are you?"

"We are. We even managed to defeat my former friends to get to you. They tried hard to prevent me from reaching you, but we prevailed."

"Good. I didn't want them to stop you. I wanted to speak to you."

"Did you now? Then why didn't you defeat them yourself?"

"Because you needed to find out the truth about who they really were." The wizard took a hard look at the young man and gazed into his eyes. "Yes, there is a determination I did not see before, strength, and fortitude where I once saw weakness and frailty. There is an intelligence I did not see, along with a newfound disposition for logic, reason, and rationality. Drawing your sword, however, may betray that notion, as it seems to indicate that you are more inclined to fight without hearing what I have to say."

"It is just a precaution," Lance growled. "Guston told me I needed to listen to you and that you'd be able to explain everything. Out of respect for the man, I am willing to do so, but it hardly means I trust you. I must warn you, I have Artus's Sword, which is said to be able to slay any of my foes. I am ready."

"Yes, trusting yet cautious, a very reasonable stance, all things considered. Perhaps knowing nothing else, it is the only rational decision you could make. I think you are ready."

"Ready for what?"

"Ready to learn everything." The wizard walked over to his globe and started spinning it slowly. "Ready for the truth. What have you been told?"

"You've already cast the spell to end the world. My blood is the only thing that can stop it."

"Oh, Lance, you're terribly mistaken. The spell hasn't been cast yet."

"What? It hasn't?"

"No. Once cast, the spell's effects would take effect immediately."

"Does that mean you don't know what the final ingredient is?"

"I've known since the beginning."

"That can't be true."

"But it is. I made quite sure the king learned that as well two years ago, though I might have given him a bit of misinformation, I admit."

"Why would you do that? So that he would try and kill me?"

"I wanted to see how he'd react. He did mostly as I expected, though his lack of understanding and his brute display of force was still disappointing. Besides, you needed time to learn, to grow, by achieving and helping others."

"I don't understand."

"Tell me, Lance. Have you given any thought as to why I

want to end the world?"

Lance hesitated before he answered. "I...I don't know. I thought it was out of malice."

"This is more or less how the king has described me—yes, the purported 'evil wizard' as he so eagerly labeled me to be. The truth of the matter is, Lance, I am truly nothing more than an agent of change, someone who wants you to grow and share yourself with the world rather than hiding yourself in this land. I wish to end the world because you no longer need it."

"What are you talking about?"

"When this world ends, a new one will be born, a new world that you will be part of. It will usher in a new era where you will thrive."

"I don't understand. You're telling me that ending this world will create a new one? How can I believe you?"

"Because of who I truly am." Al Kahim slowly moved his hands toward his head. As he did so, he revealed surprisingly bony fingers and frail weak wrists. He grabbed the edges of his hood with his index finger and his thumb and slowly pulled it down.

A face was revealed. Stern yet soft features. Soft blue eyes. A multitude of wrinkles despite the man only being approximately two and a half decades older than Lance. Not a single hair was on his head.

Lance's eyes began to well up in tears. "Dad?"

The revelation caused Alizon to involuntarily take a small hop into the air. "What?" she asked. "This man is your father?"

"My father, Albert," Lance responded. He marched right up to the wizard until he stood mere inches from the man's face, and began to shout. "That's impossible! You left me and Mom when I was just thirteen years old!"

"I know, and I'm sorry. I didn't have a choice. I wanted nothing more than to stay."

"Do you know how hard it was for me? And for Mom too? We struggled so much without you!"

"I tried so hard to put enough away for the two of you so you wouldn't have to suffer financially when I was gone. I'm truly sorry it wasn't enough."

"Is everything about money? You were our rock, the backbone of our family! Without you, we were lost! We didn't know what to do! We loved you so much! We missed you so much!"

The young man began to sob. His father wrapped his arms around him.

"We still miss you so much! What kind of world would allow that to happen to you? You were such a good man. How could you just give up like that?"

"I didn't, though there were times I almost did. I won't lie. It was hell. The pains and sickness I felt were beyond anything I could have ever imagined. Not once did I wake up thinking the treatment was doing me any good. Almost daily, I felt like surrendering. Not once did I not feel like giving up. Yet I didn't. For two years, I fought with every fiber of my being. Up until the very end. Do you know why?"

Lance shook his head no.

"For you and your mother, Lance. It was the only reason I fought."

"It still hurts. It still hurts so much."

"I know, Joe, and it may always, but you have to move on. Your mother needs you. Your friends need you. Your real friends need you, not those that pretend to be or who you wish were your friends. You have the strength and courage to make it without me. You owe it to yourself, Joe, to move on. You have your entire life ahead of you, and you can't spend it wallowing in the past or spending it here. That is why I am trying to end the world. I just cannot do it quite yet."

"Why not?"

"Because I'm missing the most important ingredient. The only ingredient. Your blessing."

"Yes. Your blessing." A familiar voice echoed from the entrance. All eyes turned in that direction. Lance let out an audible gasp when he saw who was there.

It was King Rudolph. He appeared to have changed again. He was taller, much more muscular. His expression was one of pure, unadulterated rage. It was as if his skull were aflame.

Flanking him were twelve of his elite knights. There was something in the king's hands, but the young man could not quite figure out what it was. He learned shortly.

The king rolled the item toward Lance. It made a sickening sound as it made its way across the floor and bumped into the young man's feet. He looked down. What he saw nearly made him lose his mind. Alizon screamed and shielded her eyes. Al Kahim scowled.

"That's all that remains of the 'Great' Guston," the king sneered.

Lance lifted the head and held it tightly against his chest. Tears streamed down his eyes. "I'm sorry, Guston. I am so, so sorry. I should have stayed and protected you. I never got the chance to tell you how much you meant to me. No one has ever helped me as much as you. You were the best friend I ever had. Thank you for everything."

Al Kahim gently took the head away from the young man and put it elsewhere out of sight.

"You monster!" Lance screamed. He charged the king. He did not go far. His arm was being pulled. The young man looked behind him. Al Kahim held his wrist.

"Easy, Lance. You have to calm down so you can fight him with a level head," Al whispered. Lance's eyes remained transfixed on the king. He opened his mouth to protest but decided better of it. He nodded and wiped the tears from his eyes.

"How could you do such a thing?" Lance demanded.

"It is the fate of all who defy me," the king sneered. "You shall suffer the same for yourself soon enough."

"You lied to me!"

"Of course I did. When I learned that your blessing was all that was needed to end the world, I needed to make sure you were dead. Of course, that wasn't exactly what I was told by my messenger. He informed me that the world was safe because Al Kahim had killed the only one who could possibly end the world. His head now rests on a pike outside my castle."

"I didn't mean for that to happen," Al Kahim muttered.

"What does it matter to you? You want the world to end, which means the death of this world, which means the death of everyone."

"This world has served its purpose. It was created for Lance, but now it is no longer needed. It is time for it to end."

"Why should I believe the words of a madman?"

"I am not mad. I simply want the best for Lance, unlike you."

"Regardless, I'd like to continue from where I was rudely interrupted. We never found your body, Lance, so I came up with a contingency plan, though unfortunately, you saw right through it, with a little help from that old man. Guston, was it?"

Lance growled incoherently in response.

"My favorite part was those women," the king continued. "Just bar girls from The Wretched Swallow that I dressed up for the occasion. I had to make you feel like I had a royal welcome prepared for you. Now it's time for a royal farewell. Men, attack him!"

"Alizon and I can take care of the knights, right?" Al Kahim said, looking toward Alizon.

"Ah, right."

"I want you to focus on the king. Think of this as your final test."

Lance nodded.

King Rudolph drew a broadsword from his waist. Lance stared for a moment. The blade seemed familiar.

"That's right, Lance," the king said as if he could read Lance's thoughts. "It's your old broadsword. I think I'll give it back to you, blade first."

He lumbered toward Lance. His knights followed him lockstep. Alizon and Al Kahim immediately cut the knights off and began their assault, which allowed Lance to concentrate on the king.

The king smirked. "I suppose they didn't want them to get in the way of our little dance. No matter. I will destroy you myself."

Lance said nothing and swung his sword. The final battle commenced. Swords clashed. A struggle ensued. When Lance believed he had the advantage, the king countered with swings of his own. Each strike was parried. Each thrust was pushed aside. Several times the tip of the king's blade was at Lance's throat, only for the tables to be turned.

The knight observed his King Rudolph's every movement, meticulously analyzing for any opportunity, for the slightest fault that would allow him to press the advantage and win the fight. He saw it. Whenever Lance attacked King Rudolph's left, he would counter by crossing his right arm over his chest. It left his middle open, if only briefly. A thrust followed by a downward swing would penetrate, but only if the sword wielder was quick, only if the blade was strong, and only if it could be done in one quick motion. Luckily for Lance, all three were true for him.

His sword became a blur. The king's blade flew up to counter, and as it flew slightly in the air, Lance turned his wrists and arms and struck downward. Artus's Sword found its target.

To his shock and horror, the blade failed to penetrate. Again and again, the knight struck with increasing desperation and frustration. Realizing he could not be hurt, the king laughed uproariously. He no longer even bothered to use any defensive efforts. No matter what he did, Lance failed to make the blade penetrate.

"Keep swinging. It'll do you no good," the king sneered.

Lance continued with increasing desperation. As hard as he tried, he could not get his blade to penetrate. He wasn't prepared for this. He didn't know what to do.

Eventually, the king grew bored. He grabbed the sword from the air with both hands and smiled. "I was worried you had it all figured out, that you figured out the way to defeat me. It turns out you are the same fool you always were."

The young man was tossed with such force that his body shook the building when it collided with the adjoining wall.

"What are you?" Lance wheezed.

"Your executioner. Savior of the world."

"Are you a Taka? Did Artus fight your kind?"

King Rudolph did not respond. Instead, he slowly approached. As he did so, his smile grew wider such that it displayed his crooked, fang-like teeth.

"Lance!" a voice cried out to him. Through his blurred vision, he could make out a white silhouette running behind King Rudolph.

"Alizon, go away," Lance cried as loudly as he could.

The mage did not listen. She cast an illumination spell to blind the king.

He didn't even notice.

Multiple other spells were cast rapidly in succession. None had any effect. Nothing seemed to be able to stop him.

The king raised his sword and struck down. Lance countered, though his arms felt considerable pain when he did. King Rudolph was slow to strike again. He was toying with the lad, savoring every moment. Alizon became more desperate. She conjured whatever spells she could think of.

Distraught and with none of her spells working, she turned to Al Kahim and screamed, "Why don't you help us?"

"I'm afraid even my spells would have no effect," he said. Alizon felt a chill upon hearing these words.

All hope seemed to be lost. Lance's arms began to ache. He was able to parry each of the king's blows, but there was no telling how long he'd last. Soon King Rudolph would be through playing his depraved game of cat and mouse.

Lance looked over to Alizon, silently asking her for forgiveness, for all he'd done and all the ways he'd hurt her. How it was unfair the two would soon be separated again so quickly after reuniting. He thanked her for everything, for her support, for being there whenever he needed her, and for her love.

The woman began to glow. A fitting last image of his life, Lance thought to himself.

Then he noticed it. Alizon wasn't glowing, not her entirely

at least. Only her feet glowed.

Alathea's Enchantment. It was Alathea's Enchantment that caused the illusion. It was glowing, not Alizon. It was what Guston's family had protected. What allowed Artus to defeat the Takas. What would allow Lance to defeat the king.

"Alizon, give me the vial at your feet!" Lance screamed. The young woman looked down.

The king turned around. "No, give that to me!" He reached out for it and the mage.

In one smooth motion, Alizon reached down and slid Lance the vial. The king got his fingertips on it, only to find it slipping out of his hands.

Lance hastily opened the vial and recklessly poured it all over his blade. King Rudolph charged and screamed incoherently. He was so manic that his mouth foamed. His sword was raised. He swung it down with all his might. King Rudolph was too slow.

Artus's Sword penetrated King Rudolph's heart before he could land his blow. The broadsword fell from his hand. His eyes met Lance's. There was nothing but pure terror.

On that blade, he convulsed terribly. Soon after, the king let out a horrible scream. A few attempts were made to free himself, violently initially but with decreasing force. All of this effort was ultimately in vain. He died slowly and painfully at the tip of that blade.

Lance peeled the man off his sword, quickly and rashly, giving the man's body the respect it deserved. After the king was removed with a disgusting squelch, the knight tossed Artus's Sword aside. He hoped to never have to carry it again.

Lance turned toward Alizon. Her hands held her knees as she attempted to catch her breath. The last few hours had been quite an overwhelming ordeal for the young lady.

"You saved my life again," Lance said after he gave the mage a chance to recuperate. He then gave her a warm embrace and kiss, which she affectionately reciprocated.

"You have done well, son," Al Kahim said. "The king has been defeated. Now no one stands in your way." The wizard walked around the couple and patted the young man's shoulder. "You know the truth now, son. You now know why this world must end. I think you are ready to move on. Now is a perfect time."

He gazed into his love's sincere brown eyes and then stared at the wizard. He paused for a moment before he could manage to find the right words to say. "Will she be in the next world? Will she be where I am going?"

"Of course, son. She will be there. All your friends will be there, even some of the townsfolk you met. Even the people you adventured with will be with you, though whether you still should consider them friends is up for debate. Personally, I wouldn't associate with them if you paid me."

This prompted the couple to smile. His father continued. "They may not be in the exact form as they were here, but you will recognize them. This new world will feel more real to you than even this one. It is up to you to make good decisions about your relationships, your goals, your dreams. Everything will be up to you. I am sure you will be able to handle all of it, son."

Lance gulped. "Will…will you be there, Dad?"

Al let out a heavy sigh. "No, I will not be. Not physically, at least." The young man peeled off the mage to allow his father to give him a heartfelt squeeze. "In your heart, though, Lance. I will be with you always in your heart and spirit."

A few tears fell from Lance's face. When he was ready, he

let go of his dad.

"Okay," Lance stammered, "Okay, then. If the world must end for the betterment of myself and everyone here, so be it. I give you my blessing, Al Kahim. Dad. Please end this world. I no longer need it."

Reality began to crumble. Visible cracks emerged in the air which they breathed. Lance and Alizon tried to shout. Al Kahim seemed to say, "Don't worry. Everything will be all right," but sound itself seemed to have disappeared.

Everything shook. The foundation of the building cracked. The ceiling collapsed. A large piece of debris fell on Lance. The world turned black.

James Kirst lives in the Evergreen State in a humble little abode within the forested city of Dupont. There, he earned his Master's Degree at the University of Washington. Commuting up north to Tacoma, he has worked as a senior programmer and software development lead for almost ten years.

With a borderline obsessive interest in the paranormal, James has conducted intensive study into the subject. To that end, he has visited some of the most haunted places in the United States, including Salem, the LaLaurie Mansion of New Orleans, and his personal favorite, the Shanghai Tunnels of Portland, Oregon.

As an avid fan of mystery both in fiction and in real life, he has done extensive research into police procedurals, the machinations of detective work, and life as a private investigator.

A big sports fan, James is sure to either be watching or

participating in one when not writing about or educating himself in one of the aforementioned subjects. In fact, he has won multiple championships in bowling and slow-pitch softball and has made several appearances as a softball All-Star where he was given the privilege of playing in Cheney Stadium. He is still seeking that elusive kickball title, however.